ABOUT THE AUTHOR

James Wheatley was born in the North of England and has worked as a roofer, a labourer, a financial and business risk analyst, and a market researcher. He currently lives in Yorkshire, England, where he divides his time between writing and playing guitar. *Magnificent Joe* is his first novel.

JAMES WHEATLEY

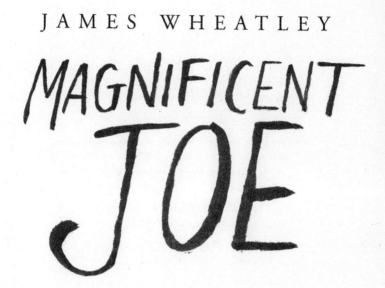

MAGNIFICENT JOE

ONEWORLD

A Oneworld Book

First published by Oneworld Publications 2013
This paperback edition published by Oneworld Publications 2014

ISBN 978-1-78074-369-1
eBook ISBN 978-1-78074-119-2

Text designed and typeset by Tetragon, London
Printed and bound in Denmark by Norhaven A/S

Oneworld Publications
10 Bloomsbury Street
London WC1B 3SR
England
www.oneworld-publications.com

Prologue

There is a body in the lane. They caught him at a break in the high hedgerow and did it by moonlight. He lies crumpled, like casually discarded clothes. The search is over, and all around me the night is suddenly vast and cold. I watch, I breathe, and then I run the last few feet and drop to his side.

'Joe.'

I grab the arm of his coat and roll him over. He flops onto his back, all limp.

'Joe.'

He makes a weak sigh, but his eyes are swollen shut. I touch his face.

'Joe, please.'

'Jim, help me.' It comes out low, with a soft spray of blood.

'Oh God, Joe. Hold on, hold on. It's going to be all right.' I know that it is not going to be all right. His whole body has caved in. He will die soon. I have no phone, and no help, and if I leave him now, he will die alone.

'Why?'

'Oh Jesus, Joe. You know why.'

'They wanted to hurt me.'

'They're gone. Just hang on for us.'

'Will you look after me?'

'Aye, Joe. I'll look after you.'

But what can I do – first aid? It's hopeless, and what if I did actually save his life? I thought that I wanted to, and that's why I charged out here after him, but now this has happened, it would be better to let him reach the end. He is going to die, but at least I will be here with him.

'Joe, I love you.'

———

I have watched TV archaeologists disinter bodies in the name of science. They work with care and the skeleton emerges slowly. The last layer of soil is brushed away from the surface of the skull, from between the tibia and fibula, from between the radius and the ulna, and from between the vertebrae. We dig up the past, we carbon-date it, and then we gawp at it from behind the glass. It is supposed to tell a story. This is our story.

I got a letter from Geoff:

Hello Mate,

I hope your all right. I'm doing well I've lost two stone. Its the climate. Your probably angry with me. They never suspected a thing they thought I was just a hairy arsed builder! I am sorry if you feel riped off but it wasnt exactly millions. I could'nt see the point of shareing it when there was so much I wanted. I think of you when I am having a drink off an evening and I rise a glass to you. I know that you fucked her but I have the hole truth now and I forgive you for every thing.

Cheers,

        Geoff

ps She told us about Joe. Im sorry he was just mental and should of been in a home.

Of course, there's no return address. It's a local postmark too: he must have sent it to someone else first, inside another envelope. Maybe he had the presence of mind to retain a lawyer here, just in case. There's no point in any detective work, though; like he says, it wasn't exactly millions. Besides, he's probably spent most of it by now.

Geoff doesn't give a shit about Barry, and neither do I. I can't imagine that hateful bastard received a letter of his own. He's so bitter he'd treat it as a clue and try to send it for forensic analysis or some such shite. Not that anyone would listen to him now. I think Geoff knew that, fundamentally, I wouldn't care about the money. Money was never my problem.

Now when I look back on the things that have happened, I can hardly believe I was there. If I couldn't hold the evidence in my hands, I wouldn't know if any of it was real. There is no one now. Mrs Joe, Joe, Geoff, and Barry are all gone in one way or another. For a while there was Laura, but then Geoff sent for her. She gathered up her stuff in the middle of the night and I never saw her again.

Part One

Part One

1

OCTOBER 2004

A Friday morning. The weather is cloudless but chilly. It's a halfway decent day, at least; there's no rain, but it's not warm enough to really sweat. I stand on the edge of the loading bay and look down as the teleloader drives up to the pack of concrete blocks below. From the cab, the driver waves at me and I raise my thumb to him. The diesel engine picks up again and the forks extend under the pallet, then lift and carry the blocks towards me. I wave the driver on and step back as the pallet slides onto the scaffold. The fork withdraws and I begin to rip the plastic off the pack. I don't rush. Geoff and Barry still have plenty to be going on with; looking down the platform, I can see them laying blocks.

They stand a few feet apart and move along the wall a couple of steps at a time. Barry leads with one course of blocks, and Geoff lays the course on top of that. They work with smooth, unflustered concentration. Even when one of them picks up a cracked block that falls in half as he lifts it, he chucks the pieces away without a second look and only the barest of murmured curses. The bits of concrete sail groundward and thump into the mud, easily capable of killing anyone they hit. Despite this, some of the men still save their hard hats for official inspections only.

We're building a temple, as a matter of fact. Barry has plenty to say about this, but he doesn't really care – none of us do. We'll never even see the finished thing; as soon as the walls are up, we'll clear off to the next job. We might go even sooner if we get pissed off, or kicked off. To be fair, though, it's a long time since we were kicked off a site. We're a good crew, whatever that means. Besides, getting kicked off a site involves fucking up royally, and we're all well past that sort of nonsense. There's a twisted pride to be had in doing a decent job, even though you hate the work.

If you wanted to, though, you could really make a mess: a mess so bad that a man, maybe several men, could die. All you'd have to do is look serious when whichever idiot in a hi-vis vest and tie walked past. He might stop and have a look, perhaps even get his tape out, and then maybe say something like, 'It needs to come up five mil by that end,' but he wouldn't notice that anything was seriously wrong, he'd just keep walking.

These thoughts linger, unsaid, in the silence of the cabin at lunchtime, until someone breathes, 'Thirty-odd more years of this shite,' and then everyone's lottery fantasy comes tumbling out, warming the place, and even the most pig-ignorant sod on the site can achieve a certain eloquence in the telling of it, because they get plenty of practice – the same story day after day, slipping through clumsy mouths like worn rosary beads through arthritic hands. 'Ah well, live in hope, eh?' someone says.

I load blocks into my wheelbarrow, two at a time, stacking them neatly to get as many in as possible. It takes a bit of grunt to get it rolling, but once it's moving, it goes easily – stopping is the harder part. I guide the barrow down the platform, towards Geoff and Barry, and then squeeze behind them to draw up slightly past where they're working. I load out, starting a stack for each of them so they can move along and continue the course.

Geoff looks over. 'All right, Jim. They getting any lighter yet?'

'No fucking chance.'

'Ah well, live in hope, eh?'

I grunt at him and go back for more.

———

Under the strip lighting of the Co-op everything takes on an unnatural glow. It gives me a headache, further adding to the bafflement I feel when trying to shop. I'm surrounded by groceries and I can't make a single decision. This shouldn't be so hard for a man of thirty, but apparently it is for me. I hate it. I'll live on tinned tomatoes for days rather than go to the supermarket, so this expedition does not constitute an ideal Friday evening. Sadly, I really do need to be here – I've run out of toothpaste, soap, whisky, and food, and I need a packet of sixty-watt light bulbs.

Despite knowing all this, any sense of purpose I had deserted me as soon as I stepped through the automatic door and now I'm completely fucking zombified. In truth, I'm close to tears. I mutter, as I do every time, 'I should have made a list.'

I grip the trolley and start to stride up and down the aisles, hoping that when I pass something I need, it'll trigger my memory and I'll pick it up. It's a hopeless situation, though: how are you supposed to know what you want when you're surrounded by signs and labels telling you that you want something else and there's fifty per cent extra free? And now, as if I wasn't confused enough, Joe is walking towards me.

'Hello.'

'All right, Joe.'

'What you doing?'

'Erm…I'm shopping, Joe.'

'Me too – look.' He brandishes a list in front of my face and then turns it round and begins to read, 'Milk! Bread! Potatoes! Cheese! Beans! To—'

'All right, Joe, I understand.' I'm mildly surprised, but I shouldn't be. I know he can read, and I know he can count, and I know he can use a shop, because he kept me in beer and fags during my early teenage years. But still, actually seeing Joe do something normal always surprises me. He's a slow shambles of a man. Even in my childhood memories of him – at which point he was in his twenties and considerably slimmer than he is now – he plods and lumbers like a sleepy elephant. Slow or not, he's making a better job of shopping than I am: his trolley already contains several items, while mine is painfully empty. I suppose he's had plenty of practice in dealing with this sort of thing, because the way I feel in a supermarket must be the way Joe feels all the time.

His gaze turns to a display of cakes in the bakery section and a big grin lifts his chubby, crumpled old face. 'It's magnificent, in't it?'

'Aye, Joe, it's fucking magnificent.' Actually, they don't look that bad. Joe is pleased that I agree. 'Are you going to get one?' I ask, knowing the answer.

'It's not on the list.' Joe frowns.

'So what? Just get a fucking cake if you want one – it's your disability benefit.'

'No! They're not on the list.'

'All right.' His mother will have made the list, and Joe will have received strict instructions. Joe's mother is too old and too ill to leave the house herself. In fact, she's too old and too ill to be alive, but she refuses to die because Joe has no one else. 'I'm going to get one.'

'Which one?'

'The chocolate one, there.'

'I love chocolate, me.'

'Me too.' Joe and I approach the bakery display and I pick up the cake. It's in a cardboard box, with a cellophane window on top. The icing looks creamy and delicious. The price tag says,

'Two pounds ninety-nine,' and, 'Lovingly handmade at the in-store bakery.' We gaze at it together and I lay it in my trolley.

'Looks lovely,' breathes Joe.

'Aye, it bloody does.' We push off, to continue our shopping together. 'Joe, what's the difference between a supermarket trolley and a blonde?'

'Dunno.'

'The trolley has a mind of its own.'

'Oh. Righto.'

'It's a joke, Joe.'

'Oh.' With Joe to talk to, the shopping becomes much easier and I feel in control again. He sails through all the crap, picking up exactly what he came for, and I follow his example. At the checkout, Joe has his money counted out before it's even his turn. Joe's mother has been doing things the same way for a very long time indeed, so Joe shops from a rather limited slate of items and has had time to memorize their price. I can imagine his consternation on the occasions when something has gone up, but this evening all is well and Joe hands over the money without a word, takes his change, and waits for me patiently. Special offers, piped music, point-of-sale advertising are all powerless against his unyielding regime. His idiocy is his force field; he stands astride the aisles like a simple-minded colossus.

Finally, I get my groceries bagged up and breathe a sigh of relief. 'All right, Joe. Do you want a lift home?'

'Aye, that's magnificent, that.'

'Howay, then, as long as you make a brew – I can't eat all that cake myself.'

'Aye, you'd be a right fat bastard if you did.'

I shoot him a sidelong glance and realize that he knew all along. Sly bugger, he's never quite as daft as you think he is.

———

Joe and I chomp chocolate cake and slurp tea in his mother's kitchen, run-down but spotless. Loud snores emanate from the front room, where Joe's mother has fallen asleep in front of the blaring TV.

'Fucking hell, Joe. How does someone so small make so much noise?'

'Who's small?'

'Your mam. She sounds like a fucking elephant.'

Joe giggles. I shake my head, bite cake, and slug at my tea.

'You've got chocolate on your face,' says Joe.

'You what?' I pick up a teaspoon, to see my reflection, but Joe is already reaching over to dab at my face with a bit of kitchen roll, motherly concern on his face. 'Fuck off, man. I can get it myself.' I push his hand away.

'Just helping,' he says matter of factly.

I grunt a reply and wipe my mouth with the back of my hand, leaving a chocolate smear near my wrist. I lick it off.

'You're a mother hen, you,' I tell him.

Joe thinks about this for a moment, and then starts to make chicken noises and flap his elbows.

'I'll wring your neck like one in a minute.' But it's too late, I'm already laughing at him – his eyes bunched up, his bottom lip pushed out, and his cap pulled low over his brow. Joe stands up and begins to parade back and forth across the kitchen, clucking. 'You're crackers! Sit down!' I shout, through my laughter.

'All right, keep your hair on,' he says, sitting.

'Keep my hair on?' I snatch his cap from his head. Joe suddenly looks bereft, separated from his hat. I inspect the embroidered logo. 'What the fuck is Chicago Bears?'

'Dunno. Bears, I think, in Chicago.'

'Where's that?' I ask, out of mischief.

'Somewhere down South. Near London.'

'Oh, you been there?'

'No. I bought it off Sharon. Nine ninety-nine. Mam said I needed a new hat.'

'Sharon?'

'Aye, the lady in Allsports. She's got a badge.'

'Oh, the one that says, "Hello. My name is Sharon"?'

'Do you know her?'

'Aye, I've had her.'

'You what?'

'Nothing.'

There's a stirring from the other room and the snoring has stopped. I hand back Joe's cap as his mother shuffles in.

'Hello, Mrs Joe,' I greet her.

'Hello,' she replies, with a slight suspicion that could lead me to believe that she doesn't remember who I am, though I know that she does. She's stooped and looks groggy from sleep. 'You woke me,' she says.

Quite frankly, I regard this accusation with some scepticism: nothing Joe or I did came even remotely close to the volume of her television. 'Oh, I'm sorry, Mrs Joe.'

'Doesn't matter. I shouldn't have fallen asleep there anyway – it's bad for my back.'

I don't know what to say to that, so I look around the kitchen. 'Your lino's coming up in that corner,' I inform her.

'Is it?'

'Aye. I'll come round tomorrow and stick it down for you.'

'That's very kind. Have you eaten yet?'

'Yes, I have.' That's not quite a lie, since I did manage a couple of slices of toast before I went to the Co-op.

'Oh, I made some shepherd's pie earlier. There's some leftovers. Are you sure I can't tempt you?'

'No, thanks, Mrs Joe. I'd better get going actually.' Barry and Geoff will be in the Admiral already. It's Friday night and I'm ready to start drinking.

'Well, I'll see you tomorrow, then.'

'Yes, you will. Goodnight. See you later, Joe.'

'See you later, alligator!' Joe smiles at me, replete with chocolate.

'In a while, crocodile.'

I pick up my jacket and make for the kitchen door, but Joe calls after me, 'Don't forget your cake!'

'That's all right – you hang on to it, Joe. I'm watching my figure.' I step out into the October night and catch the smell of burning leaves. A slight drizzle has set in. I sigh, turn up my collar, and walk back to the car.

———

'You're a bit late.' Barry squints up at me through the smoke of his cigarette. These days, everything he says seems to come with a sneer. From above him, I can see the beginnings of a bald patch in his curly brown hair. The three of us are the same age and work in the same places, exposed to the same elements every day, but Barry looks at least ten years older than Geoff or me.

'I had to go shopping.'

Barry snorts and pretends to check his watch. 'Who for, a fucking army?'

'Never mind. You all right for drinks?'

'Yeah,' says Geoff. 'We just got 'em in.'

I dump my jacket on the back of a free chair and make my way to the bar. I buy a drink – shit bitter, given the illusion of substance by a thick nitro-keg head. Normally, I would resort to lager when faced with such a dismal choice, but this is my local, and a man shouldn't have to drink lager in his local. There are two other pubs in the village, and the Admiral is the worst of the three. We frequent it out of habit. We're ingrained in this place just like the dirt and the fag ash. None of us has ever suggested that we drink elsewhere.

I get back to our table and sit. The pub hums with Friday-night bitching and belching.

'They're taking over, the black cunts.'

'Aye, Barry, they're taking over.' Geoff nods with bland sympathy and rubs the back of his head as if he were polishing it. Immigration is one of Barry's favourite topics and I hear exactly this crap from him several times a week. His fleshy lips are shiny with spit and beer, and his face is red with alcohol and argument. Geoff, with his shaved head and impressive beer belly, looks like a lucky Buddha in jeans and T-shirt. At any rate, he is the centre of contentment around which Barry's fury can flow without meeting much resistance. Barry likes it that way.

'We should drop a fucking nuclear bomb on the lot of them.'

'A bit extreme that, Baz,' Geoff says amiably.

'Aye, it is, but they're extreme themselves, aren't they? It's what they understand.' Barry takes a big gulp of his beer, as if he's wetting his whistle, the better to continue a debate.

Geoff takes advantage of the pause to light another cigarette and then turns to me. 'Y'all right?'

'Aye, not bad, mate – just knackered.'

'Get that beer down you, then. You've catching up to do.'

'The point is, Geoff, they're all over there, chopping each other to pieces and fucking up their own countries, and then they want to come here and get a fucking hand-out. In the meantime, us three are working for a living, and what do we get for it?' Barry floats the question over the table as though he expects something profound in response.

'Fuck all, mate,' sighs Geoff.

'Exactly! Fuck. All.'

'Well,' I join in, 'it pays for the beer, like.'

Geoff snorts, but Barry looks at me as if I'm an idiot. 'Look, it's all right for you,' he huffs. 'You're free and single, but I've got a family to raise and this country is going to shit.'

I fail to see what raising a family has got to do with it – apart from the fact that Barry always wants to act as if he's older and wiser – but I just shrug and take a drink of beer. There is no point in stirring him up. Besides, I've got nothing to prove to Barry.

Geoff nudges me in the ribs. 'Here comes trouble.'

I glance over and groan. Sinister Steve – the local one-stop shop for anything knocked off or bootlegged – has slipped through the door. He looks at us. The pub is crowded, but Steve moves through the throng like smoke and arrives directly behind Barry. He taps him on the shoulder.

'Fucking hell!' Barry twists in his chair.

'All right, mate?'

'You fucking sneaky bastard. I almost dropped me pint.'

'Yeah, good evening to you too.' Steve nods at me and Geoff, then pulls over a stool and sits down next to Barry, too close. Barry stiffens slightly, but he stays still and lets Steve talk into the side of his face. I can't hear their conversation, but it doesn't last long before the pair of them get up and leave together. 'Back in a minute,' says Barry.

'What's that all about?' I ask Geoff.

'He's banned from selling fags in the pub, so he does it in the car park instead.'

'Right. Are you ready for another?'

'Aye.'

'Go on, then.'

'Fuck off, it's not even my round. Anyway, you both owe me for the lottery, and you're the worst – you're two fucking weeks behind. If we win, I'll keep it for myself.'

'All right, all right, calm down. It was worth a try.'

I go to the bar and buy another round. When I return to our table, Barry is back with two large cartons of cigarettes wrapped in a plastic bag.

'Got what you wanted, then.'

'No, I was hoping he'd have some frilly knickers in stock.'

'Well, we had our suspicions.' I lean over to put the drinks down, and as I do so, I get a whiff of something coming from Barry's direction. 'Have you stood in dog shit?'

'You what?'

'Something smells.'

Barry leans to one side and checks his feet. 'Fuck.'

'Is it?'

'Bollocks. I was only in the fucking car park.'

'Well, you'd better go back there.'

Barry shakes his head like a man who has become accustomed to having every noble principle crushed. 'Modern Britain, eh?' He lets it hang there, as if we all know exactly what is wrong with the world.

2

On the last day of Jim's almost-life, summer filled the village with a warmth that made men and women want to loll like cats. Old couples dragged dining chairs into their front yards and read the Sunday papers. They turned the pages with languor and exchanged soft commentary on the stories of the day, sometimes shuffling back inside to make tea, fetch a packet of biscuits, or spend a penny. Kids zipped past on bicycles and played football in the streets, and when they swore, the old folk glanced up and clucked. The kids played on. Jim walked past them all, head down, hoping not to be noticed.

At the end of the terrace, Jim turned left and tramped up the main road that led out of the village. He felt more free there, away from the houses, with no busybodies who might call out after him, 'How, Jim lad! What's in the bag?' Jim especially didn't want to run into his father. Jim's father thought that Jim was indoors, revising for the exams he desperately wanted Jim to pass because he never got the chance to take them himself. Jim was the only chance, because Jim was an only child.

He walked faster, and with each step his rucksack jogged and made a dull clunk. His T-shirt darkened at the armpits. The rucksack chafed his shoulders. Jim stuffed his thumbs under the straps to take off some of the weight, then leaned forward for a moment of relief. The rucksack slid up and smacked him in the back of the head.

'Fucking hell,' Jim hissed, and shook his head. 'The bastards had better be grateful for this.' He put his hands on his knees and stayed still, just breathing. Then a movement in the hedgerow entered his periphery and he turned his head to look.

There was a crane fly caught in a fragment of cobweb. Its legs were trapped, pulled together like those of a roped animal. Its wings were free, though, and they beat hard. The insect strained so much that Jim wondered if its legs would tear off. No spider came. The web must be old, Jim thought.

Jim looked between his legs, back down the road, to check that no one was watching him like this: bent double, staring into the hedge. The upside-down street was empty, except for some younger kids on roller skates trying to play street hockey with bamboo canes and an empty can. They weren't looking at him. Jim raised his head again to watch the crane fly; it struggled on. It would probably keep going until it dropped dead and twisted there in the breeze. Jim briefly considered freeing it, but why should he?

The hedgerow teemed with life: flies of different shapes and sizes, the odd bumblebee, caterpillars, butterflies, and wasps. There were a lot of wasps; perhaps there was a nest nearby. Jim hated wasps, hated the noise they made, their colour, their shape, and their bad-tempered sharpness. To be so close to them made his spine tingle. He chose to stay, though. He felt none of the blind panic that made his world blur and his body burst ahead of his thoughts when one buzzed him at head height or landed on his arm. Jim thought of a B-feature he saw at the pictures in which people dived with sharks. He felt like that.

One of the wasps floated closer to the crane fly and hovered there as if it too was a spectator. Suddenly, the wasp darted at the crane fly and mounted its back. The crane fly kept beating its wings and pulling against the web back and forth and side to side, so that the wasp seemed to be riding it in a desperate rodeo. Then the wasp arched its body into a crescent shape and jabbed its stinger into the crane fly over and over again. Jim held his breath. The crane fly was still fighting, but the wasp curled itself tighter, brought its hard black mandibles over the crane fly's head and chewed. The crane fly dropped, and for a moment both it and the wasp dangled on the end of the broken web. Then the wasp flew away.

'Predation,' Jim whispered to himself. 'Predation is the word.' He stood up. A car rattled past. Jim shuddered and walked on.

———

Geoff stood at the edge of the beck, where the water ran slow and green, and formed a long pool bedded with silt and rocks and clotted with pondweed. He turned a flat stone in the fingers of his right hand and looked across the water. Jim said that this pool was manmade, the header of an old millrace. Geoff didn't know what a millrace was, but he liked the sound of the word and the way the little fact nestled in his brain. He felt good under the sun, and as he wound back his arm, he knew that this would be a great throw.

'Are you watching?' he called out.

'Gerron with it, you fucking pansy,' Barry answered from behind him.

Geoff narrowed his eyes, breathed in, and whipped his arm forward. The stone flew out, oblique to the surface of the water, and then hit it in a dash of spray, burst up, came down, skipped again, and again, and again until it died out in a series of tiny bounces too rapid to count. Ripples spread over the pool.

'Five good ones,' announced Mac.

Geoff turned round and smiled at them.

Barry shook his head. 'You're a lucky bastard, you.'

'Nah, that was pure skill, that,' Geoff laughed. He felt the glow of an action performed smoothly and correctly. Barry opened his mouth to retort, but Mac broke in.

'Jim's here.'

Barry and Geoff turned to look down the path and there was Jim trudging towards them with a cloud of midges around his head. He glowered at them and swatted irritably at the insects with the back of his hand.

'Y'all right, Professor? You look a bit sweaty,' Barry said.

'Get fucked, Baz. Take this pack off us.' Jim wriggled out of his rucksack and let it thud to the ground, then he walked straight past them and sat under a tree.

'Temper, temper,' chided Barry, but he went over and picked up the rucksack anyway. 'Fucking hell, this is a bit heavy. How many's in here?'

'Twenty-four.' Jim gave a short snort of laughter. 'Joe had them all in plastic bags. He reckoned his arms were going to fall off.'

'He'd be a proper flid, then. Fucking loony.' Barry walked over to the tree with the rucksack.

'Leave it out – he's sound.'

'Oh, aye, sound as a pound,' said Barry, as he squatted next to Jim and fiddled with the straps of the rucksack. 'Can't fucking open it,' he grumbled.

'They'll be pulled tight from the weight. Give it here.' Mac took over and quickly got the rucksack open. He stuck his hand inside and with a look of religious contemplation withdrew a four-pack of lager, which he held above his head. 'All hail!'

Geoff giggled. Barry shook his head and chucked a stick at him. 'Shut up, you big div.'

Geoff caught the stick and dropped it. 'You're a proper cunt, you.'

Mac ignored them, twisted out the first can, and handed it to Jim. 'Nice work, Jim.'

'Thanks, Mac. There's fags in there too.' Jim smiled and opened the beer. He grimaced as he drank. 'It's a bit warm. We should put the rest in the water.'

'Good idea.' Mac grabbed the rucksack and slung it over one shoulder. Before he walked away, he nudged Barry in the side with his toe and said, 'Drink your beer and stop being a bastard.'

'Who elected you fucking president?'

Mac ignored him and took the rucksack to the pool, where he removed each of the five remaining four-packs one by one and carefully lowered them into the water. Barry glared at Mac's back for a little while and mouthed the word 'dickhead', but then did as he was told.

Geoff sat opposite Jim and opened his beer. 'So. GCSEs next week, Jim. Are you nervous?'

Barry grunted and said, 'I bet he's shitting himself, aren't you, Professor von Einstein?'

Jim turned to face Geoff so that he had his back to Barry. 'I'm prepared.' He paused and added, 'I think.'

'Aye, that's the best way.'

'Yeah.' Jim didn't really want to talk about it. Barry and Geoff were supposed to be in the same year as him, but they'd already given up on school and had no intention of turning up for their exams. It made him feel out of place. Still, it was better to have this conversation again than listen to Barry whinge, so Jim asked Geoff, 'What about you?'

'Still haven't found a fucking job yet. Mac reckons he knows a bloke, though. Building.' Geoff squeezed his can so that the sides crumpled in.

'That's not bad.'

'Aye. Mebbes.'

Jim drank his first beer quickly and retrieved another from the beck. The water hadn't made it any colder, but at least it wasn't any hotter. He opened it and sucked up the foam before it ran down the sides.

'Bring some over for us, mate,' said Mac.

'Yes, my lord.' Jim made a stiff little bow like a costume-drama butler, but Mac didn't even notice; he'd turned back to the others. Jim realized that he didn't have a clue what the three of them were talking about, because he'd spent the whole time thinking about his revision.

'Fucking hell. I need to get drunk,' he said to nobody in particular, and downed the whole can in seven big gulps. He tossed the empty into the bushes and helped himself to a new four-pack.

Jim handed the cans round and sat down again, poking at the earth with one end of a stick. Mac gave him a shove in the back. 'Jesus Christ, Jim lad. Relax.'

'I told you,' said Barry. 'He's fucking bricking it. I don't know why you bother, Jim. All this just to go to college and hang out with a bunch of fucking benders.'

Jim gave him a wink. 'You're right. I could stay here and hang out with benders, couldn't I, Baz?'

Geoff and Mac laughed. 'He's got you there!'

'Yer fucker,' said Barry, but he was laughing a little bit too, and it was good to see the bugger smile for a change.

Jim fell on his back, spread his arms, and let the sunlight pour over his face. 'It's all fucking mental, lads.'

'You're fucking mental.'

Another beer later and Jim felt drunk in the heat. They were talking about their dream motorcycles. Geoff wanted a Harley Davidson. Mac wanted some Jap superbike. Jim suggested Barry should stick to mopeds. Mac said, 'A moped? Are you mad? It's a pushbike he wants. You can't trust him with something motorized.'

'He needs stabilizers and all,' said Geoff.

'You're all cunts,' said Barry, and stumbled off for a piss.

They were listening to him splatter a tree trunk when a deep voice called from up the path, 'How, Baz! Is that you down there?'

Jim looked, but he couldn't make out who it was. 'Who's that?'

Barry reappeared, fiddling with his belt. 'Settle down – it's me brother.'

'Oh fucking hell.' Jim stuffed the beer can into the space between the small of his back and the trunk of the tree. Geoff took a huge gulp from his and then lobbed it away. The dregs spun out of the can and glittered in the sun.

Mac ran a few metres up the path for a better look and then scuttled back muttering fucks like a park-bench wino. 'Aye, it's Martin all right, and he's got that dickhead Gary Scruton with him.'

'He's all right,' said Barry.

'He fucking isn't. Hide your beer – they'll nick the lot if they cotton on.'

Barry just shrugged. Mac glared, ripped Barry's can from his hands, and tossed it into the undergrowth. Barry shook his head and then looked up as his brother drew close. Martin loomed over him and rapped him on the head with his knuckles, as if he were knocking on a door. Barry blinked twice and then stared into the ground.

'All right, shit for brains,' Martin said. 'Are you lot having a party or something?'

Jim looked up. It was difficult to see Martin's face because the afternoon sun was right behind him, but his size was evident. Martin was a big lad – as tall as Jim, but broader and stronger – and had a reputation as a scrapper. His hands rested, open and still, by his thighs. Jim could see black dirt engrained in the lines on his knuckles. The nail of his left ring finger was badly discoloured. There was a thin blue scar just above his wrist.

'Nah. We're just sitting around,' Mac spoke out.

'That's funny – there's a can of lager right there.' Mac's beer, unopened, lay in plain sight. Jim felt a hard knot of fear in his guts.

'We had some earlier. That one's left over.'

'You're too young to be drinking, you lot.' Martin squatted down and reached for the can. 'There's four of you. How come there was one left?'

'It's mine,' said Mac. 'I wasn't thirsty. You can have it if you want.'

Martin was already opening the beer. Mac looked down.

Now that Martin was squatting, Jim could see over his head. Gary skulked in the background with his hands stuffed in his pockets, and occasionally kicked out at the undergrowth. Jim wondered if he was looking for something.

'What's in the bag?' asked Martin quickly, and without waiting for an answer, he grabbed one of the rucksack's straps and dragged it over. He pulled the top open and looked in. Jim's leg twitched. 'Fags. Brilliant. I've run out. Do you mind?' Martin took a cigarette, produced a lighter from his pocket, and lit up. He exhaled through his nose and tipped his head back. 'Thanks, lads.'

Gary got closer to the water's edge. Jim closed his eyes.

'Here, Martin, the fucking beck is full of lager.'

'Look, just fuck off, will you.' Mac burst to his feet and began to stride towards Gary, but Martin stuck out his leg. Mac tripped and fell headlong.

'Watch where you're walking, mate,' said Martin casually.

'Look at this.' Gary was walking back towards them, with a dripping can of lager clenched in his fist.

Mac pushed himself up onto one knee and looked Gary in the eye. 'Get off 'em, you cunt.'

'What did you call me?'

'You fucking heard,' hissed Mac, and got to his feet.

'OK,' said Gary with a smile. 'I'll get off 'em.' Then he brought up his arm, twisted his body, and threw the full can of lager straight into Mac's face.

The can exploded in a shower of foam and Mac's head flicked back on his shoulders. He weaved for a moment, then his legs went and he fell to his hands and knees. Blood poured down his face.

There was silence.

'Fucking hell, Gary,' Martin breathed.

Jim glanced at the other two. Barry was looking away; Geoff was plain rigid with fear. Jim stood up.

'Do you want some?' said Gary.

Jim cocked his head as if he were considering this and then said to Martin, 'Is your mate offering me a blowjob? I didn't realize he was that way inclined.'

'You little fucker.' And Gary rushed at him.

Jim ducked and slipped under Gary's reach. Gary skidded into a turn and Jim danced backwards and away. He felt bright and fast. 'Come on, sweetheart,' he cooed. 'If you catch me, you can bum me.'

Now Gary roared out loud and came on like a bull. Jim dodged him again. Gary just managed to stop himself from running into the beck; his feet skittered dust and stones into the water. Gary turned, but this time Jim didn't skip away. He was waiting with his best straight right – the one he'd seen in all the western saloon brawls – and he unwound it straight into Gary's head.

Gary splashed down hard on his back in the shallow water and there was a loud crack from somewhere. Jim was shouting now, 'Have that! Have that, you fucker!' He walked into the water and stood over Gary, and saw the smoky cloud of blood gather around Gary's head. It billowed and ribboned out down the stream. Gary shuddered and twitched, and finally someone was shouting, 'Get an ambulance! Get an ambulance!'

3

OCTOBER 2004

I step out of my door. The day is clear but cold. I need a coat. I lay my tool bag on the step and go back inside. In the kitchen, the light is murky, diffused through the blinds I haven't opened. I can't see my jacket slung over the back of any chairs or lying on the floor, so I pick my way to the cupboard under the stairs and fumble inside for the light switch. The light comes on, uncomfortably bright, and as my vision returns, I see my jacket hanging limply on its hook. I grab it, slap off the light switch with the flat of my hand, and leave the house.

Standing on the step, I pull on the jacket and heft up my battered and over-full tool bag. For the job in hand, I don't need all this stuff, but it's better to be prepared in case you discover some problem, or fuck up and have to repair your own mistake. And there's always plenty to do at Mrs Joe's house. I didn't enlist for this responsibility, and I don't do it out of the goodness of my heart. I inherited it from my father. Carrying on the good work is the only thing I can do for him now.

At the kerb, I stop by the car. The wing mirror is askew; probably some drunk walked into it on his way home last night. I consider twisting it back into position, but am overcome by the futility of the gesture. Anyway, I decide to walk.

We call this place a village, but it could just as easily be a small town. The main road cuts right through from west to east and the village follows it, long and thin, as two parallel lines of redbrick houses broken here and there with convenience stores, newsagents, and takeaways. There is no real centre, but the library and the post office are next door to each other, so I suppose that counts as one. If you were driving through on your way to somewhere else, that's pretty much all you would see, except for the park.

Behind the road, on either side, there are terraced rows of old tied housing, built a century ago for the men who worked the now long-gone mine. Those streets are narrow, and when you walk down them, the houses loom in and you feel almost as if you are underground. We all grew up in these terraces – Geoff and Mac next door to each other, and Barry and me on the two streets either side of theirs – but none of us lives there now. Mac doesn't even live in the village anymore. We never see him these days.

Then there are the two council estates, one on either side of the village. I live in the one to the south. They were built in the 1960s, when the local factories and engineering firms were still in business. A good one-third of these houses are boarded up now, sheets of metal over the windows and doors. The council estates and the terraces blend into each other at the edges, but the modern developments – of which there are three or four – stand apart by design. They're turned in on themselves – all closes and cul-de-sacs – as enclaves of relative wealth for people like Barry and Geoff who have trades, and the others who do God knows what desk jobs in Teesside, Sunderland, and Newcastle. Maybe I would live in one of those houses now, if it hadn't been for the conviction. More likely, though, I would be miles from here.

But here I am, and there's a quality in the light today. Every object seems precisely defined as if embossed on the world: mountain ash, rhododendron, iron railings, paving slabs, chip trays, dog shit. I tramp past it all, out of the estate and along the main road, where cars glide past me, breaking up the morning sun and throwing it back in glints of silver. A bus thunders by, leaving me and a gap-toothed parade of shops in its sooty wake. Twice I have to veer round pools of last night's vomit, splattered on the flags.

I fork off at the lane, into relative peace. Some modern houses back onto it with their panel fences, but it is a half-hearted encroachment, and after a while they stop abruptly where the scrubby grazing begins. A pair of stocky horses stand quite still. The lane bends, bridging a beck to run parallel to the old train line. A hedge shadows the road, so here and there the potholes still have a sugar-pane of ice. My arm aches from carrying the tool bag.

Mrs Joe's house is at the end of an isolated terrace of railway cottages. Of course, there was once a station nearby, but this is now nothing more than some suggestive bumps in a field where sheep graze. The houses are Victorian, well built, and must be worth quite a bit. I'm sure Mrs Joe knows this, but I'm equally sure that she doesn't care.

I go round the back and knock. There's a shuffling from within. After some time, during which I studiously avoid noticing that the wall is water-damaged and needs repointing, Mrs Joe opens up.

'Morning. I've come to fix that lino for you.'

'Come in, son.' Mrs Joe smiles tiredly.

There are breakfast smells in her kitchen, but the evidence has been cleared away. There is no sign of neglect in her housekeeping. The offending linoleum curls up in the corner of the room. I hope that no damp has spread under the rest of it.

'Would you like a cup of tea?'

'Not yet. I'll get to work first.' I kneel and begin to peel back the lino, which comes away with unhappy ease. Clearly it is completely fucked and there's barely any point in trying to stick it down again. 'How are you?' I ask Mrs Joe.

29

'Oh, fine apart from the usual complaints.'

'Joe not here?'

'He's gone out walking.'

It was a pointless question: Joe plods the local footpaths for hours every day. Maybe he has a plan – a timetable of routes that he follows – but it's not one I've ever fathomed. He just appears here, there, or anywhere – shoulders hunched, hands thrust into coat pockets. He has been this way for as long as I can remember. Once, people would recognize him and give him the odd wave or very occasional jeer, but these days, nobody knows him. Perhaps they assume he's a tramp.

I fold the loose lino all the way over on itself and weigh it down with my tool bag. Mrs Joe stands at the other side of the room, watching me. 'Is it bad?'

'Aye. We'll just have to do our best.'

'You sound like your father. "Do our best." That's what he always said.'

I rummage in my tool bag for a scraper with which to remove some of the old adhesive.

'He used to do bits for me too, you know, after my Johnny died.'

'Aye, I know.'

'That's right, you came with him sometimes.'

'I did,' I say, and feel as if I've been shown a photograph of myself that I don't remember posing for. 'It was a long time ago.'

'It only seems that way to you.' She stands there, one claw-like hand resting on the work surface, and looks down at me. She probably remembers a lot of things.

Mrs Joe was almost a surrogate mother to my father. He had no parents of his own, or any other family. He grew up in a children's home, and when that was over, he got a job as a trainee welder, where Johnny – Mrs Joe's husband – was his foreman. One day, Johnny cottoned on that my dad had no tea to go home to and brought him here. It was because of this relationship that my dad eventually moved to the village, where he met my mother. I suppose I have Mrs Joe's cooking to thank for my existence.

Of course, this was back in the 1960s, before Johnny died, when Mrs Joe was just Mrs Sally Briggs. Before there was nothing left to define her life but her idiot son.

I turn back to my work, but the scraper proves ineffectual. I need solvent. It doesn't really matter. The lino, like almost everything else in this house, is well past it. There is no point in sticking it down again, but there's equally no point in replacing it. Mrs Joe is old, can't afford it, and in a couple of years this house will be occupied by some Audi driver who will put tiles down anyway. Best bodge it, then. I am prepared for this eventuality – I pull out a tube of strong glue I nicked from work a few weeks ago and hack off the nozzle with my knife.

'Is that special lino glue?'

'Er…not really, Mrs Joe. It's…all purpose.'

'Is it going to work?'

Of course it's going to work. I pity the poor bastard who has to scrape this shite off.

'Aye, there's no doubt about that. You sometimes have to be a bit creative when you're dealing with the older houses.' I try to sound like I know my stuff as I ram the tube into my caulk gun with authority.

'Not everything in here's shagged out, son.'

I feel the tight heat of a smile like the first crease across dried-out Monday-morning boot leather. 'Oh, aye, there's plenty of life in the old place yet.'

'Don't you forget it.'

'No danger of that, Mrs Joe.'

I twist to face her again; she looks less tired now. She smiles back at me. 'Well, you're better mannered than he was, despite it all.'

'Who?'

'Your dad.'

'Oh.'

'You look like him.'

'What?'

'You do.'

Her eyes are focused elsewhere. I realize that she is seeing something in the past as if there were nothing between then and now. I have to turn away from her and stare at the exposed floor. A white slug lands right in front of me with a faint *putt*. Glue. I glance at the caulk gun in my right hand. I must have squeezed the handle; the stuff oozes from the nozzle like thick, plastic toothpaste. The spot on the floor resolves itself into a shallow dome the size of a tuppence and I feel stupid.

'Yeah, I know.'

She is quiet now. In my hand, a longing stirs at the fingers and ripples up my arm, in one of those strange urges for a cigarette that suddenly come from nowhere even though I gave up two years ago. It was the best thing I ever did.

———

After her moment of reverie, Mrs Joe went and sat in the living room while I stuck down the lino. In the end, it didn't take me very long, but when I looked in on her, she was asleep. So much for my cup of tea. There was no sign of Joe and I left quietly, but I didn't want to go home, so I left my bag just inside the gate and set off the wrong way.

I tramp over the fields. This path is familiar to me, but it must be years since I last walked along it. I'm not a big walker, and I don't have any of the other reasons – a dog, someone to walk with, or a place at the other end where I need to be – so I've never really been out here again. When we were kids, though, me, Geoff, Barry, and Mac used to play out here all the time. At least, that's the way I remember it.

The field is pasture and a little boggy, so I can see footprints on the path. I didn't come looking for solitude, or even expect it, but the evidence of human activity hauls me into the present. The cold wind blusters around my face and cuts through my jeans. Two fields ahead of me looms a large stand of trees, and I see that although I set off with no particular destination in mind, I am walking to the ponds. I stop. From horizon to horizon unbroken grey cloud flows across the sky, but I feel that it will not rain, so instead of turning back, I carry on.

It doesn't take me long to cover the distance to the copse. I follow the path through the trees and then I'm there. The surface of the water is covered in dead leaves; sycamore and oak spread out flat and slick in an oily yellow skin. Even with this wind the place smells strongly of their decay. Surrounded by bare trees, all the omens are of death, but I know that really the pond is alive; I used to come here as a kid to collect frogspawn.

Through a break in the leaves, I see that there is something in the water: a bicycle. I can't understand how or why anyone brought a bike out here. Any way you come you'd have to lift it over stiles, ride across broken ground; it would be quicker to walk. I move the leaves away with a stick. It's a child's bike and the story becomes obvious: nicked from a smaller kid and dumped when it wasn't funny anymore. I wonder if I could get it out of there and I stretch out further with the stick, but I can't quite reach it.

'What are you doing?'

Words from behind me. I almost lose my balance and plunge into the water, but manage to drop the stick and flap my arms until I can stand up straight. I turn round and it's Laura, Geoff's wife, with her ash-blonde hair whipping in the wind.

'Uh…there's a bike in the water.'

'It's been there for ages.'

'Oh. Really?'

'I see it every time I come down here. God knows what else is in there. It's kids, isn't it?' She shrugs and looks at me with her head cocked to one side. I notice that she's properly dressed – stout shoes, fleece jacket – and quite clearly came out for the specific purpose of 'taking a walk'.

'Is Geoff with you?'

'It's Saturday morning. He's on the sofa watching cartoons and nursing his hangover.'

'Oh. OK. You're just having a walk?'

'Yep.'

'Your usual route?'

'Well, it's the closest thing to a beauty spot there is around here. Are you going to interrogate me all morning?'

'No, sorry. Just surprised to see anyone, that's all.' In the distance I hear the faint crack of an air rifle – probably someone after rabbits. 'Sounds like we're not the only ones, though.'

She starts to walk along the path and passes me – closely – as if she expects me to fall into step beside her. Without thinking I do just that and we amble alongside the edge of the pond. It's not a big body of water, but it's big enough to take a few minutes to get round, and she's walking slowly.

'What's your excuse, anyway?'

'What?'

'For being out here. Geoff says you don't do anything except read and go to the pub.'

'Yeah, well.' I look over the water for a few moments. 'I just felt like being outside for a while. I used to come here when I was little.'

Another long pause, during which she stops and sits on a stump. She looks up at me, actually fixes me with her gaze. 'Were you reminiscing?'

34

'I try not to.'

She laughs and her smile is wide and bright. 'We don't see much of you.'

'I don't think Geoff considers me house-trained.'

She shifts over and gestures me towards her. 'Sit down.' The stump is big enough for two and I am careful to leave space between us, but then she reaches out and touches my arm. 'It would have been easier for you just to tell him, in the long run I mean.'

'It wasn't the right thing to do.'

'But you didn't know that then. You didn't really know me.'

'I could just tell.'

'Thank you, anyway.'

'You don't need to thank me. You don't owe me anything.'

I look into her face. I always thought her eyes were green, but now I can see that they contain flecks of brown. A gust of wind and a few of the last leaves give up and are carried away.

'I'll leave you to it, then,' she says.

'Yeah.'

Suddenly, she leans over and kisses me on the forehead – just above my eye, right on my scar – rough and tender at the same time. Then she gets up and walks away, quickly, without another word. Soon she disappears beneath the trees. I feel a vague breath of regret under my sternum; I wonder what it would be like to have someone I could talk to about anything I wanted. Laura is the worst possible choice, though, and anyway, that's all bollocks: a problem shared is a problem doubled.

I kick out at the ground and turn up a stone. I bend down and pick it up. It's muddy, but what does that matter? I straighten my body and aim for the water, then see movement on the other side of the pond: a man, with a rifle and a satchel. He hurries away, but I recognize his walk and his lank black hair.

'Steve!'

He doesn't hear me, and I can't catch up with him from here even if I wanted to. The shifty bugger probably couldn't see who I was and decided to scarper for fear of getting caught shooting where he shouldn't. I throw the stone. It hits the water with a satisfying splash.

4

FEBRUARY 1996

Barry was waiting outside the prison just as he'd promised, and when Jim walked over, he opened the car door for him.

'All right?'

'Aye, I'm all right.' Jim paused and looked at Barry, who didn't move but looked straight back.

'Get in, then, unless you want to hang about here.'

'No. No, let's go.'

When Jim was seated, Barry closed the door on him and walked round to the driver's side. Jim watched him through the windscreen; as he passed, he dragged his fingertips across the bonnet. Then he got in and started the engine.

'It's not mine. I've borrowed it for the day.'

'Right.'

'We're buying a van, like. For work.'

Jim nodded and looked out of his window. Barry reversed out of the parking space and they drove off.

When they got onto the dual carriageway, Jim began to take notice of the road signs because they weren't right. They didn't point home, to the village.

'Are you taking me to Middlesbrough?'

'Aye.' Barry kept his eyes on the road.

'Why?' Jim felt suspicious. If he had allowed himself to imagine anything, this would not have been it.

Barry smiled thinly. 'You'll see.'

'For fuck's sake, Baz, I've only been out for twenty minutes. Can we not just go to the pub?'

'There's plenty of time for that.'

Jim felt uneasy. The heater was on in the car and the air was close. The jeans they had given him didn't fit properly – too tight on the thighs. Barry smelled of aftershave. Jim started to feel carsick.

'Stop. I'm going to throw up.'

On the hard shoulder, Barry didn't stay in the car, but got out and stood almost near enough to Jim to have his shoes splashed. Jim disgorged his breakfast in a long stream, and when he was done, he hooked his tongue through his mouth to pick up the pieces of half-digested food and spat them into the grass. Some of the sick was in his nose and he dislodged it with a hard snort; the chunks spidered to the ground in a thread of mucus. Jim watched them fall, then wiped his mouth and stood up.

The traffic hurtled past them. The air-wash of the trucks was strong and it made the car rock on its suspension. Jim looked around. There was just the road, the embankment, and then, probably, fields.

'Are you finished?'

'Yeah. What the fuck are we doing?'

'Trust us.'

Barry turned to walk round the car, and Jim shouted after him, 'But I don't fucking trust you!'

Barry spun back to Jim and threw his arms out to the side. 'What else have you got? Are you going to stand here? Are you going to walk home?' Jim couldn't answer. They faced each other, like that, at the side of the road until Barry spoke again, calm this time. 'Get in the car, man,' and Jim did.

———

Later, they sat in a café on Linthorpe Road, and Jim could see people everywhere, just doing things: walking, shopping, eating, drinking. Eventually, he had to stare at the Formica tabletop so Barry wouldn't see that his head was spinning. It was the women, mainly. Jim knew that he was supposed to find them attractive, but he wasn't prepared for the colours of their make-up. He thought they looked like Chinese dragons. Nothing had seemed this vivid on his pre-release outings, but now there were no limits.

Jim realized that his right leg was jiggling and he tensed the muscles, clamped his heel to the floor. He wanted to turn over the table, grab Barry by the shoulders, and scream into his face, 'What are we doing here? Take me home!' but he knew he had to ride it out, humour Barry, because without him he was stuck: no lift, nowhere to stay. He shredded a napkin.

Food arrived, and tea in a big stainless-steel pot. Barry had ordered them a fry-up each, without even asking Jim what he wanted. Barry tucked in. Jim watched him chew.

'Howay, get that down you.'

Jim sawed off a piece of sausage and put it into his mouth. He held it between his teeth for a few moments before he could work up the will to bite down, but then he got going and it calmed him.

They were half-way through before Barry spoke again. 'I'm sorry about your parents.'

Jim shrugged, tried to keep eating.

'Your mam especially. It wasn't fair.'

'It was just cancer, Barry. It could have happened to anyone.'

'Are you angry with your dad?'

'For killing himself?'

'Yeah.'

'No. He's dead. What's the point? Can I just eat in peace?'

'Suit yourself.'

The food wasn't going down well now, though, so he pushed the plate away. 'I can't afford to eat out, Barry. The money they gave me, it's fuck all.'

'Don't worry.' Barry looked sly. 'I'll take it out of your wages.'

'What wages?'

'There's loads of work on at the moment. Me and Geoff could do with another pair of hands.'

Jim started to feel the dizzy anger again. He didn't understand what was going on. 'What?'

'Well, you'll need a job, and we're your mates. It just makes sense.'

'Don't fuck me around, Baz. I don't know anything about bricklaying.'

'You don't have to know anything. We just need a labourer. Think about it. We've got loads of work. You'd be well sorted.' Barry spoke casually, but his eyes were fixed on Jim. Jim stared at the tabletop and pushed grains of salt around with his fingernail. Barry watched for a few seconds and then asked, 'What else are you going to do for money?'

Jim muttered, 'I don't know,' and he really didn't. He had no plan at all.

Barry spread his hands and said, 'Well then,' as if it was all settled.

Jim looked up and couldn't find any comfort in Barry's smile.

———

Back in the car, Barry chatted at Jim and told him things he already knew from Barry and Geoff's occasional visits – that he didn't have to worry about the Scrutons because they'd moved away, that Martin was with a different crowd now and had no interest in opening old wounds, that Geoff still lived with his parents and was fatter than ever, that Mac 'the gobshite' was in Spain building hotels, that Barry couldn't understand how the council had buggered up Jim's housing, because no fucker else wanted to live in the village anymore.

'Thanks for letting me stay with you,' Jim managed to say. 'They might have kept me in otherwise.'

'Least I could do. But tread carefully, 'cos wor lass is pregnant and that pisses them off.'

'Congratulations.'

Barry just sniffed. 'Stupid cunt messed up her pills.'

'Oh.'

'Never mind. It has to happen sooner or later,' Barry said with a sigh, and fumbled to light a cigarette. He took a couple of heavy drags and wound down the window. 'Look, have you heard from your uncle?'

'No. You saw him at mam's funeral. He wouldn't even look at me. Thought it was my fault. You know, that she didn't have the strength to beat it.'

Barry nodded, thin-lipped. 'So he didn't tell you.'

'Tell me what?'

'He packed up, Jim. Took his family to live in Australia. They're gone.'

'Right. I see.'

So that was it. Jim did not have a single blood relative left to call on. And he saw what Barry had really meant by 'What else have you got?' Then, as if he were reading Jim's thoughts, Barry said, 'Don't worry – me and Geoff will look after you.'

Still Barry did not take Jim home. Instead, they drove deep into a grid of terraced houses just outside the centre of Middlesbrough. 'You should get yourself a woman: it helps calm you down. You could do with a bit of calming down,' Barry said.

Jim ignored him. He let his head loll over the back of the car seat and stared at the roof, but then Barry was braking, veering to the right, and winding down the window all at the same time. Jim looked to see. The car drew level with a black man who was walking down the street. Barry took a last, deep drag of his cigarette and flicked it hard out of the window. It hit the man in the side of the face. Barry sped up again and through a cloud of smoke said, 'Fucking niggers. We're being over-run.'

Jim scrambled to look out of the rear screen; the man was staring after them, with his hand to his face. Then they turned a corner, and Jim slid back into his seat. 'Are you trying to get me sent down again?'

'Relax.'

'Don't fucking tell me to relax. Where are we going?'

'You've never had sex before, have you?'

Jim twisted in his seat. 'Are you looking for a smack in the mouth?'

'All right, all right. I'm just making conversation.'

'I don't want a fucking conversation.'

'Aye, I can see that. Anyway, we're here.' Barry pulled over and turned off the ignition.

It was just a narrow, terraced street, identical to the ones they'd been driving through. Some of the houses were boarded up, others were obviously lived in, and the rest fell somewhere in between. Here and there the road revealed great patches of cobbles where the tarmac had broken up. The lamppost at the corner listed dangerously, and about four feet up it in white marker someone had scrawled, 'NF.'

'This is a fucking shithole. Why are we here?'

'She's waiting for you,' said Barry.

'Who?'

'In there.' Barry nodded at the house they were parked outside. The paint on the door was blistered; the brown curtains were drawn; the downstairs window was broken at the corner and patched with cardboard and electrician's tape.

Jim felt the sickness return, and with it realization. 'Have you paid a prostitute?'

Barry smiled. 'No money has changed hands. I've just called in a favour.'

'I'm not doing this.'

'Don't be stupid. Every man needs to fuck and you've waited longer than most.'

Jim was still and silent for a moment. He thought of the women on the street and in the café, the hairspray and eye shadow, and the plump waitress with her top buttons undone and her tits cupped in a red bra. Then he scrambled for his seatbelt. 'Fine, I'll do it. Satisfied?'

'Good lad.' Barry grabbed Jim's arm. 'Look, you're not going to regret this, take it from me. Don't let the state of the house put you off – she's a good-looking young lass.'

Jim could tell that Barry wasn't lying about this, at least, so he just nodded and got out of the car. He stood on the pavement for a little while and breathed fresh air until he heard Barry's muffled voice behind him. 'Go in!' Jim walked to the door and opened it.

There was darkness and a strong odour of damp. Jim saw that he was at the bottom of a staircase and that there was a door immediately to his left. It was very quiet. He went through the door and found himself in what might have been a living room. There was a little more light there. It came through the curtains, and from inside Jim could see that they were made of sacking. At the back of the room was another doorway, slightly ajar. The only furniture was a broken-down sofa covered with a twisted heap of blankets.

'Is that him?' a man's voice came from the room behind the door. He sounded sharp and angry. Jim lifted his hands, ready to make fists.

'What?' A low voice was there in the room with him. Then movement, and what Jim had thought were just blankets on the sofa resolved themselves into a person. Jim could only see half her face, the other half was covered by her hair. She squinted at him for a few moments, and then whatever fear or curiosity had motivated her to move seemed to slide away and she sank back into the cushions without saying another word.

'Ignore them. You're looking for me.' Another voice.

Jim turned round. It was a young woman. She wore a thin dressing gown. She had blonde hair and was barefoot. Jim had never seen a prostitute before, and despite what Barry had said, he'd expected someone older. He didn't know what to do, or even how to speak to her.

'Follow me.' It didn't occur to Jim not to obey her, and she led him upstairs and into a bedroom. It was fresher and lighter than downstairs. The sheets looked almost clean.

'Sit down and get ready. I'll be back in a minute.' Then she disappeared, closed the door behind her.

Jim was alone in the room. He sat on the edge of the bed. What did 'get ready' mean? He thumped his leg. 'This is fucking ridiculous.'

After a few minutes, she came back, raised an eyebrow at him. 'Are you going to get undressed?'

There was nothing to say, so he did it. Then she dropped her dressing gown and she was naked. She climbed onto the bed with him. Jim grabbed a fistful of sheets. Her hands were very cold.

———

'Jesus Christ!' Barry tapped the clock on the dashboard. 'I expected you to be in and out within ten minutes. What the fuck did you do to her?'

Jim shrugged.

'You didn't ask her to talk, did you?'

'No.'

44

'Good. How do you feel?'

'Just drive, would you.'

'Suit yourself.'

They drove in silence for a few minutes, until Barry punched Jim on the shoulder. 'You're not feeling guilty, are you? You'd better not have caught fucking religion.'

'Of course I haven't.'

'Well then, smile, you twat. You're a man now.'

'I didn't ask her what her name was.'

'Does it matter?'

Jim shrugged again.

'She wouldn't have told you her real name anyway.'

'Right.'

'Look, do you want this job or not?'

'Aye. All right, then.'

'That's the spirit. Let's get you home and get you drunk.'

5

Jim slept badly and his dreams were weird. They jolted him awake in the early hours and he couldn't sleep again. He'd get up and clean, read, smoke, do press-ups – anything to clear his head – and in the morning he went to work.

Work was where he lost himself. Work and drinking after work. Jim took to it. He wasn't skilled like Barry or Geoff, but he was strong and reliable, and he could handle the labour. Barry was the leader now. He bullied and cajoled the other two and usually got his own way. Geoff and Jim just got on with the job. Now and again, Jim would catch Barry watching him as he humped buckets of mortar or swept up. Barry looked satisfied. Jim didn't care anymore.

Out in the village, Jim kept his head down and tried to ignore the human shapes that flickered in his peripheral vision. Even so, he couldn't help finding himself face to face with people he used to know. Geoff's family looked right through him; they blamed him for getting 'their boy' involved in all that 'nastiness'. His old neighbours smiled sadly. Barry's big brother, Martin, gave him one solemn nod and never acknowledged him again. It was always hate or pity, and Jim didn't want either. One day in the pub, though, Mac's dad said, 'Welcome home, son.' Jim accepted a pint.

Old school friends were the worst: they asked Jim questions, but he didn't want to talk about any of it. Some of them had good jobs, a few were starting families, and one or two had even been to university. Sometimes when they talked to him, Jim felt anger welling like hot vomit in his throat and he had to turn on his heel and walk away before a fight happened. Eventually, he shaved his head and then fewer people recognized him. And that was better.

When he talked to his probation officer, Jim smiled nicely and told him everything was going well.

That summer, Jim passed his driving test and bought an old car. He opened his UK road atlas and looked at the country. It was all made of places that he'd never visited. He thought about going somewhere, Scotland maybe. He planned a route and he could imagine himself driving it, but after that all he could see were the things that might go wrong. Truth was, he had no idea where to start. No idea how to find rooms, or campsites, or any of the other things he would have to arrange. Christ, he'd barely managed to arrange furniture for the house: one dining table, two dining chairs, and a sagging armchair were the best he could do. Upstairs, he was still sleeping on a mattress on the floor. His mother would have called the place 'a bloody shambles' and told him to pull his socks up.

Worst of all, if he went away, he would be alone. Alone in all those places where everyone else would be together. Jim closed the atlas and went out for a walk.

————

Later, Jim was walking across the park when he saw a familiar figure coming his way. Jim stopped and smiled. The surprise of smiling made him smile even more. At first, the man didn't see Jim, because he was staring at the ground. The day was warm

– Jim was in his shirtsleeves – but the man was wearing a duffel coat, buttoned up all the way. He still hadn't seen Jim, but then he looked up and stopped too. They faced each other for a few seconds.

'Joe!'

'Howdy, partner.'

'"Howdy, partner"? It's been years! How are you?' Jim felt a bizarre urge to hug Joe, but fought it and put his hands in his pockets for good measure.

'I'm magnificent.'

'I'm glad to hear it. Have you been hiding? I haven't seen you at all.'

'No. I've seen you. You didn't notice me.'

'Shit. I'm sorry, Joe. I've had my blinkers on.'

'Your what?'

'Since I got out. Eyes front. I only see in corridors.'

'But we're in the park.'

Jim laughed. 'Yeah, we're in the park. So how's your mam getting on? Are you still up at that house?'

'Aye. She says it's falling down around our ears.'

'It can't be that bad.'

Joe looked at his toes. 'I'm going back now. Do you want to come for a cup of tea?'

Jim scratched the back of his head and sighed. 'I don't think your mam would be glad to see me, Joe.'

'She won't mind.'

'Another time maybe.'

'Suit yourself. See you later, alligator.'

Jim watched Joe shuffle away, across the park and down the road. He hadn't changed a bit. 'Daft bugger,' Jim muttered to himself, but he was still smiling.

———

One Friday night shortly afterwards, Geoff, Jim, and Barry went out together. It was one of their 'big nights'. Usually they just went to the Admiral, but now and again they went into town and did a proper bar crawl. They caught a bus – nobody wanted to be the driver – and sat on the top deck. Jim looked out of the window and watched fields and villages trundle past as the other two chatted. He was nervous. Going out like this always made him feel anxious; all those people chatting and dancing and flirting and he had no idea at all how to join in. It was ridiculous; he was with *Geoff and Barry*. They were the same age. They'd grown up together. Jim had known the pair of them for longer than he could remember: he should feel comfortable in a pub with these men. They should be mates, out having fun together, but Jim felt like the Tin Man. Some clanking monstrosity. He thought he looked foolish to everyone, and warmed up only after a few drinks. Then he enjoyed himself, until oblivion set in.

Barry poked him. 'Brighten up, Jim. You'll pull no birds with that face on.'

Jim wished for a tart comeback but just said, 'Don't worry about me.'

'Aye,' said Geoff. 'Tonight'll be your lucky night. Finally.'

'Piss off,' said Jim.

The other two laughed at him.

When they eventually arrived, they found that the pubs were full way beyond the usual Friday-night crowds. Barry identified the problem immediately.

'Fucking students,' he said.

'They'll have finished their finals,' said Jim. 'It's that time of year.'

'They're a bunch of cunts at any time of year.'

Jim went to the bar and found it at least four deep for its entire length. It was only eight o'clock and the floor was already slippy with spilled drink. He was crammed in with a group of girls in tiny skirts. He winced as his elbows unavoidably collided with their tits, but they didn't even notice. He smiled at one of them and she smiled back. Then she turned away, but it was better than a kick in the balls and it gave him a kind of hope.

He bought bottled beer, because there was no way he'd get back to the others with pints intact. As he turned away from the bar, though, one of the girls stepped into him and knocked the bottles out of his hands. They hit the floor, rebounded like skittles, and sent up a triple fountain of foam. The girl danced out of the way, but Jim caught a jet of beer all up the leg of his jeans.

'Sorry,' she mouthed, with outspread hands.

Jim just looked at her. He had nothing to say; he was still in the blank, calm time before emotions respond to events. She slipped away and he lost sight of her in the crowd. It was the same girl who'd smiled at him earlier.

'How, watch what you're doing. You've fucking soaked me.' Some lad, shouting in Jim's ear. Jim gave the lad a brief glance and without thinking about it reached out and shoved him off his feet.

Geoff appeared beside Jim, linked arms with him, and steered him towards the exit. 'Let's go somewhere else. It's too busy in here anyway.'

They emerged onto the pavement under the summer evening sun and Barry was already there, waiting. Jim looked at his jeans and said, 'I'm all wet.'

'Let's get some tinnies and sit in the park for a while. You'll soon dry off,' said Geoff.

Barry marched off ahead of them, setting the pace, eager to get out of the area. Geoff walked next to Jim and said, 'You need to settle down, mate. You can't keep doing things like that.'

Jim ground his teeth. 'Fuck that. You saw that bloke. He was looking to start something.'

'You have to let these things go, Jim.'

Jim turned and stopped right in front of Geoff. 'Look at this.' He pointed to the scar bisecting his eyebrow. 'This is what you get when you don't stand up for yourself. It was my first week inside and someone had a point to prove. I was so scared I just stood there and let him do it. I never let it happen again, and I'm not going to start now.'

'It's different out here. You're not in prison anymore, and I don't want to see you go back there. You need to leave all that stuff behind.'

Jim stuffed his hands into his pockets and looked at the ground.

'Come on, Jim. It's over now.'

'Thanks. I'll bear that in mind.'

———

Later that evening, they'd all had a lot to drink, and they were in a club. Jim leaned against the bar and watched as Geoff danced self-consciously. He was trying to bump 'n' grind with the girls, most of whom looked horrified and quickly left his vicinity. Eventually, he found a fat bird who didn't mind his attentions and soon they were frotting in a corner.

Barry was propped up next to Jim, insensible with drink. He still had a pint gripped in his hand and looked like he was trying to climb into the glass headfirst.

'It always ends up like this,' Jim muttered to himself. He thought glumly of the cost of the taxi home, and decided to drink more to take the edge off it. Then he became dimly aware of a tugging at his sleeve.

Jim looked round and blinked, trying to focus on the face in front of him. He was drunker than he had thought.

'Hello. It's me.' It was a girl. She was shouting to be heard over the music.

'What?' Jim leaned into her so that they were ear to mouth. She smelled of perfume and vodka.

'I spilled your drinks. I'm sorry.'

Jim squinted at her. He recognized her now and tried to smile. She tried to smile back. She was supporting herself with one hand against the bar. 'It's all right,' he yelled. 'I'm dry now.'

She motioned towards the dance floor and took him by the hand.

———

Later, Jim would be unable to remember how they got to her house or even what her name was. He woke up at dawn, huddled in a bus stop, with a vague sense that something unpleasant had happened. There was vomit on his jeans that he knew wasn't his own. He looked at the timetable; he could get a bus home.

When the bus arrived, the driver looked at Jim sceptically. 'Rough night?'

Jim just paid and went and lay down on the back seat. There was hardly anyone else aboard, and the thrum of the engines lulled him back into a drunken doze.

When he got home, he went straight for a piss and saw himself in the bathroom mirror. There was a mark under his eye. Not quite a bruise, but something or someone had definitely hit him there. Then he remembered the girl throwing him out of the flat.

'Fuck,' he said, and sat down on the toilet seat. Had they had sex? They must have. Mustn't they? He remembered seeing her naked. He'd said something funny about her nipples and she'd laughed. But then later, she was angry with him, and Jim couldn't fit the two scenes together. Somehow he'd screwed it up.

'Fuck,' he said.

———

That Monday morning, Barry and Geoff picked up Jim from the corner as usual. He climbed into the van and sat silently, knowing what was coming. It was Geoff who said it.

'Are you seeing her again?'

'No.'

They drove on for a few minutes.

'Never mind,' said Barry. 'It's better to have loved and lost than to live with the stupid cunt for the rest of your life. Take it from me: I know.'

Jim told him nothing.

———

That night, Jim was ejected from sleep at about 3 a.m. He stumbled downstairs into the kitchen and smoked at the table, drinking instant coffee. He felt unco-ordinated and numb. His hands shook and it was hard to roll cigarettes. He got tobacco everywhere. He felt like shit, and he couldn't think of a single good thing.

'There's got to be more than this,' he said out loud.

———

In the morning, he didn't go to work, but got dressed and walked through the village and along the lane to Joe's house. Jim hadn't been there for years, but the route came automatically to him.

When he arrived, he went round the back and stopped as he walked into the yard. There was a car there. He recognized it, but it used to be serviceable and parked at the front to be driven occasionally – and inexpertly – by Mrs Joe. Now it was up on blocks and the dark, dry stain on the cobbles said all its oil had long leaked away. There was no one here to maintain it, thought

Jim. The last person to do any work on it was probably his own father. Jim slipped past it and knocked on the back door. He felt like someone forcing themselves to step out into space.

She answered after a while. To Jim, she'd always looked old. Now she looked a bit older than that. She peered at him over the rims of her specs.

'He told me you were back,' she said.

'He says the place is falling down around your ears.'

Mrs Joe sighed. 'You'd better come in.'

6

OCTOBER 2004

We roll onto the site through a thin, damp mist. It's Monday morning, it's eight thirty, and I've got that cold-start feeling where every joint in my body seems to grate and squeal, and the week hasn't even started yet. I get out of the van and the cold comes through my sweater immediately. I shiver. I reach back in and grab my boots, then trot over to the cabin. Of course, the door is locked.

'Who's got the key?'

'I have – hold on.' Geoff climbs out of the van, followed by Barry. 'Bollocks, it's colder now than it was when we left.'

'Stop moaning and bring us the key.'

Geoff wanders over and rummages in his pocket for the key to the cabin. 'Fucking bastard.' He separates it from the crap, gripping it precariously between two fingers. Flakes of old tissue paper float to the ground, and a packet of tobacco almost follows. Eventually, he fumbles the key into the keyhole and lets us in.

'Put the fucking kettle on, then,' says Barry, and throws himself into one of the plastic seats. He lights a cigarette immediately and sucks in the smoke with relish.

The cabin is dank from being closed up all weekend, and stinks of the mud that coats the floor. Soon, though, Barry's cigarette smoke cuts through the damp, dirty smell. Geoff has settled into his own seat and is proceeding to roll himself a fag. I presume, therefore, that the command to put the kettle on was directed at me. I fill the kettle in the filthy sink and brew up as the other two tap fag ash onto the floor.

'Fuck.' My heart sinks. Last thing I need on a Monday morning.

'What?' asks Barry.

'There's no fucking teabags.'

'There was a whole fucking packet of PG Tips on Friday.'

'They were that fitter's. He took them home.'

'Stingy cunt.'

We look at each other shiftily. I sigh.

'You'd best go and get some,' says Barry.

'Money.' I hold out my hand. The other two reluctantly cough up a quid each.

'Get some milk as well.'

———

Fifteen minutes later, I return to the site bearing a plastic bottle of semi-skimmed milk and a box of eighty teabags. As I trudge up the access road, I see a silver 4x4 parked right outside the cabin. It looks quite posh and not very old, and I've never seen it here before. I wonder, glumly, if some kind of manager has come down to check up on things, but as I get closer, I hear Geoff's giggle through the door. Something must have cheered him up.

As soon as I get inside, I am enveloped by stinking blue cigar smoke, and as I cough, I see something that gives me such a shock I almost choke on my own spit.

'Fucking hell.'

'All right?' Mac grins at me, grips his cigar in his teeth, and shakes my hand mightily.

'Christ. It's been a while.'

'Three years. Geoff's wedding.'

'What are you doing here?'

'Working.'

'Really?'

'No, I just travelled two hours for a cup of fucking tea. Yes, really. There's six of us; the rest'll be here in a minute.'

'Fucking hell. Well, it's good to see you again.'

Barry grunts and lights another cigarette, but Geoff smiles brightly. 'Aye, it's going to be just like old times.' Barry shakes his head and looks out of the window.

'Anyroad, are you lads going to show me the ropes or what?' Mac takes a long drag on his cigar and pauses expectantly.

Geoff and Barry look at their cigarettes and continue to smoke without moving from their chairs. Mac keeps looking at us.

I sigh. 'All right, Mac, I'll give you the fucking tour. Just let me get my boots on.'

'Good lad.'

I sit down to change my shoes. Being called 'good lad' by Mac is a bit rum, since he's only a year older than me. On the other hand, he's probably earned the right. He stares down at me from beneath his thick black eyebrows. 'Been keeping yourself busy?'

'Not really. Just the same old shite.' I finish lacing my boots. 'You must be, though, judging by that fancy motor.'

'Aye, business is good. I'll need a fucking secretary soon.'

Barry snorts loudly.

Mac grins. 'Do you need a tissue, Baz? You should keep one up your sleeve, like your granny used to.'

'All right, Mac,' I say. 'Let's go.'

We walk out. The mist is gone, but the sky remains grey. I lead Mac over to the jagged building. 'This isn't my job, but anyway, there it is.'

Mac stands with his arms folded and takes in the view. Judged solely by his constituent parts – the timeshare tan, the belly, the moustache, the tremendous eyebrows – Mac should look ridiculous, a Mexican bandit gone to seed – but he doesn't. He just looks like Mac, and Mac is solid and reassuring.

'Well, let's see now.' He strides to the hole in the wall that will one day hold the side door and extends his head into the darkness within.

'The leccy's just inside, to your left,' I say, and Mac is swallowed up. I hear the scraping as he swings his foot over the floor, feeling for the distribution box, and a heavy clunk as he connects with it. There is a brief fumbling and the temporary lights flicker on. I follow him in, but he just stands there amid the dust and assorted mess, looking around him quite casually.

'Geoff and Baz were saying this is a fucking shambles.'

'It's just the usual bollocks – you know, one thing after another. There were four other brickies to begin with, but they fucked off weeks ago. They found some replacements, but they were coming all the way from Wales and buggered off the minute they got something closer to home. Then it rained for a week and the site flooded.'

'Jesus. Well, I'll soon get it shipshape.' He gives me a wink.

'Fucking hell, don't take that attitude with Barry – he'll kick off.'

'Don't worry. You stick to your walls, my lads'll take mine, and I won't interfere.'

'Good, because you know what he's like when he thinks he's got something to complain about.'

We hear the sound of vehicles drawing onto the site.

'That must be my lads,' says Mac. 'I'd better go and let them know the score.'

We splash through the mud back to the cabin and find it suddenly a lot more crowded. Mac is true to his word – six men – and though there are enough seats for everyone, the seats in question are small, very close to one another, and bolted to the floor. Things look pretty cosy. I slip onto the seat next to Geoff, opposite Barry.

'Full house now, then,' I say to them.

'Aye.' Geoff smiles. 'Mebbes they'll liven the place up a bit. It's got to be better than spending all day with you two miserable bastards.'

I give Geoff the benefit of a laugh, but Barry just snorts again and violently shakes open his newspaper.

'What's up, Baz?' Geoff asks.

'Nothing,' says Barry without looking up from his paper.

Geoff winks at me and then calls out, 'Here, Mac, do you remember that motorcycle we did up?'

Mac looks over from where he's sitting and smiles broadly. 'Yes, I bloody do. One of the best summers we ever spent that, wasn't it?'

'Aye, it were.'

'I remember when Baz went over the handlebars. We thought we'd lost you there, until you got up and started staggering around like a drunk.' Mac laughs at the memory. Barry shakes his head and pretends to read.

Barry doesn't like Mac. There is the inevitable clash of characters, but really it all goes back to the motorcycle. Mac got a couple of weeks' work one summer, helping out on a local farm. All he did was clean out a big barn – hard labour and not in the least exciting. It was the motorcycle that made it worth doing. Under a tarp he found a wretched old C15. It was ancient even then, and in need of serious attention, but in Mac's imagination it gleamed and roared. An agreement was reached that when the job was finished, Mac could take the motorcycle.

It became a shared project, and the four of us worked on it for weeks that summer. Whenever the weather was fine, we'd be in Mac's back yard puzzling over the repairs and arguing about the best way to do things. Sometimes Mac's dad would stand in the doorway, drinking tea and smoking. Usually he just laughed at us, but occasionally he offered advice.

Against the odds, we got the bastard running, and spent the remainder of the summer taking turns to rip around the fields and lanes. Naturally, Mac was the best rider, but at the end of the summer, he sold the bike and took the money.

That's when the recriminations started. Geoff and I had always considered it Mac's bike, and though we were disappointed that he'd got rid of it, we didn't bear any grudges. Barry, on the other hand, was furious: he felt we had a stake in the bike and deserved some of the money. It was ridiculous – Mac had paid for the rebore, and we'd siphoned all the petrol we used out of his dad's car – but Barry remained implacable.

Anyway, by the time I got out of prison, Mac was gone – off in Spain building hotels. 'Best place for him,' Barry would say, and from Barry's point of view, that was true: without Mac around he could finally be the boss. A year or so later, however, Mac came home with new skills and big ideas, and hostilities flared again. He went into business for himself, and not just as a self-employed brickie like Barry and Geoff, but a *proper* business with a balance sheet and his name on the van. And then his name on the truck. And then his name on the register of company directors. One day, he knocked on Barry's door and offered us work. Whether Mac did it out of mischief or genuine need I'll never know, but Barry turned him down flat.

By then, Mac had married and moved away to the countryside of North Yorkshire, so we saw him less, and then hardly ever. Still, Barry couldn't forgive him. 'That fucking John McCluskey, always out for the profit and fuck the rest of us,' was his constant refrain and judgement of the man. Barry would have done the same, though, if he'd had the wit.

'Could you shift over, mate?' A man stands over Barry with a mug of tea in one hand and a half-eaten egg and bacon McMuffin in the other. Barry looks up and inspects him slowly. His disgust is palpable; the man has fashionable hair.

'Have you nicked one of our fucking teabags?'

'Fuck's sake, Baz, let the lad sit down.' Geoff kicks him under the table, but the man is already lowering himself into the space, leaving Barry with no choice but to move over.

'Cheers, mate,' says the man. 'No, I haven't, actually. We brought our own.'

'Good.'

'It's your milk, though.'

Barry slaps his newspaper down on the table.

'Only joking.'

'He doesn't have a sense of humour.' Mac, from behind. He places his hand on the man's shoulder. 'Our Barry is an iron man, aren't you?'

Barry just looks out of the window.

'Anyway, lads, this is Lee. He's my right-hand man.'

'Hiya,' says Lee. We're all introducing ourselves when the Irish cunt walks in.

'That's the site engineer,' says Geoff in a low voice. 'He's a right bastard.'

'You new boys, sign these fucking forms,' the Irish cunt brandishes a clipboard at the nearest man.

'Have you got a pen?'

'Find your own fucking pen. Which one of you is John McCluskey?'

'Over here,' says Mac slowly.

'I need to see you in the office to go over the plans.'

Mac looks at the Irish cunt, takes a drink of tea, swallows, and then carefully places the mug back on the tabletop. 'I'll be right there, once I've finished my brew.'

'Well, I haven't got all day.' With that the Irish cunt turns to us and looks as if he's about to ask why we aren't working when it's gone ten, but from outside comes the deep growl of a truck engine and the hard beep of a reverse signal. 'Fucking hell,' he mutters, and bustles out of the cabin.

Barry gives Lee a grim smile. 'Welcome to our world.'

I don't think I can listen to any more moaning today. I close my ears and look out of the cabin window. Outside, the Irish cunt is involved in a heated argument with the man who delivers our mortar.

———

Van, work, van, home, pub, bed. As Barry pilots us around the long bend that leads into the village, the knowledge that it's only Monday night squats in my thoughts. We left the site early – the mortar was the wrong mix and everyone was thoroughly fed up – but it's October now, so it's already dark. A whole day murdered for nothing, and four more to go. Geoff snoozes in the passenger seat, his left cheek making a wet slap against the window every time we hit a bump. He has farted several times since drifting off, but we are thankful for the fact that he has not started to snore. I'm in the second row of seats, staring at my reflection in the side window. At first, it is solid and lifelike, but is obliterated as we enter the village and the shapes of buildings and parked cars loom up under the streetlights.

I sense a movement and turn to meet it; Barry is looking at me in the rearview mirror. Our gazes lock, briefly, on the glass.

'What fucking day is it?' he asks.

'It's Monday, Barry.'

'Fuck. Four days.'

I grunt some sort of sympathy, some sort of common feeling. There is a sudden discomfort in the realization that I share thoughts with Barry. Somehow it just makes it worse.

Ahead of us, I can see the back of a pedestrian as he walks down the street: shopping bag in hand, heavy gait, and slight stoop. It can only be Joe.

'Pull over, Barry, I'll walk from here.'

He doesn't argue. 'Suit yourself.'

'I will.'

The van stops and we are still some way behind Joe. If I walk slowly at first, Barry will have driven off before I catch up with Joe, and won't see us. I needn't have worried, though. Barry is away the moment I slide the door shut. I set off briskly and draw up with Joe.

'All right, Joe?' He turns his head towards me, then looks ahead again. He doesn't stop or slow down. He's on a mission.

'Hello,' he says. Not without warmth, but he's obviously concentrating on other things.

'Been running errands?'

'Aye.'

'How's that lino?'

'It's magnificent.'

'Glad to hear it. Your mam all right?'

'My mother has a bad back, arthritis, and diabetes. If she turns blue, I've to call an ambulance.'

'Good plan. What's diabetes?' I can't resist, and anyway, his mother does it too. You have to laugh occasionally or it would be a hard slog.

'It's when your body can't digest cake.'

'That's shite. What does she eat instead?'

'Weetabix.'

'Right. It looks the same when it comes out, you know.'

Joe chuckles. Shit jokes: they never fail.

'She got stuck on the toilet. I had to wipe her bum.'

'Fuck.' I'm genuinely horrified. I stop walking. Joe carries on. I trot back up to him. 'Can't she get a nurse or something?'

'The council says she has to sell the house first. She doesn't want to.'

'Oh, right.' We're passing the pub. 'Fancy a pint?'

'I've got to take the shopping home.'

'Righto.' We keep walking. 'Joe, do you remember when I was little?'

'Aye, I saw you the first day you came home from the hospital.'

'Really?'

'Aye, my mam was cooking for your dad while you were getting born. You were a canny little baby.'

'What else do you remember?'

'Loads. I've wiped your bum too.'

'Oh. Well, I hope I took the opportunity to shit on you while I still could.' Fucking hell – Joe has changed my nappy. No wonder I can't use the urinal with other men next to me.

'You're a dirty bugger.' This is said with a vehemence that surprises me.

'It's not me, it's society.'

'That's mumbo-jumbo, that.'

I laugh a little. 'Well, if I've turned out scum, it's your fault for buying me all that beer when I was a kid.'

Joe lurches to a halt and turns on me fiercely. 'Shhh! Don't tell! Don't ever tell them anything! They'll send me to prison!'

Shit. It's been a long time since I've seen Joe have an episode, but I can sense that one is impending. To the unaware, they explode like a bomb blast on a busy street. You have to be firm and sound like you know what you're talking about. I fix him with the best direct look I can muster. His eyes are wide open, and a thick string of saliva, launched from his furious mouth, hangs across his chin. He looks like an angry child in the body of a fifty-something man.

'Jesus, Joe! Calm down, man. No one's sending you to prison.' Not quite the calm authority I was aiming for.

'They would if they knew.' His eyes bulge and the muscles in his neck stand out; his face is turning red.

'No. Joe, look, you don't go to prison for that sort of thing. It's not a serious offence.'

'It got you into trouble!' Joe breathes hard and stares at me. 'Big trouble!'

'That was nothing to do with you. You weren't even there.'

'You were drunk because of me.'

'No, Joe, I wasn't drunk.' We face each other. Joe is close to me and I can smell his breath. It's bad.

'You weren't?'

'No, I wasn't. And nobody cares about that anymore. Come on, mate. Forget about it. You're all right.'

Joe seems to relax, and roughly wipes up the spit with the back of his hand.

'You're not lying?' he asks quietly.

'No, Joe. I can't lie to you.' There's an aching void where my stomach should be and I identify the feeling as guilt.

We're at the point where I would turn off to go home, but I don't. I walk him all the way to the top of the lane that runs behind the terrace.

He stops and says, 'You coming to the fireworks with me this year?'

'Course. We always go. What time do they start?'

'Seven. It says on the poster.'

'Well then, I'll see you there.'

He grins. 'Magnificent!'

'They'd better be: I put a fiver in the collection. G'night, mate.'

I watch him recede into the darkness towards his back yard and then hear him grunt past the old car, but I wait for the sound of the kitchen door closing behind him before I go.

7

It's 5 November – it falls on a Friday this year – and some of the blokes are discussing it at lunchtime when Mac looks up from a pot of rhubarb yoghurt and asks us, 'They still do a display up the Admiral, right?'

'Aye,' says Geoff. 'It's not a bad 'un either.'

'Well, I'll pop along after work, then. Have a few beers. For old times' sake, like.'

'I won't be around,' says Barry. 'I'm taking the kids to the big display at the arena.'

Normally, he would say something like that the way a condemned man might say, 'I'm being shot at dawn,' but right now he sounds quite pleased with himself.

'Never mind. We'll manage without you, won't we, lads?'

Judging by Mac's smile, he doesn't expect Geoff or me to disagree with him. Cheeky bastard. I'm tempted to tell him I have other plans – just to be awkward – but Geoff gets in first and says, 'I'm supposed to be going with Laura.'

'Then bring her along, son. It's ages since I've seen her, and we could do with a bit of eye candy.'

'Mind how you go,' I say. 'He gets jealous.'

'I bloody don't.'

'Well, he's definitely a lucky man,' says Mac, with a wink. He turns to me. 'I suppose you're still single?'

'Yes, I am, thank you, Mac.'

He takes a big toke on his cigar, leans back in his chair, and through an almighty curtain of smoke utters, '*Ploo sa chonge*, son. *Ploo sa chonge*.'

———

Later, I'm changing into a decent shirt in preparation for going down to the pub when there's a knock on the door. Who the hell is that? Then I remember. 'Shit.' I go down and answer it.

'All right, Joe.'

'It's Bonfire Night!'

'I know.'

He stands there and watches me like a dog that thinks it's going for a walk. He's got his wellies on.

'Put your coat on. It's cold.'

'All right, just give us a minute.'

I wrap up and then we walk down to the pub together. I feel a bit anxious about Mac and Geoff. It's not that I'm ashamed to be seen with Joe – although he can be an embarrassment – but it isn't the best mix of personalities. My phone beeps with a new text; apparently, they're already in the pub. Oh well. With any luck, they won't see Joe and me in the crowd, and I can join them inside after the display is over and Joe has gone.

When we arrive, the bonfire is alight, but the fireworks haven't started yet. People still trickle out of the pub's side door, across the car park, and onto the piece of wasteland where the fire burns. Beyond the wasteland is the old factory, a black hulk of shadows. The firelight licks at it and reveals ripples of crumbling brick, shattered glass and the straight edge of an asbestos roof. Joe doesn't say anything to me. That's the good thing about him:

he doesn't need conversation like some people. If you shut up, he will too.

A few metres away, I see a couple standing together. At first, I think they're strangers – the firelight keeps the shadows mottled and moving on their faces – but then I realize that I know them both from school. They're called Mick and Donna, and I used to fancy her in a distant and thankfully unnoticed way. Geoff fancied her too, but being the ever-hopeful sort, he was far too obvious about it and all her friends ridiculed him. Barry said he had heard she was a slag, so Geoff should just wait for her after school and do her in the bushes. And Barry was the first of us to find a wife. Jesus.

I didn't even know Mick and Donna were an item, but that's the way of things: lives just diverge, even in the same village. I haven't spoken to either of them for years. They happen to look towards me and I give them a smile and a nod, but the gesture just melts away without making the connection. I realize that they don't recognize me. Maybe they've both forgotten entirely the fact of my existence, and I find this possibility a source of perverse optimism.

The flames catch the Guy's feet, but no one really watches; he's not the main event. More people are coming out now, some grip hot dogs, hamburgers, and pints of beer. Wrapped-up kiddies hold little bottles of pop with brightly coloured straws, while teenagers shiver in their tracksuits. A tap on my shoulder. I look round and it's Laura.

'Oh.'

'Hello, you,' she says.

'Hello.' No sign of Geoff and Mac.

'They're indoors,' she tells me. 'Already well away. They'll be watching through the window at this rate.'

'Can't say I blame them. It's perishing out here.'

She holds up her hands and wiggles her mitten-clad fingers at me. 'Mac's still as loud as ever.'

'Oh, you noticed that, did you?'

'It's hard to miss.'

'He's a sound bloke, he's just…'

'An enormous gobshite?'

'…forceful in his personality.'

I don't hear her response to that, because Joe nudges me in the ribs and hisses, 'Is that your girlfriend?'

'No. Shut up.'

She turns to face him. 'Hello, Joe.'

'Oh.' Recognition floods his face. 'You're Laura, big fat Geoff's wife.'

I step on his foot, but just get the void at the end of his welly.

She laughs. 'That's right.'

I stand between Joe and Laura, and we wait for the display to start. The crowd is tense now, and expectant. Then, with a sudden whoosh, three rockets score parallel lines of fire and smoke into the sky. They burst hard in the air above us and bloom into great, incandescent carnations.

'That's magnificent, that.'

'Aye, Joe, it's magnificent.'

As the light fades, Joe turns and beams at me, and then says, as if the pyrotechnic thrill has just jogged his memory, 'I'm in the panto!'

Joe takes part in the local pantomime every year, and every year, without exception, he plays the back end of the horse. It was his mother's doing; she could sew costumes and presumably Joe's involvement was part of the bargain. He's been a fixture of the event ever since, and no one has the heart to kick him out now.

'That's great, Joe. I'll come and see you.' I even manage to smile at him, but he keeps looking at me like he has something else to say. At that moment, the display begins in earnest and I turn my attention back to the night sky. It's full of gold and red, and the thuds are so loud that I feel them right through the soles of my shoes. I stuff my hands into my pockets and give myself over to the light and sound, but then Joe is saying something that I can't make out. 'You what?'

He leans close. 'I said you'd build the set.'

'What do you mean?'

'The set for the panto!'

I skid back into the reality of cold night, acrid smoke, and damp feet. 'Why the fuck did you do that?'

'Mr Green had a stroke. He can't even lift a hammer.'

Mr Green. He was my games and geography teacher at school. He retired when I was in third form, but I remember him well – principally for his insistence that we refer to rugby as football, and football as association football, and the fact that he hated small boys. He was also the mainstay of the village pantomime. He built the sets and did most of the hard work, and I imagine that having a stroke has somewhat curtailed this.

'You dickhead, Joe. That's the last thing I need.'

'All right, keep your hair on. Mr Green's still in charge, like. He says you won't have to use your brain, just your muscles.'

'Thanks. That makes it all better.' Too late I remember Joe's ambivalent relationship with sarcasm.

'Great. I knew you'd be pleased!'

In front of me, a little girl drops her hot dog and starts to cry. I don't know whether to join her or laugh.

When the display finishes, Joe slopes off, and Laura and I wander into the pub to meet Mac and Geoff. We find them in the deep conversation of men who are already half-way pissed.

'Here he is!' cries Mac, as we walk over.

'What have you been doing with my wife?' asks Geoff.

'We've been watching the fireworks,' Laura answers for me. 'You missed them all, you daft buggers.'

'Never mind about that,' says Mac. 'We've important drinking to be done, and important matters to discuss.' He brandishes a twenty at me. 'Get a round in, son.'

'Thank you, Your Majesty.'

I take the money and buy drinks. Judging by the head of steam Geoff and Mac have built up, it's going to be a long night.

———

One pint blurs into the next and by nine thirty I have no idea who keeps going to the bar, but beer keeps appearing and I keep pouring it down my throat. I'm hammered, but I'm having fun. Mac might have a big mouth, but drinking with him is a damn sight more entertaining than drinking with Barry. We try to play darts; my aim feels true, but they just won't hit the board. Mac is explaining the game to a teenager with a bottle of blue WKD and a troubled expression.

'You don't just chuck the dart, right. You stroke it towards the board. Don't chuck, don't flick, stroke! A smooth movement from the chest. Stroke, my son. Stroke!'

The lad slips away while Mac is distracted by lighting a cigar. I find myself dancing with Laura in the space between the pool table and the wall. I haven't danced in years. She laughs at me, but I laugh with her and it's all OK. Then Geoff reels towards us, and I can't work out what the hell he's on about till he holds his phone out to me.

'It's Barry,' he shouts.

I put the phone up to my ear. 'Hello.' Nothing.

'No, it's a text!'

'Oh…right.'

I look at the screen: *U lot still down pub? Cd do wiv a pint. C u in a min. B.*

Bollocks. Barry's back from his outing, his family are doing his head in, and now we're his least bad option, even with Mac in tow.

I hand the phone back to Geoff. 'Shit,' I say. 'Just when I was starting to enjoy myself.'

Laura leans over Geoff to look at the screen. 'I don't want that grumpy bastard to come out: he spoils everything.'

Mac comes over and we give him the bad news. He stands for a moment, exaggeratedly stroking his moustache. 'Well, there's only one thing for it.'

'What's that?'

'We leg it.'

'You what?'

'We leave before he gets here.' He looks at me. 'All back to yours, son. It's the only way.'

No one ever comes to my house. No one except Joe. I'm embarrassed for a moment and then relieved when I remember, 'But I've got nothing to drink.'

'No problem – the Spar's open till half ten,' says Geoff.

It looks like this is my night for getting myself into things. I shrug. 'All right, then.'

The four of us sink the last of our drinks and file out of the side door into the car park. We're just crossing it when Mac hisses, 'Shit!' and ducks behind a parked car. The rest of us follow him and we huddle together in a pool of shadow. 'I saw him coming round the corner,' whispers Mac.

Footsteps approach.

Laura starts to giggle. I clamp my hand over her mouth.

The footsteps stop. 'Fucking kids.' Barry. 'I'm not scared of you, you know.' Then the footsteps start again, faster than before, until they're swallowed by the sound that spills out from the pub door.

'Run,' says Mac, and we do.

We pelt it down the street, hooted at by the lads in the bus shelter and honked at by passing cars, until we arrive outside the shop laughing and gasping for air. I look around to see everyone. 'Where's Geoff?'

Geoff is still struggling up the road, listing forward with his right hand clasped to his side. He lifts his feet and swings his free arm as if he were running, but actually moves at the pace of a slow walk. We cheer him as he comes close.

'Yer bastards,' he pants, bent double. 'I'm not fit.'

'We could've told you that for nowt,' says Laura, and kisses him on the back of the head.

We go into the shop, buy an excessive amount of beer, and walk back to my house. I'm not used to visitors, but I'm drunk enough not to be embarrassed by my mismatched furniture and the horrible brown carpets. Anyway, they must have known it wasn't going to be palatial. On arrival, Mac goes through my CDs but finds nothing to his satisfaction, so he turns on the radio and tunes it to a local commercial station. It's their Friday-night show: house music. It's cheap, but I'm cheerful and soon we're dancing again.

Mac and Geoff are trying to hold a conversation about some property-development deal Mac is involved in, but they're both so drunk they keep forgetting what they've said and repeating themselves. Geoff starts smoking and I try to tell him to take it outside, but instead I somehow end up smoking myself. Geoff and Mac go upstairs for some reason. The last thing I remember is sitting on the couch with Laura.

I wake up and find myself staring into the side of Geoff's head. He's leaning over the couch and talking to someone, but not to me. There's a heavy weight on my body and a bad taste in my mouth.

'What's going on?' I ask.

'Gotta go home, mate. 'S late.'

My vision clears. The weight on my body is Laura. Geoff shakes her.

'C'mon, pet. It's home time.'

'Let me stay,' she moans.

'Can't sleep here,' he says.

He tries to pull her up, but she's a dead weight and he's way too drunk to do it. I give up on them and fall back to sleep.

In the morning, they're gone, and Mac stands over me shirtless and hairy-chested, with a mug of tea in each hand. 'Wakey, wakey.'

'Fucking hell.' My head hurts.

He gives me his sunniest grin. 'It was a bloody good night, son. A bloody good night.'

8

'Is Geoff coming or what?' Barry held a skewer topped with a charred sausage and squinted over it at Jim. 'He's missing all the scran. That's not like him.'

'You should have waited for the flames to die down before you put that lot on.'

'Bollocks. They'll be fine.'

'It's not even seven o'clock yet. He has to go and pick up his girlfriend.'

A gust blew smoke into Barry's face. He coughed and his eyes watered. 'Fucking hell. I fucking hate barbecues.'

'It's your party.'

'It was her idea.' Barry gestured towards the back door. 'Daft bint.' Barry returned the sausage to the griddle and rubbed his face with the back of his hand. 'Has he shagged her yet?'

'Of course he's shagged her; they've been going out for three fucking months.'

'Good lad.' Barry nodded and chugged at his beer. 'How come we haven't met her yet?'

'Fuck knows. Ask him. He was probably scared you'd embarrass him.'

'I wouldn't. I'm civilized, me.'

'Are you fuck. I need another beer. Are you operating an open-fridge-door policy?'

'Aye, go for it.'

'Cheers.'

Jim hauled his body out of the orange deckchair and stood up. The warm breeze slipped over his face and arms, and he stood for a while and let himself sway in the summer air. It struck him that Barry's garden was very neat, as if it had been edged and trimmed with the aid of a set square and rule. He could imagine Barry on his hands and knees with a pair of scissors to ensure that no single blade of grass encroached over the path or the brand-new patio.

Jim's perceptions were muffled by sun and warm beer, and he walked up the garden with a sense of not really being there. This ghostlike drift ended abruptly as he stepped into the kitchen, where the coolness and dim light induced a sudden pain at the back of his eyes. He squeezed them shut and heard a click in his skull as his eyelids slid over his corneas. When he opened them again, he saw the kitchen clearly. Rows of uncooked burgers, sausages, and chicken legs sat on trays on the countertops. Jim realized that Barry expected a lot of guests. This really was Carol's idea; Barry could not possibly have wanted to spend so much money on others.

Carol was making salad at the kitchen table.

'That's a canny spread, Carol.'

'Spread? What?'

'The food. There's loads of it.'

'Oh, aye, there's a few people coming over, like.'

'Looks it.'

Carol leaned over her work. She halved and quartered tomatoes with short, swift movements. She didn't look at Jim. He didn't move, because Carol blocked his path to the fridge. He stood there until she spoke again.

'I've been on at him to have some people round ever since he finished the patio. It's nice to sit out on.' She paused. 'You know what he's like, but I finally persuaded him.'

She smiled and Jim could not tell if she was excited or nervous, so he said, 'It's a lovely patio.'

'It is. He's dead proud of it. Not that he'd tell you.' She reached for a cucumber and began to slice it too quickly for Jim's comfort. He winced as the blade swooped past her fingers, close and sharp.

Jim did not know Carol very well; in fact, he barely ever saw her. The most time he had ever spent in her company were those few weeks sleeping on Barry's sofa while he waited to be housed. That was over four years ago, when she was pregnant and they were still living in a rented house in the terraces. On those nights, the three of them would sit in silence and watch TV, until Barry would stand up and announce, 'Let's go to the pub.' There was no need for him to add that he didn't mean Carol.

Since then, Barry seemed to utterly divorce his life at home from the rest of it. Carol did not come out with them, and on the rare occasions that Jim had cause to come over, she said little or nothing. He had no idea what went on under this roof. The idea of Barry having a home life at all was faintly fantastical to him. Does he play with the kids? He must do, as they kiss him on the cheek and call him 'Dad'. Jim had seen it. Still…a party. At Barry's house. Carol must have nagged carefully, but persistently, to make this happen, nibbling at the edges until she had carved out her little victory.

'Who's this new bird of Geoff's, then?' she asked.

'I don't know any more than you, Carol.'

Jim didn't tell her the truth, that three weeks ago, drunk but lucid, Geoff looked Jim in the eye and told him that he loved this woman, loved her with all his heart, and that she was going to change his life. Jim wasn't sure he knew what that kind of love really meant, but he could see that it was powerful and that

Geoff was happy. Happy and scared that something might take the happiness away.

There were noises from within, someone entering through the front door of the house, then the sound of children getting excited. Carol raised her head and called out, 'Pam? Is that you?' Then she put down her knife and went through to the living room.

Jim seized the opportunity to get to the fridge. He took a beer and looked out over the garden. Outside, Barry squirted lighter fluid into the barbecue. The flames licked up through the grill and engulfed the food. Barry smiled. Jim shook his head and wandered back out.

'It's not fucking cooking on the inside.'

'I told you – the charcoal isn't ready yet. You want radiant heat, not fucking flames.'

'Radian teet? Is that one of your clever words?'

'Fuck off, Barry.' Jim sat down with his beer and tried to return to a state of relaxation. Barry's daughter was playing in the grass, and his younger sister was down there with her, on hands and knees. Barry's sister was wearing a summer skirt and Jim could see the line of her knickers. He tried not to look too much, but Barry caught him at it anyway and poked him in the arm with a spatula. Jim shrugged and picked at the ring-pull of his beer instead.

More people arrived and in due course Barry presented various guests with carbonized lumps of meat on paper plates, handing them over with pride. They smiled weakly. Only Jim understood that Barry was so proud specifically because the food was inedible.

'Lovely, Barry,' said his next-door neighbour. 'Very generous of you.'

'Think nothing of it, Pete. It's a value pack from Iceland. Dirt cheap. Probably made of tongues and testicles, like, but beggars can't be choosers, eh?'

Carol did her best to ignore Barry and flitted between guests refilling their glasses from a jug full of a suspicious liquid in which floated lumps of cucumber.

'What the fuck is that stuff?'

Barry glowered and then pronounced, 'Pimm's,' as if he were speaking the true name of Satan.

'What's that?'

'It's a cocktail. For benders. Stick to the beer, mate.'

Jim tried the Pimm's anyway and found it quite refreshing, though he filtered the cucumber between his teeth and spat it into the border. He became quite drunk and stumbled back into the kitchen to grab some bread. As he buttered a slice, someone entered the room and Jim turned to look. Geoff beamed at him from behind a pair of sunglasses.

'Fucking hell, Geoff. Shades.'

'Aye, they're bonny, aren't they?'

'Very stylish.'

'Jim, there's someone I want you to meet.' Geoff grinned and seemed to inflate to even greater dimensions. Jim couldn't help but smile too.

'Where is she?'

'I'm here,' chimed a clear voice from the kitchen door, and a woman stepped in. 'Laura.'

Laura had sunglasses too, but hers were pushed off her face and sat in her ash-blonde hair. She was short, slim, and delicate. Jim shook her hand almost as a reflex.

'Geoff's told me a lot about you,' she said.

'Likewise,' said Jim, and as they made eye contact, he had a sense they'd met before. 'You seem familiar.'

'Are you trying to chat her up?'

Jim realized that he was being cued. 'Well, she's very glamorous.'

'She is that. Right, let's go and introduce you to Barry.'

Laura allowed Geoff to lead her to the door, and as they left, Jim called after them, 'Don't accept any meat from him. It's raw, in a crunchy coating.'

'I'll bear that in mind,' smiled Laura.

They walked out into the garden and Jim continued to butter his bread. He sat alone in the kitchen and opened another beer, glad to be out of all the chit-chat for a while.

It struck him as he finished the first slice. 'Shit.' He was scared to look, but he had to, and when he peeked through the open door and saw her again, he was sure. Jim didn't want to be sure, so he muttered to himself, 'It's been years, man. Your memory plays tricks.' He stared at the kitchen wall and laughed to himself, but it wouldn't make the idea go away.

Jim sank the rest of his beer, opened another one, and went outside. He leaned against the wall and watched. Against his advice, Geoff and Laura were eating from the barbecue. Barry helped them to chicken legs. Jim blinked hard, but it was no use; the resemblance was uncanny. As he watched the three of them together, Jim had another horrible thought: What if Barry knows too?

Barry was stabbing roughly at sausages and burgers, and Jim saw nothing different about him. Jim tried to remember exactly what Barry had said that day, but he couldn't. For one moment of fleeting relief, Jim thought it was possible that Barry had never even met Laura before, but the feeling crashed away almost immediately.

'Of course he has. That's why he chose her.'

'Sorry, what was that?'

Jim shuddered back to awareness of the space around him and saw that Barry's next-door neighbour had caught him talking to himself. 'Oh. Um, nothing, Pete.'

'You all right?'

'I'm fine.' Jim weaved to one side and steadied himself on the drainpipe.

'You've had too much to drink, mate.' Pete put his arm around Jim. 'Come and have a burger.'

'Get the fuck off me.'

Pete leaped back as if Jim had pulled a gun on him. 'All right, all right. Just take it easy.'

Jim ignored him, because now Laura was talking to Carol, who gave her directions to the toilet. Laura went into the house. Jim waited for a few seconds and then followed her inside.

At the bottom of the stairs, Jim heard her footsteps on the landing and stopped. He waited until the bathroom door opened and closed, and then gave it another few seconds to make sure no one was coming down. Then he climbed the stairs, leaning on the rail and concentrating on being quiet. It took him longer than he expected, so when he reached the top, he only had time to belch loudly and mutter, 'Fuck, I'm drunk,' before the taps were running. Jim stood as straight as he could and waited for her to come out. When the door opened, she almost walked into him.

'I know who you are.'

'Yes, we were introduced about twenty minutes ago. You're pissed.'

'No. I know who you really are.'

'What?'

Jim scooped her into the bathroom and locked the door behind them.

Silence. She put her hands on her hips and glared at him. 'Explain yourself.'

'I remember you and I don't want to remember you, but I remember you.'

'Oh my God. Are you mentally ill? Geoff! Geoff!'

'Shh! Shut up! I need to know if it's true.'

'If what's true? Jim, this isn't making any sense to me.'

'Just stay where you are, OK? Don't move until we've sorted this out.'

'OK. OK.' She sat on the edge of the bath and spread out her hands in front of her. 'Let's get this sorted out, whatever it is.'

Jim sank onto the toilet seat. He'd expected her to see immediately what he meant; he'd thought she might remember him. Now he would have to say it out loud.

'Have…have you…?' Suddenly, Jim's mouth felt as heavy and difficult to move as his legs did in the slow-walking dreams from which he would wake with tears of frustration still wet on his face. 'I need to…'

'You're hammered.'

'No! I'm not. Well, I am, but not that bad. It's just hard to explain.'

'Try.'

'Oh God. Look, have you ever lived in Middlesbrough?'

'Yes. I went to college there.'

'Really?'

'What? Yes, really. I have an HND in computer science.'

Jim tried hard to focus on her face, but he couldn't decode it; she was too tough and he was too drunk. She just looked right back at him. Jim realized that he wasn't in control, and it made him angry. 'I've fucked you.'

Laura's body jerked. She put her hand on her forehead. 'What?'

'As a customer. Barry was too, I think.'

'Christ. When?'

'Four or five years ago.'

'What are you going to do?'

'I don't know, but if Barry cottons on, there'll be a right fucking scene. He's not sensible about this kind of thing.'

'I really love Geoff.'

Jim picked up a toilet roll and turned it over in his hands.

'It's true, I do.' She touched him on the wrist.

'I believe you. Why else would you be *here*?' Jim threw the toilet roll at the wall opposite him. 'Shit.'

'I don't remember you at all.'

'Probably a good job; it wasn't what you'd call an uplifting experience.'

'It usually wasn't. Look, I need to know you're not going to screw it up for me and Geoff. It was a long time ago, and everything's changed now.'

Jim squinted at her, tried to make sense of her. Her face was the same, but otherwise there was nothing about this woman that reminded him of that girl. She's sorted, he thought. She's been to college, for fuck's sake. It struck him that he quite liked her. He pushed his hands through his hair and forced himself into resolve. 'Geoff loves you. I won't tell him.'

'What about Barry?'

'Don't do anything – I'll deal with him. It'll be like a fresh start.'

'Oh, please. I don't need a husband to get a fresh start. I clawed my way out of the shit on my own. This isn't about fresh starts; it's about my life. And Geoff's.'

'Husband? Christ.'

'Yeah.'

'OK.'

'OK.'

They watched each other for a few moments, until the sound of footsteps on the staircase shook Laura into action and she slipped out of the bathroom without another word.

Jim stayed where he was. He heard her walk along the landing and say hello to someone as she passed them at the top of the stairs. 'Bollocks,' he muttered to himself, and decided that since he was in the bathroom anyway he may as well have a piss.

Back downstairs, Jim sat in the kitchen again. He didn't want to go outside and mingle with people, but he watched them through the doorway. Even though he kept a close eye on Barry, he didn't see the precise moment when Barry realized who Laura was. It must have been a gradual dawning, rather than the sudden floodlight that Jim himself had experienced. Still, when Barry strode up the garden, straight towards the kitchen door, Jim knew why he was coming.

'Were you just going to sit here all night and not say anything?'

'What do you mean?'

'I saw you follow her indoors. I thought, "That looks a bit funny," and it got me thinking. Then I worked out where I'd seen her before.'

Barry stood over Jim and waited for him to respond, but Jim didn't say anything.

'So what are we going to do about it?'

Jim gazed up at Barry. He wanted to pretend nothing was happening, that he didn't know what Barry was talking about, but he knew there was no point. He just shrugged and said, 'I dunno.'

'Fucking dirty bitch.'

'She doesn't do it anymore, Baz.'

'How do we know that?'

'Because Geoff said she works for the NHS.'

'She's probably lying.'

'She's not lying. He's been to her fucking office; he picked her up for lunch. He told me all about it last week.'

'She's still a slag.'

'They love each other.'

'Are you defending her?' Barry was full of genuine disbelief.

Jim paused and flicked a stray piece of lettuce across the table-top. 'Everyone's done something they regret. And he's happy.'

'He's not going to be happy when he finds out she's a fucking whore.'

'He doesn't have to know that.'

'Bollocks. I'm going to tell him.'

'Barry, don't.' Jim stood. 'Look at her – she's good for him.'

'Fuck off! Half of fucking Teesside's been through that cunt.'

'Aye, including you. So how can you judge her now?'

'What? Are you fucking stupid or something? She's been a fucking prossy.'

'Why should that matter now?'

'Of course it fucking matters. Look, you've got to be cruel to be kind.'

'Barry, they're going to get married.' Jim stepped towards him. 'Don't fuck it up.'

'Married?' Barry stood, stunned. 'Fucking hell. Well, that settles it: no friend of mine's marrying a hooker.' He turned to leave, but as he reached the doorway, Jim grabbed him by the shoulder.

'Don't do it.'

'Get off me.' Barry tried to shrug Jim off, but Jim gripped him harder and bodily turned him. Barry shoved Jim in the chest. 'Fuck off. I'm telling him.'

'No!'

'Geoff,' Barry shouted out, 'come in here!'

'Stop.'

'Geoff!' Barry roared it this time, and over Barry's shoulder Jim saw Geoff turn, look suddenly worried, and trot towards them.

Jim looked Barry in the eye and saw malice and determination. 'Fuck you,' he whispered, drew back his right fist, and punched Barry in the face. Barry fell backwards over the doorstep and landed outside, face up. His eyes were still open, staring up into the sky, and he was breathing heavily.

Jim stood in the doorway. Everyone was still and silent, until the jug of Pimm's slipped from Carol's hand and shattered around her feet. She looked down at her sodden shoes and blood-flecked ankles, put her hands to her face, and began to cry.

'I'm all right.' Barry sat up, but no one moved to help him. He looked at Jim. 'You fucking bastard.'

'Just watch your mouth.' Jim looked up. 'Geoff, take me home.'

'What the fuck was that about?'

'Nothing. I'm just drunk, and he's being a twat. Right, Barry?'

No answer. Geoff surveyed the carnage and shook his head. 'Trust you two to fuck this up.'

'Let's go.'

———

Later that night, the booze had worn off and Jim sat in his armchair with a terrific headache. He tried to watch TV, but he couldn't concentrate on the screen, so he just listened to the sound. It formed a bed of something, at least, in the room and held back the nothingness. He tried to imagine, without much optimism, what it would be like when he went to the Job Centre on Monday morning. He'd never been inside one; there had always been enough work with Barry and Geoff. But now there wouldn't be any more Barry and Geoff; Jim had fucked everything up. Even if Barry did keep his mouth shut, neither he nor Geoff would want to work alongside Jim now.

The worst part was that Jim hadn't planned, or even wanted, to hit Barry. It burst out of nowhere. Everyone had seen him do it, just like the stupid ex-convict he was, and just when he thought things were getting better. Jim put his hands over his face and sighed. 'Oh God. You fucking idiot.'

Then the phone rang.

'Hello?'

'I've just done you a big fucking favour.' Barry, in a low voice, as if he was worried he might be overheard. 'Carol wanted to call the fucking police. I told her not to be so daft.'

'Right. Thanks.'

'Nothing's broken, you'll be pleased to hear.'

'Oh.'

'*Oh*. Is that all?'

'Yeah. That's all.' There was no point giving him an apology now. 'You're a miserable cunt.'

'Well, that makes two of us, then. Goodbye, Barry.'

'Hold on, hold on.'

'What?'

'I've thought about it. Mebbes you're right. Not about her, like – she's a fucking slag – but y'know, about rocking the boat and that.'

'I never said anything about rocking the boat. I just told you not to be a twat.'

'Well, I'm saying about it now. So listen to me, you bastard. I'm not going to tell him – yet – but I've got this one on you, right? So don't fuck me about anymore.'

'Fuck you about?'

'What I mean, Jim, is that you need to remember who the fucking boss is around here, OK?'

'And that's you, is it?'

'Yes, it fucking well is. I'll see you on Monday.' Barry hung up.

9

MAY 2001

Geoff sat in an armchair in his family's living room and stared into space. The carriage clock on the mantelpiece said it was eight thirty. Geoff was still in his pyjamas, and his tea was going cold.

Jim was in the kitchen polishing the men's good shoes. Now and again he looked up through the doorway at Geoff, who hadn't moved for a while. Jim just concentrated on getting the shoes nice and shiny; right now, it seemed like the best way he could help. Not that any of them would thank him. They almost hadn't let him in the house, but Geoff insisted.

Eventually, Geoff's brother came down and roughly patted Geoff's shaven scalp. 'Cheer up, you fat fucker. You've done bloody well for yourself.'

'Yeah,' Geoff said, and then he didn't say anything else.

Jim watched them for a few seconds, blinked, and went back to the polishing. Geoff's brother walked into the kitchen and rummaged for something in the cupboard under the sink. He ignored Jim. Then he went back upstairs.

Jim finished the last shoe and called through to Geoff, 'Come on, mate, let's get a move on, eh?'

Geoff nodded slowly and stood up.

They went upstairs to the room Geoff used to share with his brother. Jim hadn't been in this room since they were teenagers. It still had the two single beds in it, although Geoff had moved out six months ago and got a place with Laura. Jim pointed with his foot at Geoff's old bed. 'Is there still a stash of *Razzle* under there?'

'Dunno,' muttered Geoff.

Jim decided that there probably wasn't, and started to pull the plastic off the rented suits.

Geoff dressed slowly, fumbled with the buttons. Jim finished long before him and sat on one of the beds to wait. Eventually, Geoff turned and said, 'Look all right?'

'Aye, like a real groom.'

'Good.' Geoff paused. 'I'm sorry you're not my best man. It's just…'

'They wouldn't like it. I know. I'm an ex-con.'

Geoff shook his head. 'Don't say that. It's in the past.' He paused. 'You're doing well.'

'There's a ringing endorsement.'

'You know what I mean.'

'Don't worry about it, Geoff. Anyway, your best man should be your brother.'

'Little bastard. I caught him perving at her the other day.'

'You can hardly blame him – she's pretty fit.'

Geoff sighed and sat down on the other bed.

'Geoff, what's wrong? You were dead happy before. You couldn't believe your luck.'

'That's the fucking problem. I don't believe my luck. I know it's fucking stupid, but I just cannat stop worrying, you know?'

'Geoff, I'm not the best person to ask about relationships. I've never had one.' Geoff just sighed again, so Jim said, 'What are you worried about?'

'About everything you've been saying, man. That she's beautiful, and she's nice, and she's just…' Geoff trailed off in a growl of frustration and hammered his fists on his thighs. 'Too fucking good for me, that's what.'

'Well, she must think you're all right. She's fucking marrying you.'

'I keep telling myself that, but then I keep thinking that she's going to get bored of me in the end. I'm fat and I'm boring.'

'Jesus Christ, man. It'll be more than just boredom she feels if you carry on like that. You've got to pull yourself together.'

'I'm serious, though. What's going to happen a few years down the line?'

'Fucking hell, Geoff. I'm no expert, but I think most people generally consider that *before* their wedding day.'

'It's not fucking funny.'

'Do you see me laughing?'

Geoff stood up and looked out of the window, his back to Jim. Jim glanced at his watch. Barry would be here at any moment, and Jim suddenly felt sick.

'Geoff, have you talked to anyone else about this?'

'No. Just you.'

'Good.'

Geoff put his forehead on the glass and sighed. 'It was all right until we said we were getting married and now I'm just fucking sick to death of hearing people say, "You've done well for yourself." Like no fucker can believe it. It makes me feel like a fucking maggot.'

Jim realized that Geoff was close to tears and he dug his fingernails into his palms in embarrassment and pity. He didn't know what to say to his friend. The sound in Geoff's voice reminded Jim of a day – years ago, shortly before Geoff left school – when a girl Geoff secretly fancied had called him 'Spotty McBlobby' to his face. Geoff had burst into tears and thrown a chair across their form room.

A mad thought flickered like a knackered light bulb in Jim's head: tell him the truth. Jim shook it off. It was far too late for that. All Jim could do now was make sure that Geoff got down the aisle without incident.

'Well, you're marrying her. You're going to get out there and you're going to show them.' Jim tried hard to make his voice sound casual, as if it was all just a matter of fact.

'Everyone'll be laughing behind their hands. Even my own bloody brother.'

'Bollocks. Anyway, who cares what they think? This is between you and Laura, and no other bugger's opinion matters.'

Geoff sat on the edge of the bed again and rubbed the back of his neck. 'Thing is, mate…I don't know if I can keep up with her. She's so' – Geoff screwed his eyes shut – '*experienced.*'

Jim laughed despite himself. 'You fucking idiot. Is that what this is all about?'

No answer.

Jim sighed. Other than the odd detail dropped into workday banter, Jim had no idea what Laura had told Geoff about her past. Jim would have to be careful about what he said, but all he could think of was, 'It's a damn sight better than marrying someone who's fucking frigid. You're sex-obsessed yourself, man!'

'Aye, but now I'm worried that I'm never going to be exciting enough for her.'

'You've been thinking about this too much, mate. You're going to drive yourself bloody crackers this way.'

'You're too late – I'm already there.'

'Come on, man, get a grip. And give her some credit – she's not stupid. She's not marrying you for a laugh, is she? She's serious about you.'

'No, she's not stupid, that's for sure.'

'Fucking right it is.' Jim's mouth was whizzing ahead of his mind now; he felt like he was cycling downhill. 'And mebbes she's had enough of that sort of excitement, eh? Mebbes she wants someone she can actually rely on, and that's why she's chosen you.'

'Yeah?'

'Yeah. You've got a fit bird who likes you just the way you are. It's the best of both worlds, mate. You're on to a winner.'

Geoff smiled for the first time all morning. 'You're right.'

'Of course I'm right.'

'I knew I could trust you to set me straight.'

Jim had no idea that he'd done any such thing, but he smiled and said, 'Let's get you married.' He desperately wanted a drink.

10

I think Barry's scowl is going to stick to his face and stay there for ever. They'll cremate him like that and it'll be a closed-coffin job, because once he stops breathing, nobody will want to look at him again.

'That fucking Mac, thinks he's the fucking crown prince.'

We've had this for days: every time the three of us have the cabin to ourselves, out it comes. It's nine thirty and Barry hasn't even changed into his boots yet. He kicks out at one of them and it skitters across the floor, coming to rest next to me. I kick it back.

'He's all right is our Mac,' says Geoff. 'He's got a big gob, but a big heart too.'

'He's arrogant, that's what he is. Arrogant.' Barry drags hard at the last of his fag, drops it onto the floor of the cabin, and grinds it into a black smear under the heel of his trainer.

I've had enough of this. I finish my tea and walk outside. It's freezing. November brought an early frost, and now it's almost cold enough to justify downing tools, but Mac negotiated a completion bonus with the main contractor, so his lads keep at it. Barry won't be shown up, so we're here too. The difference is that they're actually working, while we are sat on our arses.

I mount the ladder and haul myself to the second tier of scaffolding that runs along the section we're to work on today. This side of the building is in shadow, and dew is frozen in the folds of the hessian that protects the blockwork. I'm about to pull it back so that I can see where new stacks are needed when Mac rounds the corner and says, 'Morning.'

'Morning, Mac.' My breath clouds.

'Are them two coming out to play or what?'

'Give 'em time. They have a unique conception of what constitutes a working day.'

'Has Barry mentioned the other night?'

'No. I think he suspects something, though.'

'Miserable bastard. Why the fuck are you still working for him anyway?'

'It's not really for him, is it? We're old mates; it's just the way it's worked out.'

'Doesn't mean it has to stay that fucking way.'

'We've been the same crew almost our whole working lives, man. Anyway, it's Geoff I feel sorry for – he has to stand next to the bastard all day.'

'I'm not fucking worried about Geoff.'

'Well, don't worry about me either. Shouldn't you be sat in an office somewhere?'

Mac laughs. 'I couldn't sit down in my office even if I wanted to: it's an absolute pigsty.'

'I bet it's a damn sight warmer than out here.'

'Bollocks to the weather. I'll lead from the front. That's why my buggers are out here working, while your buggers are indoors.'

'You've got some cheek, you know. You've been gone for years.'

'You knew where to find me. You've hardly ever called. You could work with me, you know. I'd fucking pay you more for a start.'

'Mac, don't rock the boat. You haven't been here. You don't know what's happened. There are other things I've got to consider.'

'Like what?'

There is nothing I can tell him. Then I see the top of the ladder shift and Barry emerges over the edge of the platform. He looks sour, but I can't tell if that's because he heard anything or just because Mac's here.

'All right, Baz?' Mac asks with a smile.

'Aye,' Barry mutters, and then looks at me. 'Are you going to bring up some fucking muck or what?'

I'm quiet for a moment; even Barry doesn't usually talk to me like that.

'There's a tub of it right behind you,' Mac observes calmly. He's right: there is. A full tub, sat on a pallet. If I gave Barry the merest shove, he'd land in it arse-first.

Barry gives it a cursory glance. 'That'll be old.'

'Actually, it's fresh. I was on the teleloader anyway, so I sent it up for you, and a pack of blocks. You can say thanks if you like.' Mac puts his hands on his hips. Barry stares at him. Mac stares back.

'Thanks.'

'You're welcome, son.' Mac claps his hands together and rubs them briskly. 'Right, I'd best get on with some work.'

Barry watches Mac until he disappears round the corner of the building and then nods at the pack of blocks. 'They're a bit close to the edge, like.'

'Never mind, we'll soon use them all.'

'Not at the speed Geoff's moving. He's on his third cup of tea and he hasn't even put his boots on.' Barry picks up his float and trowel, and knocks them together to clear the crust. 'Lazy bastard.' He stands there for a moment and stares at the blocks as if he's steeling himself to start work, but then snorts, 'Fuck it,' sits down on top of the wall and lights a cigarette.

He smokes in silence and I don't know what to do, so I just watch. Eventually, he looks up at me. 'Was Mac giving you earache, then?'

'No, just chatting, you know.' I scratch the back of my head.

'He's full of shit, him.'

'Aye, well, he must be doing something right.' I don't want to stand here and have this conversation with Barry. 'I'm fucking freezing. I'm going to start work.'

'Suit yourself.'

———

Eventually, Geoff drags himself out of the cabin and our collective mood improves somewhat. Cold gives you a hardship in common – unlike rain, which just locks you into a personal misery – and soon even Barry is laughing at the odd joke here and there. We fall into a rhythm of work, until I feel the first edge of late-morning hunger and somehow the soggy sandwiches in my bag become a tempting prospect.

'I'm getting hungry. I think I'll go in.'

'Righto. We'll be along in a minute. Put the kettle on.'

I clamber down the ladder and begin to trudge to the cabin when Mac spots me from inside the ground floor of the building.

'You all right?' he calls through the window opening.

'Aye, just going for me bait.'

'Anything nice?'

'Potted beef.'

'Classy.'

'Oh right, because I suppose you've got smoked salmon, eh?'

Someone starts the engine of the teleloader, so I don't catch Mac's response, but I think it involved the words 'cheeky bastard'. I give him a wave and head in, and behind me I hear the teleloader's reverse pips. I have my hand on the door handle when there's a loud crash and the pips abruptly stop. That doesn't sound good. I turn round and look back towards the building, but can't immediately work out what happened. All I can see is the teleloader, which is stopped roughly where I was standing when I spoke to Mac. Then I notice Barry and Geoff, still on the second level, peering over the edge. Something is going on. I climb up the steps of the cabin to get a better view, and it dawns on me: the idiot driver reversed into the scaffolding. Thankfully, Barry and Geoff were working three bays along or they might have been knocked off.

I trot over, and as I get closer, I see that two standards have been knocked out entirely. The boards above wobble and twist. Then I see Mac; he's at the window again, and cranes out to see what's happening. He shouts, but I can't hear it, because the engine of the teleloader is still running. I can see the guy in the cab just sat there like a child caught with their hand in the biscuit tin. Mac starts to climb through the window and I'm suddenly flooded with fear, because I can see exactly what's about to happen.

'Stop! Mac! Stay inside!' He can't hear me. He's outside now and ducks under a crossbrace. I run. Mac marches towards the offending vehicle. 'Get back!' I'm too late. The first block hurtles inches past his face and slaps into the mud right in front of him. He stops dead, looks at it, looks up, and then they all come. In the split second before he is knocked off his feet I think our eyes meet.

I skid through the mud on my knees and scrabble to pull away blocks, hurling them behind me. *Just a sign of life. Just a sign of life.* But there's no way he's alive, not like that. Arms slip under my shoulders. 'Come away! It's not safe.' They drag me off. My heels furrow the mud. I see Lee's face above me. 'It's not safe.' He points up. 'There's more.' I look. The remainder of the pack of blocks teeters on the edge; then they fall.

Part Two

Part Two

11

No matter what happens, we always end up in a pub. So it is today, but my ears just absorb the conversation around me as if it were background noise. Right now, I think, Mac's body lies in a cardboard box, on a trolley, somewhere in the hidden rooms of the crematorium. Soon he'll be vaporized and the surviving few pounds of bone ground to dust. That's the industrial process behind the velvet curtain, the sterile truth around which we erect the edifice of ceremony and grief. This is the wake, and it's busy. Mac had a lot of friends.

I avoided the other two in the aftermath. It was easy to do since we couldn't go back to work while the accident was investigated, the site inspected and made safe, and whatever other formalities were undertaken. This is the first time I've left the house for days and I feel unsafe around other humans. The other humans seem to want each other, though. They talk and talk, and drink and drink. Mainly, I do the latter. There are also sandwiches, slices of pork pie, and some mini Scotch eggs.

'They told us we could go back to work next week, like.' Barry says this as if one of us has asked, although we haven't, then pops a pickled onion into his mouth.

Geoff thumps his pint onto the table and slops some over the side. 'Bollocks. May as well have been a drug dealer or a fucking pimp.'

'You what?' says Barry, still chewing.

'Working fucking life, that's what. I must be a right fucking mug.' Geoff's voice has a manic edge.

'Well, it's like what they say: life's a bitch and then you die.'

'And you fucking love it, don't you?'

'It's just the way it is, Geoff. It's hard work and it's no fucking fun.' Barry picks up a sandwich.

'Well, fuck that. And why do we have to go back there?'

'Why not?'

'You tosser.' Geoff gets up and stomps off. He is upset, but I don't know what I could do or say to make him feel better. He was right about one thing, though: we don't have to go back to that site. It hadn't occurred to me before, but why would we want to? In this market, we'd find another job in minutes.

I look at Barry. He shrugs at me and through a mouthful of white bread and reformed roast beef mumbles, 'What's his problem?'

'Fucking hell, Baz. Mac was one of his best mates, and mine too. You weren't exactly sensitive to his feelings.'

Barry laughs and a spot of chewed sandwich shoots out of his mouth and hits the side of my glass. 'Sensitive? Divven give us all that poofter's shite.'

'Why are you even here?'

'I've got to pay my respects, haven't I?'

'Respect? Is that what you call it?'

'Bloody hell, not you too.'

'Enjoy your fucking lunch, Baz.'

I leave him and go to the bar. I can't see Geoff – he has disappeared among the mourners somewhere – so I just buy another pint and stand there with it. The pub is oppressively crowded and, now I'm crammed shoulder to shoulder with them all, increasingly hot and airless. A group of four men I recognize from Mac's crew sit round a table together. They all smoke cigars. Big ones. I suppose it is some kind of tribute, but it makes the place stink. In the heat and smoke, with the taste of my own beer sour in my mouth, my stomach turns and I need to get outside. I make a break for the door. Cold air sweeps over me and I step into it with gratitude and relief.

The beer garden slopes downhill ahead of me and I'm led along it by a path of vast stone flags embedded in the lawn. The path stops at a stand of four picnic tables, but I keep walking to the dry-stone wall that marks the end of the garden. After the wall, the valley side drops away in a steep escarpment to which grass, close-gnawed by sheep, barely clings and through which sharp limestone outcrops erupt here and there. The other side rises more gently; its folds cradle tiny hamlets and even now, after midday, patches of low mist. Squat stone barns are scattered over the land.

When Mac moved out here, Barry wasn't the only one to laugh at the idea of him as a country gent; I had a bit of a chuckle too. Mac did well for himself, though, with his big gob and his genuine talent for doing business, and if he wanted to spend his spare time in tweeds, then fair play to him, I thought. Standing here, though, I can see what he saw in the place. This is tough country, what they call marginal land, and it fits him. His house is out there somewhere. I can probably see it from here, but I don't know which one it is. I never came to visit him; at the time, it seemed more important to keep the peace with Barry.

The grass is damp and my shoes are getting wet. It'll seep through if I stay here. When I turn back, I see a man sat on the picnic table nearest to me. He sits on the outermost bench, facing out, so that his back is to the tabletop. He leans forward, with his elbows on his knees, and stares ahead. He looks familiar to me, though for a few odd seconds I can't place him. Then I realize that it's Lee, who dragged me away from the falling blocks, but he looks different, with his fashionable hair slicked into something neater and more suitable for a funeral.

'Hiya.'

He nods at me. I walk over and sit down at the other end of his bench. He keeps looking out, over the valley. I sip at my pint.

'Thanks for rescuing me,' I say eventually.

'That's all right. You just charged over to him. It was pretty brave.'

'I wasn't really thinking. I didn't even realize I was in any danger.'

'It was still brave. Have you spoken to his wife?'

'No. I mean, I don't know her that well. I've only met her the few times, like. Mac sort of lost touch with us for a while.'

'I think she'd like to say thanks, at least. You know, for trying.'

'Right.'

'You and Mac were good friends, though?'

'Aye, since we were kids. He lived next door to Geoff. We all grew up together.'

Lee studies the back of his hand and picks at his thumbnail. 'Look, Mac had quite a bit of work lined up. If you're interested, there's some of those jobs we could take on. Renovations and conversions, things like that. You could ask Geoff if he fancies it too.'

I smile. No mention of Barry there. I think of the miserable fucker, sat inside and scoffing pork pies. He pissed me off today. He's been pissing me off for a long time. I wonder if it's still worth it. 'All right, give us your number. We'll have a chat about it.'

When I get back inside, I buy another drink and stand at the bar. I feel more at ease now and the beer slips down easily. Geoff comes to my side just as I finish it.

'Do you want another?' he asks.

'I'll get these.'

'Thanks, mate.'

'Look, I'm sorry I disappeared the last few days.'

'It's all right. What were we supposed to do? Have a hugging session and a cry together?'

'I thought that's what you liked.'

'No, I just get straight to the anal sex, me.'

'Well, you've always been a romantic at heart.'

I buy our drinks and we sip together, each waiting for the other to raise the issue. As usual, I'm the more drunk, so I crack first.

'I think we need to have a serious discussion with Barry.'

'Fuck him,' Geoff mutters into his pint.

'Aye, it's all right saying that, but we've actually got to do something about this.'

'It's not right, man. What he said. We don't need to go back to that shithole.'

'I know. I'm on your side.'

Geoff's shoulders sink and he leans against the bar. 'Do you think he's serious about it?'

'I think if we don't nip this in the bud, he's going to turn up in the van next week and expect us to hop in and drive back down there like nothing happened.'

'Shit.'

'Aye.' I rub my thumb up and down the side of my glass and watch the smear of grease form. I'm on dangerous ground here. This could go very wrong indeed, but somehow I hear myself saying it anyway. 'We could just tell him to fuck off, you know. Move on. There's plenty of work out there.' The pit of my stomach fizzes.

'Jesus. I don't know about that. He's a cunt, but he's a mate, you know.'

'Are you sure about that, these days?'

Geoff sighs. 'No, mate. No, I'm not.'

'Well then.'

'Look, let's at least reason with him first. If he sees that we're really serious, he might change his mind.'

'Fine, let's go and show him that we're really serious.'

I walk across the bar, to where we last saw Barry sitting, but he's not there anymore. Geoff catches up with me. 'Come on, mate, you're drunk. Mebbes this isn't the best time for it, eh?'

'No time like the present, Geoff.' Then I see Barry, on the other side of the room, talking to some people I've never met before. I feel like I don't give a fuck about anything and I stalk up to them.

'Barry, can we have a word?'

'What's up?'

'We want to talk about the plan for next week.'

He looks at me through narrowed eyes. 'How much have you had to drink?'

'Never mind how much I've had to drink. We've got a serious problem to discuss.'

'Are you two still on about that? Do you really want to talk about this here?'

'Don't you? Is that because mebbes you were thinking we'd happily go back to the site where Mac was killed?'

'This isn't the place.' He shakes his head. 'Just shut up, all right.' He turns to the group he is standing with and leaves me to stare at the back of his head. I hear, 'Don't worry about that. He just gets a bit aggressive when he's drunk.' An old man gives me a disapproving look.

My fists are clenched and I am furious now. I can hardly believe that Barry wants to play at being the reasonable one.

Geoff puts his hand on my shoulder. 'Just leave it. Not here.'

———

Laura came to pick up me and Geoff, but she didn't drive me all the way home; nobody ever does. It's a pain in the neck to drive onto the estate and crawl along the streets littered with speed bumps. I always let them drop me off by the main road and I take the footpath home. It's narrow, and it's not well lit, but that doesn't matter. Who's going to fuck with me?

There's a tufty bit of grass and a park bench along the way, and that's where I have ended up. The sky is clear, and as a bonus, it seems that I miraculously avoided all the dog shit. I throw my head all the way back, and my skull rests, painfully, on the top rail of the bench. My eyes are filled with space. This is the best kind of being drunk, and staring into the star fields is the only way to get it. You can't do it with all of the world crowding around you; you get perspective, that way, because it's all so confusing that being drunk makes sense. Only in the simplicity of vast distance can you fully appreciate the joy of being wankered.

With my head like this, every breath feels deep. The air surges through my nostrils and makes an icy grab at the back of my throat. I cry a little, but, as ever, I can't concentrate on the feeling. The sparse and pathetic tears just collect at my temples around the hairline. Soon they create a freezing sensation and I'm forced to wipe them away with my sleeve. Clearly, I'm bad at remembrance, as I can't even maintain a dignified stillness.

If there was a time to indulge a moment, it is now. I cast around for a memory, but I just smell the dust.

12

It is Saturday afternoon and Geoff has wanked himself into a deep state of melancholy. He turns off his PC with a mournful sigh and wanders into the kitchen, where he switches on the kettle and devours three digestive biscuits. The house is empty and dusk pours into the back garden. Geoff glares through the window at the purple sky. He hates this time of year; you've barely got out of bed and then it's dark again.

Geoff knows that he's been useless recently. Since Mac died, he's done nothing but sit around the house or go to the pub. Today, Laura got up and went off to Newcastle while Geoff was still in his underwear, leaving him alone to a day of porn, telly, and more porn. Now he feels sick and helpless. The kettle reaches a rolling boil and clicks off.

He is stirring in the milk when the phone rings.

'Hello?'

'It's Barry.'

Geoff mouths a silent 'shit' and looks at the ceiling. The Artex spins. 'Hello, Baz. Y'all right?'

'Can't complain. Nobody listens.'

Geoff has heard the joke a million times before and Barry gets the timing wrong, sounds false. Geoff can't find the energy for any pretence of laughter. 'Aye, that's the way,' he mumbles.

'You coming for a pint?'

'It's a bit early, Baz.'

'Divven be queer. Come for a pint, man.'

'Is Jim coming out?'

'I think we should have a chat without him. He's been a bit, y'know, funny.'

Geoff feels panic rise from his belly. He pauses to collect himself and wonders what to say next, but all that comes out is, 'All right, I'll see you down there in a bit.'

'Get a move on, then. I'm setting off now.' Barry hangs up.

Geoff returns the receiver to the cradle and swears viciously. Then he picks up the phone again and calls Jim. No answer. Geoff sighs, looks at his feet, and sees that he isn't wearing socks. He tramps upstairs to find a pair.

He opens the door to leave just as Laura walks up to it. He notices, with some relief, that she only has two bags. 'What did you buy?'

'Nice to see you too. Just some clothes.' She bundles past him into the house. 'Where are you going?'

'Down the Admiral.'

'Great.'

'It's Baz, isn't it. Thinks we need a chat. He's just being a bastard as usual.'

Laura stiffens, but puts down her bags and says, 'What's happening with you three?'

Geoff shrugs. 'I just don't want to work with him anymore if he's being like this. Don't worry, me and Jim will find something else.' Laura gives Geoff a funny look. He can't work out what it means, so he just says, 'I've got to go.'

'Are you going to tell Barry this tonight?' Laura asks, but Geoff is already walking away.

'Mebbes,' he calls back. 'I'll see you later.'

When Geoff arrives at the pub, Barry is already there. There are two butts in the ashtray, and his pint is half finished. There is one for Geoff; the head has dissipated entirely and left a scummy half-inch at the top of the glass.

'You took your fucking time.'

'Couldn't find any clean socks.' Geoff sits down and nods at his pint. 'Thanks, mate.'

'You're welcome.'

They sit in silence for a few minutes, smoking. Finally, Geoff shifts in his chair and says, 'You owe me four quid.'

'What for?'

'For the lottery.'

'Are you still putting that on?'

'Aye.'

'Fucking hell. You'll have to get it another time. I've only got enough cash for drinks.'

'Right.' Geoff looks around the pub. It's early and only the hardened regulars are in. They concentrate on their beer. Geoff will have to ride this out alone.

'I'm a bit worried about our Jim,' says Barry. 'He was proper off with me the other day.'

'Well, it wasn't easy for any of us, like.'

'He was being a right twat.'

'We don't want to go back to that job.' Geoff blurts it out, then sits back in his chair, and looks at his hands.

Barry sucks his lip. 'Look, man, it's the best thing for us. It's steady. We can get the job done.'

'Who cares? There's other jobs.'

'There are, but this is the one we said we'd do.'

'Why are you so bothered? You've said yourself you fucking hate it there. It's fucking miles away, for a start.'

'It's the principle, and we've got a reputation.'

Geoff can't believe what he's hearing and looks directly at Barry for the first time since entering the pub. He leans over the table and seems almost like he means it. 'Principle, Baz? Since when do you give a fuck about principles?'

'What's that supposed to mean?'

'You're a complete fucking knobhead. That's what it means.'

'Fucking hell, Geoff. Settle down.'

'Look, it's not just the job. It's you. In fact, it's all you.'

'Shut up, man. You sound like my wife. Don't be so daft.'

'I'm not shutting up. You've been the fucking boss for so long you don't listen to anyone anymore. I can't believe you think we're going to go back.'

'Fucking hell. It's only a job of work.'

'No, it's more than that. You hated Mac, and you hated us for being his mates. You want to rub our faces in the fact that he's dead, for revenge. You're a sick bastard.'

'Bollocks to that. You sound like Jim. You know why Jim liked Mac so much? Because he's a fucking bum boy. A closet homo. And mebbes you are too.'

'Fuck off. You've lost it. You're psycho. I'm never working with you again.' Geoff realizes that he is standing up now and that people are watching him. He feels as if the ground is tipping under his feet and he crashes towards the door.

'Geoff, don't be stupid. Come back!'

'Fuck off!' Geoff escapes into the cold darkness and doesn't stop until he is well down the street. With a sudden rush of frustration he thinks he forgot his jacket, but then sees that he is wearing it and remembers that he didn't take it off. He pats his pockets and realizes that what he did leave behind was his tobacco. 'Shit.' He needs a cigarette now.

There is a newsagent's opposite him. Geoff still has several cartons of tobacco in his garage from last summer's trip to France and normally would resent paying for cigarettes, but under his current circumstances, the light from the newsagent's window shines like a beacon of hope in a dangerous world and he crosses the road.

Inside, there is one young woman behind the counter and a long queue of people. Geoff joins the end of the queue and stands uneasily between the chocolate and the magazines. He watches the woman behind the counter. She saunters between the lottery terminal and the till as if she was deliberately trying to tease him with her slowness. Geoff feels a hot anger with her and with the idiots who always leave it until the last moment on Saturday evening to buy their lottery tickets. All he wants is a packet of fags. She's not even good-looking. He taps his foot and mutters, 'Hurry the fuck up.'

The elderly lady in front of him turns and looks him in the eye. 'That's not going to help anyone, is it?'

Geoff tries to ignore her, but she continues to stare at him. 'Sorry,' he mutters. She nods primly and turns away.

Geoff shakes his head. All this shit is turning him into a miserable bastard like Barry or Jim. Well, maybe not Jim; at least Jim has a sense of humour and is a real friend. Still, he failed Geoff tonight, left him to deal with Barry alone and now look: everything is fucked.

Geoff's mobile phone rings. He fumbles it from his pocket and checks the screen. Barry. 'Fuck off,' he hisses, and stabs at the button to deny the call. The ringing stops and the screen goes dark.

The old woman looks at him again.

'Not you.' Geoff holds up his phone. 'This cunt.'

'Men like you should be in prison.'

Geoff thinks about this for a moment: free food and no work doesn't sound too bad. He shrugs. 'Aye, you're right. We should.'

The woman clucks and turns her back on Geoff again. She pulls up her shoulders and he can tell that she intends to ignore all further evidence of his existence. Geoff feels like an idiot, and as his mood plunges deeper, another nicotine craving rises. There are still four customers in front of him. He glares over their heads towards the cigarette display and is dismayed by how much the price has risen since he last bought fags legally. Then a different set of numbers catches his eye.

'Fucking hell.'

13

'I remember Mac.'

'Aye, you would. He wasn't the kind you'd forget about.'

Mr Green looks at me. His eyes have that elderly look, of not-firm-enough jelly. It's clear to me that this will be his last panto. 'No,' he says thoughtfully. 'No, I don't believe he was.' A pause as he fiddles with some wire. 'So how did it go?'

'All right – you know, as well as a funeral ever does.'

'Well, you've seen a few.'

'Aye' – I bite on my annoyance – 'I have.'

Mr Green manages to bend the wire as he wants it and places it amid the wood shavings on his workbench. 'Well, what now, eh?'

'Are you taking an interest in me, sir?'

'No, you daft bugger. I'm talking about the bloody crowns and tiaras.'

'Oh. They need spraying. I'll do them once you've gone in; there's no point gassing you. I'll lock up the shed and post the keys through your door on my way out.'

'Oh, you think I can't handle a few chemicals, now?'

'We don't need to take any chances.'

'Well, don't forget to set the security light. It's the third switch from the left.'

'No danger of forgetting that; you need a bloody shotgun around here.'

'Now, that's not the spirit of community we're trying to encourage, is it?' His face is partially paralysed, so I can't work out how serious this question is.

'You might be right there, Mr Green.' I would add that we could do with some spirit, but there's only so much of that talk I can take before I want to crush my head in a vice. Mr Green picks up the wire frame of the tiara again and starts to fiddle. Either he didn't take the hint or he's just not inclined to move. I involuntarily scratch the bridge of my nose.

Mr Green glances at me from over his work. 'I suppose this isn't normally how you'd spend a Saturday night.'

'Making tiaras? No, not usually. But it's all right. I'm a bit sick of that lot, anyway.'

'Your mates?'

'Aye, with the funeral and that. It's been a bit stressful.'

'It's no bloody fun, is it?'

'You can say that again. Geoff took it badly, like. It proper knocked him off his perch. I think it's made him, y'know, ask questions about life and what have you.'

'Oh…life questions, eh? They're trying to get me asking them in rehabilitation – physio-bloody-therapy and all. There's no point. I was half dead before the stroke. Daft buggers. Still, for a younger man, it might be useful, mightn't it? To ask a few questions of yourself after an event like that?' He is looking at me. I avoid his eyes and try to find something to do with my hands, but he won't give up. 'You, for instance. Maybe this is the time to make something of yourself.'

I could almost laugh. 'Like what?'

'Well, you could finish your education for a start. I always thought you'd go all the way to university.'

'That was the plan, but things changed, didn't they? Instead of sitting my GCSEs, I was sitting on remand at Deerbolt Young Offenders Institution. And how can I afford to study now?'

Mr Green retired from school over fifteen years ago. Until tonight, he and I had barely exchanged a word since then. And now this. I don't know whether I'm annoyed or flattered or just grimly amused.

'Well, I can't answer that,' he says, 'but I taught you and I know you've got potential. I still remember that project you did for me on the rainforest.'

Christ. I'd forgotten about that. I had to go to Newcastle to find the books. I sneaked into the university library and I was terrified that someone would notice me and throw me out. I photocopied what I could and scarpered.

'All that was *before*,' I say. 'I came out of prison with absolutely nothing, and I need to provide for myself. No one else is going to do it.'

'I understand that, but it strikes me that you've done your time, and there's no need to keep paying for it.'

That's easy for him to say, but I don't want to argue with the old codger, so I just nod.

He grunts. 'Well, I've said my piece, and I am very grateful for your help tonight.'

'That's all right. I suppose it's something to do.'

'Good lad. I'd suspected you might just tell our Joe to bugger off.'

I smile. When Joe turned up at my house the other day and told me my presence would be required on a Saturday evening, I almost did exactly that. 'No. You can't be that cruel to Joe; it just bounces off.'

'Is he better yet?'

'What? I haven't seen him since then. Is he sick?'

'Stomach bug. Nothing serious.' Mr Green sniffs and puts the tiara aside. 'Anyway, I'll turn in, I think.'

'Righto. Well, I'll spray this stuff, then.'

Mr Green fumbles for his walking stick, but he can't lean far enough to reach it; the tips of his fingers just miss as he sweeps his arm through space. I get up and put it in his hands. He nods a curt 'thank you' and starts to haul himself to his feet. I reach out to help him, but he waves me off – 'Not dead yet, son. Save your breath' – and throws himself dangerously off his chair and into a half-crouch. I look away and soon hear him shuffling towards the shed door.

'G'night, son.'

'Aye, goodnight.' I sit still, listening. The tap-tap of the cane on the garden path recedes, and I faintly hear the back door of Mr Green's house open and close.

I'm tired. I toy with the idea of just going home, right now, but the smell of the sawdust is comforting. The paint cans are in a plastic bag, all new and unbroken from the hardware superstore. I reach out with my foot, hook one of the handles on the toe of my shoe, and drag the bag towards me, across the floor. It sweeps a path through the powdery blanket of sawdust and the smell of pine gets stronger. I grab the bag and rummage through the contents. There's a receipt; someone cared enough to spend fifteen quid.

My phone rings. I push the receipt back into the bag and look at the caller ID. It's Barry. This is the first time either of them has tried to contact me since the funeral yesterday. Geoff said he wanted a day or two to think about it; seeing me lose my temper seemed to deflate his own anger, at least temporarily. As for Barry, well…it looks like I'm about to find out. I answer it.

'Hello?'

'It's Barry.'

'I know. How are you?'

'I've just seen Geoff. He's being a fucking idiot.'

'He's not a happy man.'

'None of us are happy. He's talking about breaking up the gang – pissing off and not working with us anymore.'

'No, not working with *you*.'

'You've put him up to it.'

'We're fed up.'

'Fuck off. Get him back.'

I stare at the wall. There's a large bow saw mounted on two nails. My dad hung his tools in the same way, in the lean-to he constructed against the back wall of the yard. Between that, the coalbunker, and the bins there was barely room for my bicycle. Once my mother was gone, it was in there that he finally did it – maybe so he didn't piss on the carpet, or maybe just to die in the only space that was ever entirely his own. He must have thought he had lost everything, abandoned all over again, just as he was at the beginning of his life.

Mr Green's saw has a thin band of orange rust along the top of the blade, but the teeth are clean and sharp. 'I don't think I can do that, Barry.'

'Fuck's sake. Grow a fucking brain. He's going to ruin everything.'

'What's he going to ruin? It's time to move on.'

'No fucking way. This gang is not breaking up; we work together.'

'Why do you care so much?'

'I built this!'

'And you're in charge? And you like it? And you know you could never have this power over any fucker else?'

'Don't fuck me about. I've got enough dirt on the pair of you to ruin your lives for ever.'

'Barry, the time for that's passed. They're married, they're settled. Even you…'

'I would. I will.'

'Barry, if you do it, you'll lose anyway.'

'Right now, I've got fuck all to lose. But you aren't going to take that chance, are you? Call me when you've fixed it.' He hangs up.

I sit and stare at my phone. The light behind the LCD screen goes out. I slip it into my jacket pocket, and then without thinking I reach to the floor and scoop up a handful of sawdust. It feels very soft and dry in my palm. I open my fingers slightly and it pours out in three streams, each one like the sand in an egg-timer. At the end, it's all gone except for a thin layer stuck to my skin that makes the lines in my palm stand out. It looks like one of those kiddie's handprints that parents sometimes tape to their fridge door.

I still don't know what to do about Geoff, and I still have to spray-paint these tiaras. I decide that most of them should be silver; I never liked gold jewellery, even when it was fashionable. If Barry calls again, I can just say, 'Sorry, I've been a bit busy making Cinderella's headwear.' What does it matter now? We're all in the shit anyway.

I pick up a spray can and shake it. The little ball clacks around inside. I can feel it bounce off the walls of the cylinder. Then there's a banging at the shed door and I drop the can in shock.

'Who's there?'

'It's me.' Joe's voice. 'Let me in.'

'It's not locked.'

'Oh.' He fumbles and the door swings open. Even in the sixty-watt light of the shed he looks ill – pale face and ringed eyes.

'You look like shit, man. You should be in bed.'

'I'm bored! Bored of television!' He shakes his head vigorously and his jowls slap against his teeth in a wet rattle.

'All right, don't get agitated. How did you find me?'

'I knew you were here. I was the messenger, remember?'

'Aye, right. What do you want?'

'Can I help?'

'No. Go home and chew some Rennies. You look ready to vomit all over me.'

'Please.'

'Joe, are you really going to help, or are you just going to fuck it up?'

'I'm going to help, really.' Despite his pallor, he looks relatively certain of the fact.

'All right.'

'Magnificent!'

'But then you've got to go home: I've a phone call to make.'

'Righto.'

'I'm spraying. Here, put this mask on.'

He slips the elastic over his head and positions the white mask over his nose and mouth. At least if he pukes, it'll catch the mess. It occurs to me that I feel pretty sick myself.

14

At the moment when Geoff's mind rejoins the flow of time, the world and all its night air rushes past his head like a breaking wave. He also registers the fact that his arse is extremely cold. That numbness is his only marker of time, the marker of how long he's been sat here, for how long he hasn't moved, and for how long he's heard nothing but the creak of this swing and the blink and buzz of that broken streetlight. The marker says, 'Too fucking long.' Geoff can see the dark shadows of his feet and decides to test if he can still move his body. The sole of his right shoe scuffs across the pad of safety material under the swing. He can't tell if he is surprised or if he doesn't care.

This isn't how he imagined it, and then his phone rings. It rings and rings, then it stops. Then it rings again. Laura would never call twice, so it must be Jim.

'Hello?'

'All right, mate.'

'Hello.' Geoff repeats it for the lack of anything else to say.

'I've just had Barry on the phone. I'd assumed we were going to do it together.'

'I couldn't reach you. He cornered me.'

'Shit. Sorry. I've been out and about, like.'

'Well, it's settled, isn't it?'

There is a long pause.

'What?'

'Geoff, I think we've made a mistake.'

Geoff looks up and stares across the dark playground to the road beyond. Silent headlights flitter through the climbing frame. The corner of his mouth twitches in a stillborn smile.

'Geoff?'

'He got to you.'

'No.'

'Aye, you always give in to him in the end.'

'It's not like that—'

'Shut up. I don't care.' Geoff spits the words almost as a reflex, but when they explode from his lips, he realizes how true they are. 'I don't have to care.'

'Geoff, what's going on?'

'Nothing I want to share with you.'

'Geoff, look—'

Geoff's ears disengage. The words become sounds that mean nothing at all. Inside himself he can feel everything fall away. It's as if he suddenly remembered a long-lost girlfriend only to realize that none of it matters anymore. It has all passed and he is new again. He cuts Jim off, 'No, no, no. No. I've done enough of listening to you. I'm going to do you a favour right now, Jim lad, and you'd better hear it. You might be cleverer than me, but I've been watching you for thirty fucking years and that makes me an expert. I've got a fucking PhD in Jim studies, and my thesis says you're a cunt. You're spineless. Ever since you got out of prison you've acted as if that was the be all and end all of your whole fucking life. You're just using prison as an excuse for having done fuck all of any worth, and it's 'cos you're shit-scared. You're too scared to do anything. All you ever do is read your fucking books and spend your time looking after that nutter Joe, pretending it makes up for things, pretending you're doing something noble. Well, it fucking isn't. It's time to stand up for yourself. You don't have to crawl back to Barry this time. He just keeps you for a pet murderer because it makes him feel tough. But we can do without him. This is your last chance. Tell me you're on my side. Tell me now.'

'Geoff, there's something else…'

Geoff takes the phone away from his ear and holds it at arm's length in front of his face. All he can hear is a tinny little gabble. 'G'bye, Jim,' he says loudly, then turns off the phone.

All of the joy that Geoff knew should have been his from the very first moment floods through his body. Every other alternative is sealed, and now there is just one bright path to follow. His fingertips ring with anticipation, and he stands upright. Barry is not going to get any of this money. As for Jim, he'll see about getting a handout to him later. All Geoff needs to do now is claim his prize and then he and Laura can disappear. He slips the phone back into his jacket and grins as he brushes against the reassuring bulge of his wallet. In there, just behind his driving licence, is his ticket to freedom. Nothing I want to share with you, he thinks, then giggles. The giggles get harder and harder until he bends double and feels as if he is going to laugh his lungs right out of his mouth.

15

I knew Geoff would take this badly, but I never suspected this much bitterness. He bawls me out and pronounces each word with such a sharp, gleaming anger that I feel as if I'm under a hail of razor blades. And then he is begging me not to sell him out to Barry, but I have no choice, so I wait until he is finished and say, 'Geoff, there's something else. Just trust me, please,' but how can Geoff trust me now? I hesitate. 'It's Barry. He's going to do something bad. I know this sounds weak, mate, but I just need you to do what he says until I can sort it out.'

I can't sort this out. What have I ever sorted out? Barry will always have that strange, hurtful secret hidden away and ready for use. Maybe it would be better if Geoff knew. I don't even decide to say it. It just starts coming out.

'Look, it's about your Laura,' and then I realize that I'm talking to dead air.

My ears rush like jet engines. It must be all the solvents in here. I push open the door of the shed and get a faceful of night. I feel a lot of different kinds of guilt, and then relief that he didn't hear me say it. I need to call him back, but I hear a horrible noise behind me. Joe. I'd forgotten he was there.

'Oh shit.' The stench is immediate and vile. Joe is on his hands and knees. His mouth hangs open.

'I'm sick.'

'Jesus, Joe! You're not a fucking kid. You can't just get down and puke on the floor. Why didn't you go outside?'

He doesn't say anything; his body is wracked in spasmodic jerks like a cat with a fur ball. He dry-heaves as the pool of vomit spreads out and envelops his hands. He looks awful and my anger seeps away. I find a rag and hold it out to him. 'Here, wipe yourself off.'

He takes it from me and dabs at his hands and face gingerly. I wait for him to finish. 'I want to go home,' he says.

My phone goes off. I check the display and it's Barry. 'Shit!'

I look at Joe. I can't leave him like this. I take a deep breath, switch off my phone, and say, 'All right, mate, I'll take you home. Can you stand up?'

Before we leave, I kick sawdust over the puke.

Joe walks slowly, and I want to stick to the shadows because in my mind Barry is out prowling the streets ready to confront me, so it takes us too long to get to Joe's house. At least the fresh air seems to do him some good; by the time we walk through the gate into the back yard, he's no longer green. He turns to me as we reach the door.

'Shhh! Mam's asleep.'

I make a show of nodding conspiratorially, but we're not even inside yet and I can already hear the television. Joe opens the door and creeps in. I follow. It's dark in the kitchen – the only light comes from the living room – but I immediately realize that something is wrong. Mrs Joe's kitchen only ever smells of one of two things: fresh cooking or kitchen cleaner. Tonight, it smells of old food.

'Turn on the light, mate. I can't see a thing.'

When he switches it on, I can see the source of the smell. There are dirty dishes in the sink. The swing bin is jammed full and overflowing. Empty cans – soup, beans, corned beef – litter the worktops, which are covered in crumbs and splattered with various colours of gunge. Joe's been cooking for himself; that's probably why he's sick.

'Where's your mam?'

'Living room.' He can tell I'm worried. He watches me with the nearest thing to suspicion that he has. 'She's asleep.'

'She was asleep when you left?'

'Aye.' Then he frowns. 'She doesn't know I went out. Don't tell her.'

'I won't tell her, Joe.' I inch towards the living room. 'I'm just going to turn down the TV.'

'She's tired. She'll be angry.'

'Look, just sit down, OK?'

I go into the living room, and as I move, I can hear that rushing again. I look at the carpet and I don't raise my head until I've rounded her armchair and stand in front of her. She is very still.

I can no longer hear the television, and the rest of the room drops out of sight. There is only this chair, and the body in it. I have to squeeze shut my eyes to provoke thought, and when I open them, I slowly reach out with my index and middle fingers. Then she stirs and I snatch my hand back. She is breathing and she can't be allowed to know that I've seen her, or the house, in this state. I back off very slowly. She doesn't move again.

'You didn't turn it down.' Joe sits at the kitchen table, wary but without guile.

'I know. I've had a better idea.' I close the door to the living room and remove the dirty dishes from the sink.

'What are you doing?'

'A spot of washing-up, then some tidying.'

Joe's eyes widen and he whispers, 'She'll go bonkers!'

'That's where you come in.'

'I've come in.'

'Joe, listen to me. If she asks, tell her that you did it.'

'That's fibbing.'

'Yes, but it's a good fib.' I try to smile at him, but my lips feel as if they're made of lead.

'She might wake up.'

'I'll be quiet, and the TV's on – she'll not hear any noise.'

'And it's still a good fib?'

'Yes. I just want to help her out.'

He thinks about this for a moment, then nods his head. 'OK. You've got a deal, partner.'

'Good man.' I turn the tap on and fill the sink with water, but I keep an ear out for movement from the front room. I need more information, but I don't want to upset him. There's a window over the sink and in it I can see his reflection. He has his chin in his hand and he stares into space. Somewhere in his idiot's brain he knows something is wrong, but I'll never get him to admit it. Not directly, anyway. I start to wash up.

'Had any visitors recently?'

'Nope.'

'Did your mam get sick too?'

'Nope.'

'Oh, not catching, then?'

'Nope.'

'Good job. It'd be a right pain in the arse if you were both ill, eh?'

Joe ignores me. He zips himself out of his coat and puts it over the back of his chair. Then he catches me watching him in the window and starts to pick his nose.

I attack a plate with more vigour than is necessary. Clearly, I won't get far with Joe tonight. The pair of them have been forced to close ranks so many times over the years that now it just comes naturally at the first hint of prying eyes. Even, it appears, if those eyes occupy the skull of the closest thing to a friend either of them have. Still, I'm going to keep a better lookout from now on.

The kitchen clock says that it is almost ten and that I should be off somewhere else, worrying, arguing, and perhaps getting my head kicked in. I'd rather clean Mrs Joe's kitchen. Here is a task I can identify and complete, despite my interloper's guilt. I wash, dry, and put away all the dishes, handling them carefully to avoid any telltale clinks and clatters. I pick up the junk, take out the rubbish, and change the bin bag. I clean the surfaces and scrub the hob. Finally, I wring out the dishcloth and hang it over the tap. By the time I am finished, Joe is asleep at the table.

I took the number for Mrs Joe's doctor. It was stuck to the front of the refrigerator under some coupons and the council-tax bill. Now, it's scribbled on a piece of notepaper in my pocket and I finger it as I turn onto my street. It's a bad idea: Mrs Joe would despatch the doctor with brittle fury and excommunicate me. If she can still walk and talk, however badly, she will never accept interference. Some hapless GP doesn't stand a chance. I'll hang on to it for emergencies, but I've got a feeling that if I do come to use it, the emergency will be over.

Once I'm indoors, I remember that my phone's still off. I just want to go to bed; everything else seems futile. All I can do is buy time with Barry, so I turn on my phone and it pings into life. There are three missed calls. I don't even check them. Then it tells me I have a text message from Barry: *Well?*

At least it's to the point. It was sent hours ago and I know, as I key in my response, that I'm just prolonging the bullshit, but that's all I have the energy to do: *Sorting things out. I'll get back to you.*

I turn the phone off again and unplug my landline. Barry won't come to the house – it's beneath what he presumably regards as his dignity – so for the time being, I'm safe and the knowledge of it brings a yawn and the slow, downward creep of my eyelids. I climb the stairs, undress, and get into bed. I don't have to fight to rid my mind of the day; thought just slows and stops. I fall asleep.

There is a noise. I think I dreamed it, because I'm full of the strangeness of sleep. It happens again: a dull sound, somewhere. The memory of it stays and I compare it to the silence. The noise had substance; there is someone knocking at my door. I hit consciousness as if it were the pavement at the end of a long fall, and turn on the lamp. The room blinds me. My jeans. I see them on the floor, grab them, and scramble them onto my legs – half on, half off the bed – and then somehow find myself standing.

Thud! Thud! Thud! A long burst of knocks. They really want me to answer the door. I blink at the clock, it's almost 1 a.m. More knocking.

'Fuck.'

I slither down the stairs on jelly legs and get to the door. Keys. Shit. But they're there, hanging from the lock and swaying gently under a renewed bout of knocking. I'm about to open the door, but then I remember: I should be worried. I should have a baseball bat. Geoff and Barry have lost their fucking minds, and who knows what they'll do next.

'I can see you in the glass. Open up!'

Not Barry or Geoff. It sounds like a woman. I turn the key and open the door. She flies at me and shoves me so hard that I stumble back.

She's screaming, 'Where's Geoff? Where's Geoff?'

16

'I've got a ticket to ride. I've got a ticket to ra-ha-hide.' Geoff can't help himself. He's full of singing as he marches down the street.

'C'mon, Elvis!' someone yells, and over the road Geoff sees three lads in the bus stop punching their Super Strength in the air. He sneers and whirls his arm round, and one of the lads shouts, 'You're a wanker!'

Geoff blows him an extravagant kiss. The lad stands up, but Geoff walks on and hears behind him, 'Leave it, Wayne. He's not worth it, man.'

'I'm worth a bit more than you think, you charver fuckwits,' says Geoff, but not very loudly.

Geoff intended to head home, now that he knows what he's going to do, but when he reaches the turn-off, he decides to carry on. He'll have a little celebration of his own, while the secret is still all his. He likes holding it unsaid in his mouth. He'll go to the other pub, nobody will bother him there: it's twenty pence a pint more expensive than their local, and Barry thinks it's full of posh bastards. Geoff looks forward to being a posh bastard himself.

That's the best part, the getting one over on Barry. Not that Barry will ever know, but Geoff takes great pleasure in the idea that while he's sipping a pina fucking colada on the beach, Barry will still be slogging his guts out, ignorant and miserable. As for Jim, well, what would Jim do with a full share? Drink himself to death, probably. Anyway, isn't Geoff the one who bothered to put the numbers on, week in, week out, rain or shine, even if they hadn't coughed up their subs? But Geoff isn't the mug anymore; he's a lottery winner, and they're just unlucky.

By the time Geoff reaches the Top House, his mind steams with thoughts, possibilities, and questions. What if they find out our numbers came up? They won't: they never bothered to check before and they wouldn't start now. How do we get away without anyone twigging on? Laura will have an idea: she's a clever lass. Will she really want to leave? Of course she will: there's nothing to stay for.

He goes straight to the bar – he needs a beer just to slow him down before he goes home and tells Laura about the win – and pays with a tenner to get change for the cigarette machine. It's in the corner and he wanders over to it, pleased with the swagger in his stride, but when he comes to put the coins in the slot, he finds that his hands are shaking as if he was rattling from some drug. He has to concentrate to avoid spilling pound coins all over the floor. Finally, he feeds the machine the correct change and selects the most upmarket brand it offers.

'Classy fags, now, son.'

A couple of girls at a nearby table hear him and giggle. Geoff turns and looks at them for too long and they shuffle their chairs away from him pointedly. He shrugs, picks up his cigarettes, retrieves his pint, and takes a seat at an empty table by the window.

Geoff is about half-way through his first beer when he gets a prickling sensation. It's the feeling of being watched. He looks around the pub more carefully than he did before. There, at a table tucked away in the shadow of the fruit machine, is the source of his discomfort. Sinister Steve tips a glass of something with Coke in Geoff's direction and nods like an off-duty undertaker passing an old client in the street. Geoff tries to smile, but it feels very unnatural.

Sinister Steve gets up and walks over, but Geoff doesn't want him to. Steve gives him the shudders, with his little rat face always looking like he knows something you don't. There's nothing Geoff can do to stop it as Steve sits down with him.

'All right, Geoff lad?'

'Aye, Steve, I'm well. You?'

'Ah, nothing a good shag wouldn't cure.' Steve gives Geoff a weird, slippery sideways look. Geoff forces a little laugh, but over Steve's shoulder he can see those two girls looking at them in open disgust.

'I know what you mean,' Geoff lies.

'You looked a bit agitated when you came in, like you were muttering to yourself or something.'

'Oh, aye. It's the stress, Steve, because I'm so high-powered and that.'

Steve laughs for longer than he should. Geoff watches the tabletop.

'I saw your mate Barry the other day. He's a good customer, him.'

'Right.'

'Anything I can do for you?'

'No, Steve. No. There's nothing you can do for me.'

'Suit yourself.' Steve drains his glass. 'Well, I'd better be going. See you later, Geoff.'

'Aye. See you.'

Steve slinks out and Geoff sees him pass the window with his mobile to his ear. Geoff shakes his head – 'Creepy bastard' – then sinks the rest of his pint and buys another.

He drinks quickly and has time to buy a third pint just as last orders are called. He takes his seat again as the landlady crosses the room to close the outside door. She disappears into the vestibule, but the inside door is open and Geoff can hear her talking to someone: 'I've called time.'

'I just need to have a word with someone inside.'

'All right, but I'll be kicking out soon.'

'Won't take long.'

Geoff looks around for the gents', to hide himself, but it's too late. Barry enters the pub and sees Geoff immediately.

'Hello, Geoff.' Barry looks much calmer than he did earlier, but this does not comfort Geoff.

'I've said everything.'

Barry ignores this, sits down, and lights a cigarette. When Barry is angry or upset, he smokes in hard little puffs, as if the filter were a teat. Tonight, he smokes like he does when he's pleased with himself: wide-mouthed, deep drags that he holds and blows out slowly. Geoff is worried for a few moments, but then he remembers that Barry has no power now.

'Whatever it is, I don't give a fuck, all right? Leave us alone.'

Barry smiles, leans over the table, and stubs out his half-finished cigarette in the ashtray. 'Have you spoken to Jim yet?'

'Aye, and I told him to fuck off and all.'

'Well, that explains why he's not answering his phone, then.'

'What?'

'Nowt.' Barry waves away the question.

'Barry, have you just come to sit there to be a cunt?'

'No, Geoff. I thought since you're moving on and all that, I'd try to give you a proper fresh start.'

'I don't need your help for nowt.'

'There's just something I think you should know.'

'Fuck off, Barry.'

'Your wife's a whore.'

Geoff freezes. Even when they've been really pissed off with each other, no one has ever brought family into it. Barry just looks at him, steady as anything. Geoff stares back. Barry smiles at the corner of his mouth and it dawns on Geoff that this is more than just an insult.

'You what?'

'She fucks for money,' says Barry brightly. 'Or she used to, anyroad.' The numbness of shock stops and suddenly Geoff fizzes with anger, but Barry sees it before Geoff even moves and holds up his hand. 'Settle down. It's all true. Ask Jim – he knows all about it. They're very close, your wife and Jim.'

'Barry, I'm going to fucking kill you.'

'No, you're not, because I'm telling you the truth. If you don't believe me, ask them. G'night, mate.'

Barry gets up and swans out. He even gives a cheery wave to the landlady and the regulars at the bar. Geoff just sits there.

By the time Geoff can move again, it's nearly 1 a.m. Calling time had been a ploy: the landlady locked the barflies in and continued serving. They tolerated Geoff because he didn't do, or say, anything. They looked at him, though, sly, over their shoulders, with a wink and a nudge. Eventually, Geoff stands up.

'What? What the fuck are you looking at?'

'Get out.' The landlady points at the door.

'Fuck the lot of you!' Geoff storms out and makes for home.

The car isn't in the drive, and as he walks through the front door, Geoff feels as if his guts have gone through a blender. He is ready to start shouting now, but the house is quiet. He goes upstairs and finds the bed empty and not slept in. Laura is nowhere to be found. Geoff sits on the bed and tries to breathe himself into some sort of calm.

It could be true; in some ways it all adds up. Geoff tries to get his brain around the evidence. Laura never talks about her past except to say that she was a 'tearaway' and that she 'fell in with the wrong crowd' and had a 'rotten boyfriend'. Then there's Jim. Geoff thinks back to all the times he's seen them together, and there is always something wrong with the picture, something secret. Then, with a sudden rush of sickness, he remembers Bonfire Night and finding them asleep together on Jim's couch.

'Christ.' It's all falling into place. This is why she was so interested in what he was going to say to Barry tonight. She was worried Barry would give up the secret. This is what he has always been afraid of: he knew he was punching above his weight. He knew something like this would happen. He wants to vomit. His testicles ache.

He'll give her a chance, one chance to explain, but if it's not right, he is going to leave there and then. He'll leave and he'll take the ticket with him. He'll claim his money and he'll go somewhere none of them will ever find him again.

Geoff stands up and looks around the bedroom. His duffel bag is on top of the wardrobe. He pulls it down and stuffs it with a couple of changes of clothing, selected at random. Then he goes downstairs, to the kitchen, opens a drawer, and pulls out his passport, his counterpart driving licence, and a credit card. He chucks them into the bag, zips it closed, turns out the lights, then sits down and waits.

In the dark, he tries to imagine what it would be like to be without her, but he can't feel anything except the anger. All he knows is that if it's true, he can't stay whatever happens. He has an escape, right now, and he can't waste it.

A car pulls into the drive. Geoff stiffens. There's a door slam, and then another, and then voices as the front door opens.

'Is he in?' That's Jim. Geoff grips the sides of his chair.

'I don't think so.'

'I can stay, if you like.'

'No, me and Geoff have to deal with this ourselves. Thanks for looking after me.'

'What are you going to do?'

'I don't know. I mean, I'll have to tell him, won't I? I'll have to tell him before Barry does.'

Geoff stands up. He's heard enough and there's no point in sticking around now. He picks up his bag and slips out of the back door. He doesn't stop to cry until he is a long way down the street.

17

For a moment, as I wake up, I am warm and contented. Then I remember Laura banging on my door last night and regret even opening my eyes. I roll over and stare at the wall. The only comfort I can take is that whatever turmoil has been unleashed is now completely out of my control. All that is left to do is to look after myself, which for the immediate future means going to the Spar to secure my usual Sunday treat: a delicious TV dinner and a bottle of Scotch.

I get up and leave the house. Outside, the world seems more drab and miserable than ever. It's a cold, grey day and it looks like rain could come at any moment. I walk quickly – the sooner I can get back in and turn on the fire, the better – so it only takes me ten minutes to get to the shop. I'm about to walk through the door when the cash machine outside reminds me that I should check my bank balance; I haven't worked since the day of Mac's accident.

Predictably, I'm not well off. I never spend very much, but without an income I'll be in trouble pretty quickly. Breaking into my modest savings isn't an option. I put that cash away – bit by tiny bit – with the idea that one day I might *do something* with it. I'm not sure what that something is, but it doesn't involve sitting on my arse and spending the money on living expenses. In short, I need a new job.

I retrieve my card and stand there, tapping the edge of it against the keypad of the machine. Fuck it. I may as well call him while I'm thinking about it. I pull out my mobile and scroll through to Lee's number.

I'm about to press 'call' when I see Barry walking down the opposite side of the street. He kicks his way through some fallen leaves, hands in his pockets, head down. He hasn't seen me yet. He crosses the road and heads for the shop. I step round the corner of the building, and after a few moments, I hear the beep that happens when the door opens.

Then there's silence, broken only by the sound of passing cars. Why did I hide? Surely by now Barry has played his hand, or had it played for him. He's got nothing left to hold over me. I lean against the wall, and as its cold seeps through my jacket, I feel an even colder fury spread in my belly and the back of my throat. I want to do something, but I don't know what. The door beeps again.

I peek round the corner and see Barry walking away, back the way he came, with a folded *News of the World* stuffed under his right arm. I let him cross the road and turn right at the T-junction up the street. Then I set out after him.

When I get to the junction, he is a long way ahead of me. It's an effort to hold myself back – for some reason, I want to keep him in sight – but from here I know which way he has to go, so I measure my pace. He doesn't stop, or deviate, or look around. He knows this place – it holds nothing new for him – and he thinks he knows exactly how this journey will end.

Once upon a time – and I mean years ago, when we were all tiny – Barry was a sweet lad. When my granddad died, he made me a card with a crayon drawing on the front. He said it was a picture of my granddad in heaven. Maybe everyone is still sweet when they're that age, and maybe Barry was always destined to become a bastard, but his brother and father made damn sure they beat all the softness out of him. They wanted him to be tough and hard like them. He never quite measured up and it turned him sour.

I follow him, from a distance, until he takes the footpath that runs behind the primary school. Then I speed up to close the gap, turn onto the footpath, and slalom my body between the offset metal frames designed to frustrate cyclists. There are tall railings to one side of the path, and a hedge of bramble, elder, and hawthorn to the other. Barry and I are the only people here, and I'm closer now. I can see the frayed fabric at the hem of his jeans and the glint of his wedding ring when his left hand swings back.

The school building is new – it was finished last year – and construction debris is still scattered here and there. Broken bricks are trodden into the mud or just lie at the base of the hedge. A long piece of carcassing timber, split and rotting and tangled with weeds, runs against the railings. Then I notice an iron spike, sharp at one end and with a tight curl of metal at the other. I stop walking. The spike is pressed into the mud, but I could turn it up easily and then...

'I don't need this.' The words appear in my mouth, but feel as if they are spoken by someone else.

'Are you following me?'

I look up. Barry faces me.

'What did you say to Geoff?'

'What are you going to do? Kill me? You're the first door they'd knock on.'

I don't move. 'What did you say to Geoff?'

Then Barry smiles. 'The truth. Well, the basics. I told him he should ask you for the details.'

'You what? What does he know, Barry?'

'I don't know why you're angry. If they break up, you'll get your chance.'

'Chance?'

'Howay, man, don't act innocent. I know there was something going on with you and her. You were spotted.'

'That's not true.'

'Fuck off. I had an eyewitness account. Anyway, I've done you a favour.'

'You've ruined my best friend's life.'

'Bollocks.'

'Why?'

'The time for fucking talking was last night, but you fucked it up. I'm going now. Nice seeing you.'

The spike is still there, but Barry is walking away and whatever made me follow him has dripped out of me. I test my will, but my hand doesn't want to move.

'Leave it, boy!'

It is a dog-walker, coming up the path behind me and dragging his Jack Russell along on a red lead. He gives me a strange stare and then passes.

I walk back the way I came and emerge from the footpath. I lean against the metal frame and watch a crisp packet scuttle along the gutter. There is blankness in my head, until a sudden thought forms: I can't let this stand. I need to go and face Geoff. I may have hidden the truth from him, but I can't let him believe this lie.

———

I walk up his drive and knock on his door, but I have no idea what I'm going to say to Geoff. In the event, it's Laura who answers. She wears the same clothes she did when I dropped her off last night.

'Hello.' It's the best opener I can come up with.

'He didn't come home.'

'Shit. Has he called? What did he say?'

'He hasn't called. He's gone. He took a bag. Clothes, his passport.'

'Fuck. Laura, something bad's happened.'

'Oh really?'

'Let me in. I need to talk to you.'

She shrugs and turns back into the house. I follow her through the front room and into the kitchen. She gestures at the kettle.

'Tea?'

'Uh, no, thanks.'

She nods and then closes the door to shut out the noise of the TV. It's uncomfortably intimate; the kitchen is just a narrow galley at the back of the house and there's nowhere to sit, no social space for me to occupy. I'm standing right in the middle of her private life. I lean back against one of the worktops and focus on a band of light reflected from the rim of a plate on the draining board. Of her, I can only see the legs now, in the left of my peripheral vision. She has propped herself against the door. I keep the plate front and centre.

'So?' Her voice sounds far away.

'I talked to Barry.'

'And?'

'He told him.'

'Yeah, well, we'd guessed that.'

'I was still hoping he hadn't really done it.'

'Fat chance. He's a bitter, evil man.'

'Aye, I've been coming to that conclusion myself. Look, that's not all – he told Geoff there was something going on between you and me.'

She doesn't say anything. I manage to turn my head and look at her, but she's completely still and just stares past me, through the window. Then her lower jaw moves, almost imperceptibly, as if it was frozen and she was struggling to form the shape of words. 'I…I…' The first sounds come as a faint stutter, and then, 'I was always afraid that I couldn't really have this, but it was the truth I was scared of. I never thought anyone would have to make something up, you know?'

'Aye, I know.'

'I mean, it's not much to ask, is it? All I wanted was a normal life, nothing special. He's hardly the man of my dreams, is he? But he's sweet to me and I thought I could have a nice life with him, a good life. I just wanted to be like everyone else, and I wanted a proper home. And now the silly fat bastard's run off and ruined everything.'

Her voice tremors with the approach of tears, and suddenly there's a twist and lurch somewhere in my own insides and I'm moving towards her and putting my arms around her and my voice is saying stuff that hasn't even passed through my brain. 'Come here, pet, it's not that bad. He'll be back soon and you'll get it sorted out. He knows what's good for him.'

'He won't even answer his phone!'

'Don't worry about that. He'll have a think and he'll be back.'

'Will he? And what then? He knows what I was and it's always going to be there. It's not fair. I tried so hard to leave it behind.'

The side of her face presses against my chest, and the top of her head just brushes under my chin. 'It's going to be OK. Just give him some time. He'll do the right thing.' She squeezes me tighter. I can smell her hair and skin. I remember the last time she was this close to me and feel sick. I'm lying to her, and we both know it. I have no idea what Geoff will do, and he has no reason to believe anything she or I say. Even if he did, the truth is bad enough.

She looks up at me. 'What are we going to do?'

'You just sit tight, OK?'

I don't tell her about the eyewitness, and I don't tell her that I know who he is, but in my mind's eye I see Steve scurrying away that day at the ponds – just after he saw Laura kiss me.

18

Sinister Steve deals in many things – cash, illegal fags, car stereos – but he has a particular penchant for acquiring and distributing general knowledge. I know this because whenever I've made the mistake of being in the Admiral when the Sunday-night quiz takes place, Steve has always been there, paying rapt attention and eagerly scribbling his answers. It's for this reason that I settle myself in a corner of the pub with a pint and a newspaper.

I'm early, but I wanted to come in unnoticed, and in any case I needed a change of scenery. Sadly, there isn't much to look at except the blinking lights of the fruit machine and some sort of variety show playing on the TV over the bar. I have spent a fair proportion of my life in here, and looking around, I'm unable to see a good reason why. Still, I feel better now, although I'm apprehensive. I'm about to do something bad, but at least I'm doing something.

The TV programme ends and another, equally worthless, programme starts. I open the newspaper and half read a feature on celebrity addiction, while trying to stay aware of what happens around me. As the evening proceeds, the bar starts to fill and soon paper and pens are handed round. People form teams and sit around tables, chatting and drinking. Frank, the landlord, tests a microphone with a flick of his finger and the percussive thud of it pops from a speaker above my head. I should have sat somewhere else.

Steve isn't here yet and I become annoyed with myself for arriving here like this and expecting everything to fall into place. Perhaps he is somewhere else tonight; perhaps he's busy. Frank is going to start soon. He walks around the barroom with a clipboard and a pint pot, taking team names and entry fees. Then Steve slips in through the door.

I feel relief, and then a strange kind of excitement, even though I have no idea how I'm going to get him alone. I watch him cross the room; he scuttles through the spaces between people and slides to the bar, where he waits for service but keeps his head flicking from side to side like an animal tasting the air. I view him as an animal now, as prey, or simply a pest to be dealt with. He wears a black bomber jacket, black jeans, and white trainers. He is slight of build, and not as tall as me.

Steve buys a drink and asks for pen and paper, and then he sits alone at the other end of the room. There is nobody who would form a team with him. I have finished my pint, and an idea occurs to me. I go to the bar.

'Smith's, please, and a shot of JD. Neat.'

With the drinks in hand, I make my way over to Steve and sit down with him.

'All right, Steve?'

'All right.'

'Here, make it a double.' I pass him the glass of bourbon. I'm pretty sure it's what he takes with his Coke.

'It already is.'

'Well, then make it a triple.'

'Thanks.' He pours the shot into his own glass.

'You doing the quiz?'

144

'Aye.'

'Fancy teaming up?'

He tips his head to one side and looks at me cautiously. Then he shrugs. 'All right. Didn't know you did the quiz.'

'I never have. Just needed a diversion. It's been a funny few days.'

'Right.' He takes a drink, and then Frank appears.

'Three pounds, please, gentlemen.'

We split the fee, and while Steve digs in his pocket for change, Frank gives me a questioning look. I just smile and spread my hands. We name ourselves the Cupid Stunts and Frank sighs as if this signifies the end of civilization.

'I saw your mate Geoff last night,' says Steve once Frank has buggered off.

'You what?'

'Aye, up at the Top House.'

'That's funny. Did he say anything?'

'Not really. He was just having a quiet pint.' Steve seems to be watching a point just over my left shoulder.

'OK.' Frank's voice bursts from the speakers in a welter of feedback, followed by a bout of swearing as he adjusts the volume. 'OK. Welcome to the quiz! Round one is general knowledge.'

It takes over an hour, during which I manage to buy Steve a further three very strong Jack and Cokes, and, miraculously, keep smiling. We manage eighteen out of twenty on general knowledge, sixteen out of twenty on sport, but perform so miserably at guess the song that we finish fifth.

'I always fuck up on that.' Steve is drunk. 'It's always bloody 1960s stuff. Never heard of any of it.'

'You got Smokey, and Martha,' I observe.

'That's soul, it's a different kettle of fish. I'm talking about all the jingle-jangle shite.'

I nod enthusiastically, but I'm bored and ready to make my move. 'Steve, I've got something to discuss with you, but I can't talk here.'

'Eh?' He tries hard to focus on my face, then gives up and flings his glass to his lips, almost spilling drink on himself.

'I've got a proposition for you. You could make a bit out of it, like.'

'How much?'

'Let's just say I'm after a certain high-margin item.'

'How high?'

'I don't want to talk here. I'll meet you round the back in a couple of minutes, right?'

'Fair enough. I'll see you there.' He raises his glass to me.

'Good man.'

In the alley, I lean against the wall. It's almost pitch black out here and it takes some time for my eyes to adjust to the point that I can see objects. The mouth of the alley opens onto the pub car park and provides a rectangle of light through which I'll be able to see anyone approach. It's cold. I zip up my jacket and put my hands in my pockets.

I don't know if this is a good idea. I don't even know if I'm still capable of this kind of thing, but I'm about to find out.

A slim figure appears at the entrance. He stumbles and puts his arm out to steady himself against the wall.

'Steve.'

'Where are you?'

'Up here.'

I step out into the middle of the path and he must see my shadow because he says, 'Oh right,' and weaves towards me. 'What's this proposition, then?'

'Steve, before I begin, I want you to know something: there's nothing going on between me and Geoff's wife.'

'What?'

I clench my fists at my sides, step forward, and barge Steve into the wall. 'What did you tell Barry?'

'What are you talking about?' He pushes me, but I'm too big for him to move and I bear down harder.

'You know what I'm talking about. What did you tell Barry?'

'Fuck. Off.' He tries to wriggle away. I grab him by his jacket and slam him back into the wall.

'I'm serious, Steve. You'd better tell me what's going on.' Even as this comes out of my mouth, I know it sounds weak. I feel weak. I have no fury on my side and this is not going to work. Steve stops resisting and just looks into my face, and I already know what he's going to say.

'Or what?'

I have no good answer to that. Steve has called my bluff.

'Let me go,' he says.

But I cannot let him go. If I don't make him talk, I go home with nothing and Barry wins. My body is heavy, my limbs reluctant to do what they need to do next. I breathe in, close my eyes, and drive my knee into his bollocks. He jolts so hard that I let go of him and he bends double, gasping for air.

'What did you tell Barry?'

'Just that I saw you together and...I'm sorry. I got it wrong.'

'You're damn right you got it wrong!' I smash the point of my elbow between his shoulder blades. His arms flail up and behind him and for a moment, before he screams, he looks like a puppet on muddled strings.

I clamp my hand over his mouth and force him to the ground, smothering him with my weight. He struggles and squirms, and I put my other hand on the back of his head and twist it round until I can almost look him straight in the eye. He goes dead still. He believes me now, but I don't know if I believe myself. 'I reckon I could snap your fucking neck, Steve,' I say. 'Shall I try?'

He makes a high, yelling sound in his throat. It might be 'No!' I take my hand away from his mouth. 'I'm sorry,' he pants. 'He shouldn't have. I told him not to do anything stupid.'

'You told him not to do anything stupid?'

'Yeah.'

'Why the fuck is Barry talking to you about our business? What's going on?'

He doesn't say anything. I get up and he tries to crawl, but I put my foot on his back and press down. 'Stay where you are.' He stops moving, but he still doesn't talk. I have that feeling of a blow to the head, like I'm standing in a ghost body that only just overlaps my own. I kick him.

'Stop!' he shouts.

'Then tell me why this happened. Tell me what you and that bastard are up to.'

Steve rolls over and holds his side, breathing hard. 'It's small-time shite. It wasn't worth none of this.'

'Just tell me.'

'All right, all right.' He shuffles himself into a seated position, with his back against the wall, and looks up at me. 'You were working on that big job, right? And because it's a big job, they have all kinds of gear on hire. Sometimes it's there for days, and it's nice stuff: generators, Stihl saws, chase cutters, high-speed drills; even the fucking safety equipment's worth something.'

'You were going to rob them? They keep it in a shipping con-tainer, with fuck-off big locks on it. You'd have to cut your way in. It's in the middle of a fucking city!'

'I know, but Barry said he could sort it out. He said he could make impressions of the keys.'

'He'd have to pilfer them from the office first. He doesn't have the balls.'

'Well, apparently he thinks he does, because he's gone this far, hasn't he?'

'Fuck.'

'Anyway, I'd give the copies to some good lads I know, and Barry would keep an eye on what was coming in and out of the site. When there was enough tasty stuff inside to make it worth our while…zip. They're in and out. I fence the gear; Barry gets his cut. But then the accident happened and you and Geoff refused to go back and fucked up the plan.'

'How much?'

'What?'

'How much would he make?'

'Depends on what we got. Mebbes a grand or so.'

'A grand? He did this for a grand? For fuck's sake, if he needed money, he could have pulled this sort of stunt on any job.'

Steve shifts his weight uncomfortably and feels his ribs. 'You know Barry – he's got no imagination. He thought he was a criminal fucking genius just for coming up with this shitty little plan. He couldn't go back to square one. He hasn't got the brainpower.'

'Jesus Christ.'

'And it's not just that. He likes to talk big. He likes to be the leader. He thinks he fucking owns you and Geoff, and he wanted to make you go back to the site to prove it. He needs the control. "I'll show those two fuckers who's in charge." That's what he said to me.'

'I don't fucking believe this.'

But I believe it all too well. I'm tired and there is nothing more to say here. My leg shakes and the change in my pocket rattles. I put my hand on it to stop the sound; the movement stirs an acid feeling in my stomach that could be hunger, but isn't. I look down at the dark, huddled shape of Steve and think that I should help him up. Instead, I walk away.

19

Geoff is neither hungry nor thirsty, but to sit here he must order. The waitress taps the top of her pen against her pad. The pad is held in a stiff wallet coated with black vinyl that peels away at the spine, and there is a huge spot on the end of the waitress's nose. Geoff stares at it, unable to form any idea of what he should say. The spot is red and swollen, and looks like it will burst soon.

'Bacon butty and a pot of tea,' he mumbles, and feels relieved that she will now go away. 'Please.'

'Brown or white?'

'What?'

'Bread. Brown or white?'

'Brown. No, white.' Geoff doesn't know why he said that; he doesn't like brown bread.

'You can have a slice of each for all I care.'

It's painful to listen to other people talk, and he is sure that she is just bullying him now.

The waitress's face remains just as grey and solid as a cold dumpling. 'Do you want any tomato or mushroom?' A long pause. 'In your sandwich.'

'No. Plain. Just plain. Plain. Please.'

The waitress writes down the order and finally leaves Geoff alone, but not in peace. He checks his watch. Late. And why do they have to meet here?

The tables are in two columns along the length of the café, with a gangway down the middle to the kitchen door. Geoff is at the last one, with his back against the wall. Apart from an elderly couple near the entrance, the place is empty.

Geoff looks down and sees the way the Formica has come away in large chips at the edge of his table. They look like bite marks. Chipped Formica and peeling vinyl; he knows his tea will come in a stainless-steel pot that dribbles everywhere.

The order arrives and proves him right. Some things never change, but at least there is plenty of bacon in the sandwich. He nibbles at it, to get used to having food in his mouth again. A hot surge of saliva under his tongue surprises him and soon he eats properly in full bites. He is almost finished when he hears the door open.

This must be the man. After two days of near-paralysis in a grotty hotel room in Middlesbrough, Geoff picked him pretty much at random from the Yellow Pages, and it shows. His suit sags around him and reminds Geoff of a schoolteacher or someone who works at the dole office. His hair is thin, and his spectacles are steamed up. He doesn't look like Geoff's idea of a private investigator.

The man takes off his glasses to wipe them clean, but drops the file folder held under his right arm. Geoff looks around in panic. Look at this shithole. Look at this idiot. He pushes the last piece of his bacon sandwich away from him and focuses on his twisted reflection in the teapot, trying not to look up as the dozy cunt walks over to him.

'Hello, Geoff?'

The truth arrives in Geoff's head. He doesn't need proof, because he knows Barry wasn't lying. He doesn't need proof, because all that matters is, he's finally getting away. 'No, mate. Not me, sorry.'

'Oh,' says the private investigator. 'Well, excuse me.' He goes and sits at another table.

Geoff pays and leaves.

20

A couple of days after my run-in with Steve, there's a loud knock at my front door. I check that the cricket bat is within easy reach, put the chain on, open the door, and peer through the crack. Whoever is there is standing just out of the light. I pick up the bat.

'Hello?'

'Howdy, partner.'

'Bloody hell, Joe. I thought you were the fucking Gestapo. Why'd you knock so hard?'

'You're late.'

'What the fuck for?'

'To pick up Mr Green.'

Fuck. I'd forgotten about this. We're supposed to be going to the church hall tonight to measure up for the pantomime set. 'Bollocks. Hold on. I'll just get my stuff.'

———

When we arrive, we find ourselves in the middle of a rehearsal. Someone plays the piano, trying to teach songs to a teenage girl who may or may not be playing Cinderella but is certainly tone-deaf. Two middle-aged men, possibly the Ugly Sisters, clatter about at the other end of the hall in an attempt to learn a dance routine. There are several children running around and knocking things over. I recognize nobody, which is probably a good job. Even now, I occasionally get a frosty reception from some long-term locals, depending on which version of the story they believe.

'I'm sorry, Ronald.' A flustered woman approaches us. She stands over Mr Green's wheelchair and looks down at him. 'We could only get the hall once a week, so we sort of have to do everything at once, you see.'

Mr Green cranes to look up at her. 'Are you going to tell us what you want doing with the scenery and that?'

'Oh, yes. I've just got a few things to do first.' She notices me. 'Who's this?'

'This is my assistant.'

'Oh. Very well. Hello. Right, back shortly.' She scuttles off and begins a discussion with the pianist that involves a lot of pointing.

I crouch beside Mr Green's chair. 'What's going on?'

'Shit-shower. It's usual. Why don't you go and measure the stage?'

'Right.' I get up and am about to go across to the stage when I notice a small boy walk towards us. He stands in front of Joe, tips his head, and stares brazenly in that way kids do.

'Are you a mentalist?' the boy asks Joe.

Joe looks the boy up and down, and then answers solemnly, 'Aye.'

They stay there, looking at one another, until the boy's mother comes over and yanks him away by the arm. 'Come on,' she scolds, then looks over her shoulder and flashes Joe an accusatory glare.

I nudge Joe with my fist. 'Howay, mate, I need some help.'

'Aye, aye, Cap'n.'

He follows me to the stage, and after I've explained to him for the third time that it's imperative not to let go of the end of the tape, we manage to establish its dimensions.

'Four metres wide and three metres deep.'

Joe watches me write it down and then nods. 'That's right.'

'What?'

'Four metres wide and three metres deep; it's the same every year.'

'You knew?'

'Aye.' He smiles proudly. 'My memory is magnificent.'

'Why didn't you tell me?'

He shrugs. 'You never asked.'

I want to throw the tape measure at his head, but if he has the energy for mischief, at least it means he's no longer ill. 'You daft bastard.'

'You're foul-mouthed, you.'

'And proud of it.' I stuff my notepad into my back pocket and clip the tape measure to my belt. 'Look, Joe, is your mam all right? I thought she looked a bit ill the other day.'

'Aye, she's all right.'

'Oh good. Shall I come over tonight? We can have a cup of tea, play a game of cards.'

'No.'

'You like a game of Fish.'

'We're not receiving visitors.'

'What?'

'We're not receiving visitors.' He does not look at me.

'Did your mam say that?'

'Aye.' He folds his arms.

'Joe, did you tell her I was there the other night?'

'No.' He steps off the stage and walks across the hall. I hurry after him and put my hand on his shoulder, but he shrugs me away. 'I didn't tell!'

I stop. If I push any further, he'll go off, and I don't want to do that to him in front of these people. He sits down on a plastic chair against the back wall and assumes a deep interest in the activities of the Ugly Sisters. I give him a couple of minutes and then go and sit next to him.

'I'm sorry, mate. I'm just concerned for you both. You're my friends.'

'Don't meddle.'

'Did she say that too?'

'It's none of your business what she said.'

'All right, Joe.'

The flustered woman is speaking to Mr Green, and he waves me over impatiently.

She talks for a long time and I take notes. I learn that her name is Lydia, she's just moved up from somewhere down South, and this is her first year as director of the pantomime. She seems unsure as to precisely how she was roped into it, so we have something in common. I also learn that in addition to the headwear we've already produced she wants three sets of scenery made up and a set of castle battlements created. Once she has run through her list of requirements, she nods towards Joe.

'Who is that chap?'

'That's Joe,' I say. 'He's in your panto.'

'I don't remember casting him.'

'You don't need to cast him,' Mr Green informs her. 'He's in it every year.'

There's a short silence, so I add, 'He plays the back end of the horse.'

'Oh dear. I hadn't planned on a horse.'

'There's always a horse.'

'That's all very well, but who's going to play the front end?' For some reason they both look at me.

'No. Don't even think about it.' I turn my back on them and look at Joe. He watches everything around him intently, but I don't believe he really knows anyone here. I don't know anyone here; none of them are old faces. Nobody speaks to him. Although he is surrounded by people, he looks more isolated than ever.

———

I narrowly escaped being made the front end of the horse, at least for the time being, and now I help Mr Green home. The rubber wheels of his chair fizz along the wet paving slabs, and over his hunched shoulders I can see his hands twine and fidget in his lap. I know he wants to get out and walk, but for such an excursion his wife mandated the chair. Anyway, he knows that he's not up to it, so we trundle along in strained silence. Then he breaks it.

'Why didn't Joe come back with us?'

'I don't know. He wanted to go home.'

'I was told that he usually hangs around you like a little puppy dog.'

'I think I've upset his mam.'

'Not a good idea – she has a formidable right fist.'

Then he tells the story I've heard before, that when Joe was a kid, they tried him at the secondary school and he was bullied. One day, a teacher just stood by and watched while three lads beat Joe up, and in response Mrs Joe stormed right into the staffroom and punched that teacher out. Joe stayed at home after that.

'She did it with a fistful of loose change.'

'You what? I've never heard that bit.'

'She bloody did. It happened right in front of me. I was most impressed. I thought, there's a woman I should make a friend of, because I certainly don't want her as my enemy.'

'You've known her for years, then.'

'Aye.' He drums his fingers on the arm of his chair.

Now I wish I hadn't said anything, because he's going to ask and then I'll have to burden him with what I know. He's fragile, and it's not fair. Then again, he knows her well and it's not right to keep him in the dark.

'So what did you do to upset her?'

'I went over and I cleaned her kitchen.'

He sucks a breath between his teeth. 'Bloody hell. Why?'

'She's ill.'

'How serious is it?'

'I think she's ailing. Badly. Can't cope with the house anymore. Joe was sick because he was cooking for himself.'

Mr Green goes quiet for the distance between two streetlights and then says, 'She won't take interference.'

He falls silent, and now his fingers don't drum on the arm of the chair, but scratch at its rubber coating. I keep pushing his chair and hope I've done the right thing.

When we get to his house, Mr Green pushes himself out of his chair without waiting for me to help him and fishes unsteadily for his keys. He opens the door and then stands, haloed by the light from inside. His clothes are very slack on his body.

'Do you want me to fold this?' I motion towards the chair.

'Aye, son.'

I kick up the clips and the chair sags in on itself. Mr Green watches me as I place it in the hallway.

'We should go and see her together,' he says. 'Put on a united front, talk some sense into her.'

'How are we going to talk sense into Mrs Joe?'

'Any way we can. I'll call you in the morning.' Then he closes the door on me.

I walk towards home. I'm on my street when a grinding of gears ahead dispels my muttering anxiety; there is a car attempting a turn in the road. It wants to come back this way, so it must have driven past without me noticing it. I walk on. The driver makes the final manoeuvre too quickly and runs out of space. The car mounts the kerb, but instead of slowing, accelerates and hops back onto the road with an audible scrape as the sump guard hits the concrete. It roars up the street, then swerves onto the wrong side of the road under heavy braking and comes to a halt alongside the pavement about twenty feet in front of me. I stop. Nobody gets out. There are footsteps behind me and pain in my eyes as the car's headlights switch to full beam. I turn away, but something heavy slams into my body and I fall.

21

I've been watching the same splatter of dried blood on the wall of this room in A&E for the past God knows how long. Hours. The blood looks like a map of a cluster of islands in a sea of semi-gloss emulsion. I've studied their geography, all their bays and inlets and peninsulas. It's my only entertainment. There is no choice but to stare at them; every time I look around or move I feel sick and dizzy and the blood is right in front of me.

Some bloke goes past. I sense the blur of his body and the swish of his walk. I yell out after him, 'How, daft cunt!'

He ignores me.

I let my eyes close.

I wake up retching. Someone comes along and a bowl appears on my lap. I hang my head over it, but not much really comes out.

'You've a concussion. It's normal to feel disoriented and sick.'

I look for her face, but she doesn't stick around. She's already swishing away. Every bugger here swishes. I lean back and fall asleep again.

A clang wakes me up. The bowl is now on the floor.

'Look, don't start any trouble, OK?'

'It fell. My head really hurts.'

'That's no reason to throw things around.'

'It fell.'

'I'll get you some painkillers.'

She doesn't come back for forty-five minutes. I know because my watch is on my wrist tick-tick-tocking away. It's almost 5 a.m. I am up with the larks, but maybe it's almost 5 p.m. Two little plastic cups arrive. One with two pills in it, one with water.

'These should help with the throbbing.'

'It's more like my skull is trying to give birth to my brain through my eye sockets.'

'Just take the pills.'

Swish.

I'm in the half-place where you're not quite sure if what you hear is real or a dream.

'Get him out of my treatment room and put him in observation.'

'Yes, sister.'

Tremors in the bed and then the ceiling flows over me.

New room. No blood. Less noise. The weird seasick, drunken feeling subsides a little. I was walking home and somebody hit me. I'm not sure if I know that because I remember it or because somebody here told me. I haven't seen a mirror yet, but my face feels stiff so I know it won't be pretty. My wrist looks swollen. Maybe I landed on it when I fell. I must have fallen because they said someone found me lying on the pavement.

It is strange to realize that after all these years of keeping myself to myself, I suddenly have enemies again. The question is, which one of them would do this? And then, as if the world was moving with the drift of my thoughts, the pigs turn up.

'Good morning, sir,' says the older one.

I just stare at them. What the fuck am I supposed to say to that? At least now I know it's morning, not afternoon. Seconds pass. The younger one glances at the older one. The older one coughs, as if – despite the fact I'm looking right at him – he thinks I haven't noticed his presence.

'What do you want?' I finally ask.

'You were assaulted.'

'I know.'

His eyes narrow. I shrug and find the movement painful. He calls out through the open doors of the room to a nurse sat at a big curved desk, 'Is he lucid?'

'I don't know,' she says. 'This isn't my ward.' She returns to whatever it was she was doing.

The copper looks back to me. I can see the broken lattice of drink in his face, like a red frost under his skin. It's far too early in the morning for him, and he hates me for it.

'I'm lucid. Ish. I think. I keep throwing up.'

'Concussion.'

'Aye, they said that.'

'Could you tell us what happened?'

'No.'

'Can you remember anything at all?'

'Just being hit from behind, falling over and...that's it.' I remember a car, but I won't give them that: they might start to think they have a lead. I don't want them to get involved, not that they appear to give a fuck. The copper squeezes his jaws together. The tip of his biro rests on his notepad, but he's not looking at that; he's staring me down. I'm a thug in a hospital bed.

'What time did this happen?'

'About eight thirty, mebbes.'

'Anything taken?'

I have to pause to think about this. 'I don't know.' I feel the impulse to pat my pockets, but I'm not wearing my clothes. 'I'm not even wearing my clothes.'

'We can check what you came in with. What were you carrying last night?'

'Just my wallet, my phone, a tape measure, and a notepad.'

They go off and leave me lying here. About fifteen minutes later, they return.

'Your wallet's gone.'

'Fuck.'

'It looks like you were mugged, then.'

'Yeah. I suppose so.'

I give him the details of what was in my wallet, and he takes my address, telling me they'll be in touch. Of course, it won't really be them who get in touch – I'm not sufficiently middle class for the police to care about – I'll receive a vague letter from Victim Support and that'll be it. All of which suits me.

They're walking out when I think of something else. 'What about my phone?'

They stop and the older one says, 'It looked buggered to me. Must've been when you fell.' Then they leave.

Brilliant. No cash, no means of getting any cash, and now no phone. I don't even know which hospital I'm in. I swing my legs off the bed and shuffle my body until I sit on the edge. Movement hurts, but I think that once I get warmed up, I'll be OK. I place my toes on the floor. It's cold. I wait a few seconds. Now I shift my whole weight to my feet and feel the sticky spread of skin on lino.

Standing, the draught reminds me that I am wearing a backless gown. If I go walkabout, I will expose my arse to everyone I pass. Maybe that's what these gowns are for: to keep you where you're put. I can't remember them getting me into it – that could have happened at any time during the blur and hum in A&E – and I certainly can't remember them taking away my clothes, but maybe that happened in the ambulance. I'll be pissed off if I find out that they cut through my jacket. I can't afford a new jacket.

I pull the blanket off the bed and drape it round my body. It comes down to just above my knees and thus saves my modesty.

There are two other beds in this room. One is empty; the other has the curtains pulled around it. I've heard nothing from behind those curtains since I was brought in here. I feel the briefest of urges to peek, then tell myself to stop being silly and take my first step.

It quickly becomes clear that in my current condition the idea of walking is a bit optimistic. I settle for a shuffle and make my way out of the room. It opens out onto a corridor, along which other rooms are arranged. I stop and check the nurses' station. The one from earlier is gone and has been replaced by a male nurse engrossed in the contents of an overstuffed lever-arch file. It crosses my mind that I could just talk to him, but since my arrival here nobody has shown much interest in doing anything for me beyond the basics of preventing me from actually bleeding to death, so I decide to leave him to it.

I look the other way down the corridor. It ends at a wall, in which there is a window. Chances are I'm in Hartlepool or Stockton, and I'd recognize either of those shitholes at a glance. Therefore, if I look out of this window, I will know where I am. Having worked this out, I feel quite pleased with myself. That in turn makes the dizziness easier to deal with, so I manage to move along the corridor with only my palm against the wall for support.

There are people in the other rooms, three or four in each. They don't do anything; they're just there, on beds. One man has acquired a newspaper from somewhere, but the others simply stare into space or sleep. Some of them look worse than I feel, a few of them are attached to tubes, and all of them ignore me as I go past. I get closer to the window and I realize I've made a mistake.

I don't know why I thought I would be high up, but I'm not. It's a ground-floor window and all I can see is the backside of another hospital building and a patch of concrete littered with fag ends. There's not even a sign anywhere. The sound of a seashell gathers behind me. I'm tired. I rest the top of my head against the glass, and as the corridor starts to move, I see it stamped on the blanket that I'm wearing, 'University Hospital of Hartlepool'. Well, that answers that, but I'm sinking up to my knees in something thick and tipping over, and I just can't move in time to miss hitting the floor.

22

Geoff has stayed up North for long enough. He wants to get away. Besides, this town is too familiar; he's scared to leave the hotel in case he bumps into someone he knows. He doesn't want to answer anybody's questions. About anything. Even the 'Hello. How are you?' of the maid who came to turn down the bed this morning was physically painful to bear.

So he's leaving. He folds each article of clothing and stacks them neatly inside his bag. He leaves out only a change of underwear, his toothbrush, and his shaving kit. The train leaves at 8.51 a.m. tomorrow. Change at Darlington and then nothing to do but watch England slide past all the way to King's Cross.

It's ages since Geoff was last in London, but he knows he can lose himself there for as long as it takes to get the money safely in his hands. He remembers the filthy B&B he and Barry dossed in when they were jobbing down there, and smiles grimly at the memory of the dirty sheets and rat shit. That was ten years ago, when Jim was still in prison and before Barry turned himself into a miserable fucker, years before his time. 'Premature middle age,' Laura used to call it. Another one of her clever little jokes, the ones Geoff used to love. He kicks the minibar; the bottles inside rattle.

There's one more job to do before he leaves. It struck him today as he skulked back from McDonald's with a bagful of hamburgers, and almost shat himself at the sight of a copper. Geoff hasn't really done anything illegal, yet, but it made him think. He doesn't care what Laura thinks – let her worry, not that she probably cares – but if he just disappears and leaves her to wonder if he's waded into the sea, the next copper he sees might be one who really is looking for him. That would fuck everything up.

He sits on the end of the bed and turns his new mobile phone over and over in his hand. It would be easy enough to dial the number, but Geoff knows that if he hears her voice, he'll vomit Big Mac all over the carpet.

'Fucking hell.' He drops the phone onto the quilt and kneads his face between his hands. 'Fuck her, just think about the money.'

Anyway, he wants her to have it in writing. She can't argue with that, especially if he delivers it by hand. He'll wait until it's late, then he'll call a cab.

Just think about the money. Just think about the money.

23

A full day later and the world has righted itself. A doctor told me to take it easy, but I'm fit enough to go. Even better, there is some spare change in the pockets of my jeans. I feed a twenty-pence piece into the payphone next to the WRVS shop and stab out Geoff's home phone number; it's the only one I can remember by heart.

'Oh. It's you,' Laura says.

'Aye. Is he back?'

'No.'

'Right.' I don't know what else to say to that. To be honest, the fact that Geoff's still out of the picture will probably make it easier to get a lift home. 'Look, I hate to ask, but I need some help.'

'You need help?'

'I'm in hospital. I've been beaten up.'

'Oh Jesus.'

'They took my wallet, and my mobile's smashed. I'm stuck.'

There's a pause and then, 'Do you want me to pick you up?'

'Yeah.' I feel guilty, but I let her know where I am and she tells me that she'll get here soon.

———

In the event, it takes her over two hours. I see her first. She walks through the automatic doors and starts looking on the wrong side of the atrium. After sitting for so long, it's hard for me to get up again, so when she turns, she catches me half crouched like an old man with my hands on my thighs. She purses her lips. I straighten up and creak towards her.

'Well,' she says, 'it could be worse.'

'I think I was lucky, under the circumstances.'

She looks unconvinced by this, but doesn't argue with me. 'What happened?'

'I don't really know. I remember someone coming up behind me, but that's about it. I got knocked out. I've been here two nights.'

'Christ.'

'It wasn't Geoff, if that's what you're thinking.'

'Of course it wasn't Geoff. Come on, let's get you home.'

'Thanks for coming for me.'

'That's all right.' She links her arm with mine, and although I don't really need any help to walk, I let her do it and she leads me outside to her car. It's parked miles away from the door, but the cold, fresh air feels good after so long inside a hospital.

Once we get into the car, I feel a bit sheepish. 'I'm sorry for the bother.'

'Forget that.' She rummages in the docket under the steering column and produces a piece of paper. 'Here, read this.'

It's a sheet torn from a reporter's notebook, folded once. I open it.

Laura Im alive and well so dont bother calling the police or anything daft like that. I know evreything so Im fucking off dont try to find me. Geoff.

I fold it over again. 'Fuck. I mean, at least you know he's all right.'

She takes it back from me and returns it to the docket. 'It was hand-delivered in the middle of the night. I heard the letterbox go, but when I went downstairs, there was nobody there. I even walked outside, but the street was empty. It scared me.'

'He must have been out there somewhere.'

'Well, I wish he had the sense to come and talk to me. I just want to tell him the truth.'

'By the sound of that letter, he's too angry to listen to it. For the moment, like.'

'Yeah, well...' She trails off and sighs. 'Let's get out of here.'

'Good idea.'

We drive away and she doesn't talk again for a while. I flip down the visor and inspect myself in the mirror. My left eye is well blackened, and that side of my face is swollen and hatched with grazes. A neat row of stitches runs in a shallow crescent just below my hairline. My wrist is strapped up, and under my clothes bruises splatter my ribs.

If I hadn't been knocked out immediately, they might have stuck the boot in with even more relish. Maybe I should be grateful for the head wound. Clearly, though, the attack itself was undertaken seriously. They followed me and waited for a good opportunity to kick the shit out of me. Taking my wallet was just a ruse. It must have been Steve who arranged it; he's got those kind of contacts. Barry might have known about it, but in the end he's just a dickhead and nobody would do this kind of thing on his say-so.

'You're not going to do anything stupid, are you?'

I look over at her, but she has her eyes on the road. 'I don't understand.'

'I'm talking about what happened to you the other night. It was to do with all this mess, wasn't it? Barry and his vengeful fucking God complex.'

'His what?'

'You know what I mean.'

'I told you, I didn't see who it was.'

'Well, don't get dragged into anything, right. Just walk away.'

'I think that's the idea they were trying to impress on us.'

'Then take the hint. Please.'

I have to agree with her. I have nothing to gain by getting into a feud now, especially one I'm bound to lose. They've got back-up and I'm completely alone. Still, if I could, I'd smash out their teeth with a hammer.

'I know what's good for me – don't worry about that.'

'I hope you know what's good for you, because at the moment you're all I've got.'

I look at her again. She indicates right and checks her mirror, then pulls out to overtake a slow-moving car. 'What do you mean?'

'I mean, you're the only other person who knows what's really going on. There's nobody else I can talk to.'

'Fat lot of good I've been so far.'

'Well, you're better than nothing.'

'Thanks.'

———

When I get home, I go straight upstairs and run a bath. I need to get the filth and infection of the hospital off my skin and out of my hair. I lean over to turn on the taps and pain pulses in my body like an electric shock. The pills they gave me are wearing off. I have a prescription for some more, but no money to pay for it. I wanted to ask Laura to sub me twenty quid, but I couldn't bring myself to do it.

I shrug off my jacket and the pieces of my knackered mobile clatter in the pocket as they hit the floor. I unwind the bandage from my wrist, roll it up, and put it in the bathroom cabinet. Then

I stand there and watch myself disappear as the mirror steams up. Geoff's letter bothers me. I've known him for years and would never have believed that he might act this way. Most of those years were years of routine, though, and this is no longer routine.

I reach out and wipe a patch of steam from the mirror. I'm a six-foot-two skinhead who has obviously been in a fight. Undoubtedly, I look like a thug. And here I am, framed in the same square of glass I stand at almost every morning, while Geoff has fucked right off. 'Are you jealous of him?' I ask my beaten-up face. He's escaped and gone to do something new. It's what I should have done, except I went to prison and missed all my chances – exams, college, a proper job. So yes, if you want the truth, I am jealous. I kick away my shoes, let my jeans drop, and – with some difficulty – tease, tug, and peel the rest of my clothes from my body.

When I first get in the bath, the hot water stings my cuts, but after a few minutes, the pain drifts away and my eyelids flutter and finally close. I don't try to open them again, but slip deeper into the water until only my nose and lips break the surface. There's peace down here, with all the sounds of the world – cars going past, voices in the street, the phone ringing downstairs – muffled and changed into slow, low music.

When I look around again, orange light ripples on the tiles. It is dark, but the streetlamp outside makes a cool, watery sun in the window's obscure glass. The bath is cold. I get out, wrap myself in a towel, and go to the bedroom to find some clothes, but the phone rings again. I manage to get downstairs in time to answer it.

'Hello.'

'It's Ronald.'

'Who?'

'Mr Green.'

'Oh, hello, sir.'

'I've been trying to get in touch with you all day. It's Mrs Joe, she's been taken ill.'

Part Three

24

As we pull into the car park, I can't believe that I'm back at the same hospital I was discharged from only this morning. I'd feel sheepish if I weren't so worried. When we stop, I go round to the boot to pull out Mr Green's wheelchair, but he calls to me, 'Never mind that – let's just get in there.'

I consider this for a moment and decide that I'll have to put my foot down. I walked through this building just a few hours ago, and some of those corridors feel like they're half a mile long. 'It'll be quicker in the end,' I tell him, and just carry on with it.

I've already got the wheelchair on the tarmac and mostly unfolded when the passenger-side door swings open, propelled by Mr Green's stiff, outstretched arm. It hits the car parked next to mine with a heavy thump. I hold my tongue. When he finally gets himself upright, he sees me standing behind the chair and grunts, but sits in it anyway. I lock the car and we set off towards the hospital building.

When we get inside and ask for directions, it turns out that I was right about the chair: Mrs Joe is deep in the guts of the hospital. I push Mr Green through the corridors and try to ignore my own soreness. He is silent the whole time, gripping his walking stick in his lap. He hasn't said much since I picked him up; our longest conversation was when he asked what happened to my face, and I told him only the bare minimum about that.

We find the ward and approach the nurse at the main desk. I tell her who we're here for. She looks dubious. 'It's a bit late. Are you family?'

'Friends.'

She flicks through some papers on a clipboard. 'I shouldn't really let you. She's sedated anyway.'

Mr Green taps his walking stick against the frame of his wheelchair.

'Is her son here?' I ask.

'I'm not sure.'

'About five feet ten, in his fifties, probably wearing a big duffel coat.'

'Oh, yes.'

'Can we at least talk to him?'

'I'll let him know you're here.'

She disappears along the corridor and round a corner. About thirty seconds later, Joe appears from the same direction. He sees us and stops.

'All right, mate?' I ask him.

He stands still, watches me.

'Joe?'

He takes a step, then another, then another. His steps pick up speed and soon he moves faster than I've ever seen him move before. He lumbers towards me, his arms pump. He gets to within a couple of metres and I think, 'He must stop now,' but instead of stopping, he lowers his head and screams out, 'Yeearghhhh!'

He butts me in the middle of the chest and I fall on my arse.

The successive impacts of skull on ribcage and floor on backside amplify the pain of my injuries from dull ache to blinding agony.

I scream. Joe belly-flops onto me like a professional wrestler. I scream again.

'You called the doctor!' he bawls into my ear. 'You called the doctor and put her in the hospital! You made her poorly!'

'Joe, I didn't do anything.'

'You're lying. You called the doctor!'

'I didn't call any doctors.'

'You did! You took his number to call him. I saw you with my beady eye. You thought I was asleep, but I was watching you!'

There's a sharp crack from somewhere above. 'Joseph! Stop that at once!'

Joe's lips stretch back across his face in the ugly grin of someone about to burst into tears, and he rolls off me clutching and scrabbling at the back of his thighs.

Mr Green stands over us, walking stick aloft. 'Any more of that and I'll knock you on the head too. It was me who called the doctor.'

———

In all the rush to pick up Mr Green and drive over here, I didn't think to ask him what actually happened, or how he knew where Mrs Joe was. If I had, I might have learned the truth and been prepared for a hostile reception from Joe. As it is, I have more bruises for my collection.

'I was worried about what you'd said. I tried to call you first – I thought you were going to give me a lift over there, like we talked about – but there was no answer,' said Mr Green.

'I was in hospital.'

'Well, I know that now, don't I? So I telephoned there, but *he* answered.' Mr Green looks over at Joe, who feeds coins into the vending machine on the other side of the hospital cafeteria. 'He kept telling me she was asleep. Now, I've known that woman for over forty years and she does not sleep in the middle of the day.' He slaps his hand on the tabletop, as if sleeping in the middle of the day were a clear sign of immorality. 'So I called the surgery.'

'And they sent someone to see her?'

'Aye, but not till this bloody morning! Some emergency call-out, eh?'

'I'm surprised they bothered at all.'

'Well, I was insistent. It's about time somebody made a fuss on her behalf.'

I pick up a salt shaker and turn it over in my hand. 'So what happened?'

'They telephoned me at lunchtime, said that Mrs Joe had a collapse when the doctor arrived and she was on her way to hospital.'

'A collapse?'

'She was none too pleased to see him. I think we can both imagine how it happened.'

'Aye.'

At the vending machine, Joe watches the tea dribble in to the last of three flimsy plastic cups. When it's ready, he lifts it out of the hatch, places it on an adjacent table with the other two, and struggles to gather them all up between both hands. I'd better help him or there'll be third-degree burns to add to the growing list of devastation. I go over and take a cup from him. He doesn't say anything, but he follows me back to the table and sits down with us.

There's a moment of silence and then Joe pushes the change across the table. 'Thanks for the money, Mr Green.'

'You're welcome, Joe. Do you have anything else to say?'

Joe stares into his lap. 'I'm sorry I went mental.'

'I'm glad to hear it.'

'But you shouldn't have called the doctor. It was meddling.'

'Bloody hell, Joe. Don't you see that someone had to meddle?'

'She doesn't like it!'

'Look, Joe,' I break in, 'I know she doesn't like it when people stick their noses in her business. And normally when that happens, she tells them where to go, right?'

'She bloody does!'

'Exactly. But this time she couldn't do it, could she?'

'She was really angry, but she couldn't talk.'

'That's not normal, is it, Joe?'

'No.' He shrugs and looks back at his lap.

'So mebbes she does need some looking after, eh?'

'Mebbes.'

'Then drink your tea and stop being a daft bastard, right.'

Joe takes a slurp of the grey tea and curls his lip. 'It's not as good as me mam's.'

'Nothing ever is, son,' Mr Green tells him.

25

By the time we've finished our tea, Joe looks better. He fidgets, but is otherwise back to his default, out-of-phase rationality.

'Missed *Coronation Street*,' he says glumly.

I look at my watch. 'You missed your bedtime too, mate.'

'I don't have a bedtime. I'm an adult.'

'Too right. You're bloody ancient, you.'

'My mam says I'm in my prime.'

'She would. Do you want a sandwich?'

'Not hungry.' He folds his arms.

Unfortunately, I am, but I don't want to be the only one sat here eating. I look at Mr Green, who flares his nostrils impatiently. 'Let's get back up there and find out how she is,' he says. 'If Joe can refrain from brawling this time.'

I squeeze Joe's shoulder. 'He's all right. We've got it sorted, haven't we, mate?'

Joe shrugs my hand away, but nods. 'All sorted. It's magnificent.'

'Howay, then.'

I get up and manoeuvre Mr Green past the tables and chairs to the exit of the cafeteria and out into the corridor. The smell of grease and stale mash subsides, and with it any feeling of ease:

I'm in a hospital, again, and the news is bound to be bad. Joe shambles beside me, just a step behind.

'Did the doctor say anything to you?' I ask him.

'He said hello. He said his name was Dr Ahmed. He said—'

'Joe, did he say anything about your mother?'

'He said she was on strike.'

I give up and we walk the rest of the way back to the unit in silence.

When we get there, there is nobody at the desk. I almost wait like a good little boy, but Joe keeps going, so we follow him. He stops at a room and looks through the doorway.

'Is she in there?'

He nods.

The curtains are drawn around the bed, but I can see at least three pairs of feet moving in the gap at the bottom. There are voices too, low and urgent. All I catch are numbers, and medical words I don't understand.

Joe makes for the curtains, but I grab his coat and haul him back. 'Just let them do their job, mate.'

'Who is it in there?'

'It's the doctors, you nugget.'

'Bollocks to that – she hates the bastards.'

Joe swears approximately never, so I don't notice him unbutton his coat and walk out of it until it's limp in my hand and I'm standing there like a dickhead.

'Joe, don't go in there.'

But it's too late. He barges into the curtain and pushes it up and over his head. Before it falls behind him, I see the nurse from earlier turn in shock from her work at Mrs Joe's bedside.

'What are you doing to her?'

'Get out!'

'Leave her alone!'

'We're trying to treat her.'

'You perverts!'

'For God's sake' – another voice, a man – 'I've been through this with you already. Wait outside.'

I step out from behind the wheelchair, but Mr Green blocks my path with his walking stick. 'Don't make it worse, son. We're in enough trouble as it is.'

Suddenly, the curtain bulges and Joe is steered out by a young Asian doctor with both hands clamped firmly on Joe's shoulders. Joe struggles a little, but the doctor spins him round so they're face to face. 'Go and sit outside and stop playing silly buggers.'

Joe doesn't have his mother's balls; if a figure in authority looks him in the eye and tells him what to do, he does it. He slopes out and brushes past me without an acknowledgement.

The doctor pushes his hair out of his face and sees Mr Green and me. 'Who are you?'

'We're…uh…friends,' I say.

'Of him, or her?'

'Both,' says Mr Green.

The doctor keeps looking at me. 'Are you mentalists too?'

'Not usually.'

'Good. I'll see you in a few minutes.'

He goes back behind the curtain.

We find Joe reading a magazine in the unit's common area. He flicks through the pages and mutters to himself. On the other side of the room, a woman and a man huddle with their backs to us. She sobs into his shirt. I resist the urge to smack Joe round the head; instead, I wheel Mr Green to one side of him and sit down on the other.

'What's this season's colours, then?'

'You what?'

I lean in to see what he's reading. *FHM*. 'That shit'll rot your brain.'

He holds it closer to his face. 'It's all right,' I hear him mutter from behind the cover.

I snatch the magazine away from him and chuck it onto a nearby end table.

'How! Give it back!'

'Shut up,' I hiss. 'You're not the only person in here with problems.'

He butts his forehead up against mine and stares into my eyes from under knotted brows. 'You're rude.' His spittle splatters on my chin and lips.

I want to shake him hard. I glance at the other people. The woman's face is still buried in the man's chest, but he has noticed us. He watches nervously over the top of her head.

I slide down the chair so that the man can't see, grab Joe by the collar, and drag him down with me. 'Get off!' he squeals.

'Shut up – you're disturbing people.'

'You're disturbing me!'

'Why are you pretending that you don't understand what's happening?'

'You're a nutter, you.'

'Joe, I know you're not this stupid.'

'What are you on about?'

'Your mother's seriously ill, man. She might die.'

He twists out of my grasp, stands up, stomps across the room, and lets himself drop onto a soft chair in the corner. He is very still for a moment, but he can't hold it in. His lip twitches and his eyes shine, and then he covers his face.

'Oh brilliant,' says Mr Green.

'I got through to him, didn't I? It's better than a fucking spaz attack every five minutes.'

Mr Green shrugs and looks away.

'Sorry,' I say.

I watch Joe cry. I'm just too tired to walk over there and do anything about it, but a growing fear buzzes in my fingers and toes. The doctor appears.

'There you are. I need a word.' He stands in the doorway.

I get up and take the handles of Mr Green's wheelchair. The doctor holds up his hand.

'Just you will be fine. We don't need to hold a conference.'

'Oh, but—'

Mr Green stops me. 'Just go and find out what's happening. I'll stay with *him*.'

I follow the doctor to a small room. He closes the door behind us. Although there are chairs, he does not sit down. I ache, but I don't want to have a conversation with his crotch, so I remain standing too.

'You're a friend of the family?'

'Yes.'

'Her son…' He gestures with his right hand – half a question, half an alternative to stating the obvious.

'…is a bit soft in the head,' I finish for him.

'Quite. He can't continue to behave that way or he'll get himself thrown out of the hospital.'

'He'll be all right now, I think. It's dawned on him that things are serious. Look, how is she?'

'Yes, I was coming to that.'

'So?'

'Well, she's very ill. It seems she had a small stroke recently, maybe more than one.'

'On strike,' I mutter. 'I get it.'

'I'm sorry?'

'Nothing.'

The doctor furrows his brow. 'She was in a bad way when she arrived: very weak, very dehydrated, obviously hadn't eaten for several days.'

The fear bursts. I feel sick. I could have done more, should have done more, but I was too wrapped up in all my other problems. Even when I did pay attention, I was more concerned with protecting her dignity – and now that dignity could cost her her life. 'Right,' I say.

'Now, we've put her on a drip and we've made her comfortable, but frankly it's too late. I think you'd better prepare for the worst.'

'Neglect. She's dying of neglect.'

'You could say that. It's quite common, actually.'

'How long?'

'Difficult to say, but not long. Hours, perhaps. He can sit with her, but you shouldn't expect her to be responsive.'

There's nothing to say. I want to go outside; the fluorescent lights make my eyes ache.

'Well, I'll leave you to it. Just ask at the desk if you need anything.' He leaves and I stand in the room and watch the carpet. I don't know how to explain this to Joe, but then, what's to explain? He's going to see for himself soon enough.

26

By morning it was all over. She was so thin and white against the white of her pillow that we could see the faint pulse of life under her skin. And then we couldn't. I drove Joe and Mr Green home; there was nothing else to do. We were monosyllabic with tiredness and defeat, and as I finally slumped through the door of my house, it felt like a place I had lived in a long time ago.

I try not to think of Joe. I don't want to remember the slope of his shoulders as he walked from my car to his home or the dazed rattle of his key until he realized the door had been left unlocked. Of course I didn't go in with him; I could barely lift my own head. There's a limit.

I'm about to climb the stairs to go to bed, when a piece of paper catches my eye. It's just inside the door, on its edge up against the skirting board. It could be a flyer, but then I see that one side is ragged, as if it was torn away from something. I pick it up. It's a note:

> I hope you're not at the pub; you should be taking it easy the state you're in! I just popped round to check that you're OK, but you've buggered off. I thought you'd be resting. Ring me if you need anything.
>
> Laura

God knows why she bothered – she has enough problems of her own – but as I read the evidence that someone cares, even a little bit, I feel a small warmth in my stomach. I walk towards the phone, but the idea melts before I get there. It is 8.45 a.m., I haven't slept, I can't even begin to approach the task of explaining what happened last night, and the only other thing I have to say is, 'Thanks for giving a fuck.' It won't do at all. I go to bed.

————

Later, I am woken by the sound of the bin men. I check my watch. It is 1 p.m. If I close my eyes I'll fall straight back to sleep, but if I do that I'll end up nocturnal. I stare at the ceiling for a couple of minutes and it dawns on me that I'm absolutely starving: incentive enough to get up and go downstairs.

In the kitchen, I use a knife to dig the mould patches out of a couple of slices of bread. Then I put the bread in the toaster. I haven't had the chance to clean in here, or buy food, for over a week and the general squalor makes me think of Joe again. He'll need to learn to look after himself, but to do that he will have to accept that his life has changed for good. Dealing with change is not one of Joe's strong points. For that matter, it's not one of mine.

The toast pops up. I manage to scrape enough margarine out of the almost-finished tub to cover both slices, just about. They taste like shit. Never mind Joe, I'm going to peg out myself if things carry on like this. I have no idea what he's doing right now – on his own in that house – but he'll have to cope without me for a little longer. I have things that need to be done.

I gently prod at my ribs; they still hurt. I circle my shoulders; moving still hurts. Clearly, the best thing for me is the couch and a quantity of Scotch, but it cannot be. I still have no cash and I still haven't reported my card stolen, so I have to go to the bank. That accomplished, I will have to go to the petrol station because the car's almost empty. And if I'm at the petrol station, I may as well go into the supermarket. The alternative is starvation.

I brush the crumbs off my T-shirt and start looking for my keys.

———

My bank balance is not encouraging, so I buy only half a tank and my food shopping is even more frugal than usual. In the supermarket, shoppers swerve to avoid getting close as I rummage through the bakery shelves for the cheapest possible loaves of bread, black-eyed and hissing to myself as the bending and stretching prompts new parts of my body to remind me that I'm not in the best of health. There's nothing for it but to crash on through the day, and do what needs to be done. I let the rest of the world blur past me. If I stop to think, I'll seize up, or worse.

I pay and get everything into the car. I've probably forgotten a lot of things I need, but at least I now have some food that's fit for human consumption. I sit behind the wheel and tear into a packet of sausage rolls. I'm hungry enough that even cold they taste good. The fat coats the roof of my mouth. I eat all five. I feel sick. I wind down the window and drive away.

The freezing air makes my eyes water. I let the tears flow all the way home.

———

Back at the house, I put away the shopping. It doesn't look like much once it's in the cupboard, but it'll satisfy my needs for a few days at least. The kitchen is still a tip, but my visit to the bank has reminded me that I have a greater priority – namely, to secure gainful employment. I pick up the phone. I'm going to call Lee and press him about these jobs, and I'm not going to let anything deflect me from the task…except for the fact that I don't know his number. It's stored on my mobile; automatically I reach into my pocket. My mobile is not there.

'Oh shit.'

It's not in my pocket because it's on the bathroom floor where I left it, completely fucked. I slam the receiver back into the cradle and wince as the shock of the impact travels through my sprained wrist.

'Fuck.'

I don't know his last name, so the directory is useless to me. Then I see Laura's note, next to the phone where I put it. I pick it up and read it again: 'Ring me if you need anything.'

———

By the time I knock on the door, I feel a bit daft. There was no real need to come all the way to Geoff's house; it would have been quicker to ask a neighbour, some of whom have started actually speaking to me in recent years. It was just the momentum of the day that brought me here; the signs all pointed this way and I followed them. She opens the door.

'You look terrible.'

'Thanks,' I say. She turns back into the house and I follow her to the living room. 'Have you heard anything from Geoff?'

'No.'

'Have you tried his family?'

'They won't talk to me,' she sighs. 'He must have told them. Why are you up and about, anyway?'

'I didn't have much choice in the matter.'

'Well, it's your funeral. Do you want a drink?'

'No, thanks.'

We stand in silence for a few moments and then she looks at me and smiles. 'You wanted to borrow my phone.'

'Please.'

She hands me her mobile and watches as I take it apart and replace her SIM card with mine. 'Is it an important number?' she asks.

'Aye, pretty important – someone who might have some work for me.'

'Oh. Just temporary?'

'Sounds like it could be long term. If it works out, like.'

I turn her phone on, and as it plays its little welcome jingle, I look up at her. I'm about to say, 'Thank you,' when suddenly I understand the look on her face. 'Fuck. Laura, I'm sorry. It's just I'm completely skint. I cannat afford to wait for him, y'know? It doesn't mean I don't think he's coming back.'

She sighs and sits down on the couch. I'm left, awkward, in the centre of the room. I sit next to her.

'I'm sorry,' I say again.

'It's all right. You've got to get on, I suppose. Everything's changing.'

'Aye, it is.'

'To be honest, I'm surprised how well I can imagine carrying on without him.'

'Well, it's like anything; you just find a way, don't you.'

'Hark at you,' she says. 'You should be one of them self-help gurus.'

'Thanks. Well, there's at least one thing you've still got in common with Geoff.'

'What's that?'

'That I can rely on you to take the piss.'

'I'm glad I'm still amusing to someone.'

'Oh yeah. It's a laugh a minute around here.' I sink back into the sofa, and with relaxation comes a resurgence of fatigue and then a long yawn. 'Sorry. I'm shattered.'

'I was going to ask if you'd been sleeping. You look absolutely knackered. Even the eye that isn't black is black.'

'Something bad happened last night.'

'How bad?'

'Really bad,' and I tell her the story of Mrs Joe's death.

She doesn't interrupt me as I talk, but when I have finished, she gives me a sad smile and says, 'Well, I'm sorry to hear that. It sounds like you were very fond of her.'

'Aye, I suppose I was. She's always been around, y'know? Ever since I can remember.'

It's cold in the room, and without a word Laura gets up and turns on the gas fire. Blue flames burst into life over the fake coal and incandescent prickles of light spread into a vivid blush. Laura shuffles herself back onto the sofa without quite standing up again, and I find myself talking more than I'd meant to.

'I felt like she was the last link to my parents. Well, my dad.' I did feel that, but I didn't know that I felt it until now. 'She was the only person who knew them that I could talk to. Well, talk to sensibly, anyway. But I didn't, really. There was so much more I could have asked, but I was too embarrassed.'

A long pause. Laura reaches out and touches my hand. 'Look, Mrs Joe probably told you more than you realize, and you shouldn't dwell on the things you regret.'

'That's easier said than done. I feel guilty.'

'Guilty?'

I stare into the fire.

'It wasn't your fault; she was an old woman. She's not your responsibility, she never was.'

'It's not just that. It's my dad. Looking after them is about the only thing I've ever done that he would have been proud of, and I've buggered it up.'

'But what about her family? Where are they in this? Don't they have some responsibility?'

'She has a younger brother. At least, I think he's still alive; I didn't hear of anything happening to him. He hasn't lived around here for years, though. I don't think I've ever met him.'

'You'll need to get in touch with him. There's arrangements to be made – all the talking to undertakers and solicitors and that.'

'I hadn't thought that far on yet.'

'Well, you shouldn't have to, especially the state you're in.'

'It's not that bad.'

'It's not that good either. And you've got Joe to keep an eye on.'

'Aye. No one else is going to do it.' I look into my lap and see that she holds my left hand between both of hers. I hadn't noticed her take it. She squeezes my fingers and it makes me smile. 'Thanks,' I find myself saying.

'Are you sure you're all right?'

'I'll manage.'

'You're so full of optimism.'

'That's what keeps me grinning.'

She pats me on the knee and stands up. 'I'm going to put the kettle on.'

I watch her walk into the kitchen, then hear the noise of the tap. Outside, it's getting dark. I should write down the number, go home, and make my call, but I don't want to move yet. I'll drink my tea and then I'll go.

———

My route back from Laura's house takes me past the end of Mr Green's street. I pause. Laura was right about the things that are and are not my responsibility, and knowing that makes everything seem easier to think about. I turn towards Mr Green's house. The light in the front room isn't on, but there is one on upstairs. I'm about to knock when I notice a glow at the end of the side passage, so I go round the back.

I find him in the shed. The door is slightly ajar, so I tap on it and he turns round with a start.

'Oh, it's you.'

'You found something to work on, then.'

'There's always something to work on.' He sniffs. 'You didn't finish all the tiaras, did you.'

'No, I didn't. Something came up.'

'Aye, he confessed to me at the last rehearsal.'

'Sorry. I'd have cleaned it away, but I needed to get him home.'

'Come in, would you. It's chilly.'

I pull the door closed after myself, unhook a folding chair from its place on the wall, and sit down. He lowers himself into his own chair. I notice that the pantomime tiaras are approximately as I left them; whatever he's doing out here hasn't involved much actual work. The air is thick with the warm smell of paraffin; an old heater burns in the back corner. It wasn't lit last time I was in here. I point at it with my foot.

'That thing's lethal. You should get an electric one.'

'It's a bit late for me to worry about health and safety now.' He gestures vaguely at his walking stick, propped in the corner alongside a split pickaxe-handle.

'You still have a wife,' I say.

'I think it would be a relief for both of us.'

'Bollocks to you, then.' A little pan-flash of anger.

He watches me steadily from beneath an arched eyebrow. 'You sound like you need some sleep.'

'Sorry. I managed some earlier, but you know what it's like when your routine's buggered up.'

'Aye, well. We're two grumpy bastards together, then.' He tips his head towards the heater. 'You can fill it up for me, if you like. I'll just spill the bloody stuff everywhere.'

There's a can marked, 'Paraffin', on the shelf above my head. I get up and swing it down with a heavy slosh; then I take it over and squat next to the heater. I can't see a funnel anywhere, so I pour slowly.

When I'm finished, he's still sitting there, staring into space and massaging the knuckles of his left hand between the thumb and fingers of his right. I put the paraffin back, and he looks at me as if he'd forgotten I was here. I sit down.

'We'll have to sort out the arrangements,' I say.

'Her brother's dealing with it. He'll be here the day after tomorrow.'

'Oh. I didn't know you were in touch with him.'

'I am now. I called Joe and got him to find his mother's address book.'

'Right. So it's out of our hands.'

'Aye.' Mr Green shrugs. 'He did little enough for her during her lifetime…'

'How did Joe sound when you talked to him?'

'Glum, I would say.'

'I just dropped him off this morning. I haven't looked in on him or anything.'

'Well, we can't babysit him, can we?'

'No, but—'

'Look, son, we'll keep him on the straight and narrow, right? Keep him involved in the panto and all that, and keep an eye on him until we know how things are going to turn out. We won't leave him to rot – don't worry.'

'Yeah.' I find myself agreeing with him, and it doesn't seem to matter that he can't even get down the lane to Joe's house under his own steam; it's good enough to know that someone else is with me on this.

'He'll be all right,' says Mr Green.

'Aye, he'll be all right.'

27

When I get in, I go to the phone and call Lee immediately. I shouldn't put it off any longer. I don't want to work – I've never wanted to work – but I have to, and this is the only offer I have. It seems to ring for a long time, but eventually he answers.

I tell him it's me and he cuts me off in a flurry of speech: 'Fucking hell, man. Where've you been? I've been trying to reach you for days.'

'Eh…' I gulp back my surprise, and say, 'Sorry, my phone's knackered. I only just managed to get your number off my SIM card. I meant to call you before, but I've been in hospital and all sorts.'

'Hospital?'

'Aye, I was pissed and I had a fall. Just a bit battered, like.'

'But you're all right for work?'

I circle my wrist; it's stiff and sore. 'I'll be fine.' I'm going to need some painkillers. 'So what's the plan?'

'Tomorrow morning, mate, bright and early. We're working the weekend to catch up.'

'Tomorrow?' I will definitely need painkillers.

'Good news, eh?'

'Aye, it's great news.'

He gives me all the details. I scribble down directions on the back of the envelope the phone bill came in. It's in the middle of nowhere, out in the country, but at sixty quid a day the money's good enough to make that worth my while. Better yet, it's cash in hand. We'll be working on the conversion of some old stables into a pair of houses, which makes a change at least. All in all, it sounds a lot better than I had any right to expect.

'I'll be there,' I tell him.

I put the phone down and wonder if I could get away with a couple of cans of Special Brew in celebration. No. I have to deny myself. I have never before started a new job with entirely new people, and I'm surprised to find myself wanting to make a good impression. The bruises look bad enough, but rocking up with a foggy hangover to boot would definitely be bad form. The feed-me-booze voice gets quieter but doesn't shut up entirely, and to take my mind off it, I walk into the kitchen and switch on the radio. It fills the room with information from Iraq: sixty-eight killed in a marketplace here; US Marine blown up there. The usual shit, but I leave it on because I know there's a real programme in the next time slot. Anyway, the world could do with fewer US Marines. If I'm not going to drink, I need some dinner.

I'm looking at the contents of the fridge when I realize there's a problem. If I go to work tomorrow, that means leaving Joe on his own for another day. I don't know if he's ever been alone for that long in his life. Without someone to impose routine upon him, someone to stand between him and whatever random events ricochet in his direction, sooner or later he'll spaz out. And why not? We've all got a breaking point.

I decide that I'd better have a word with him, at the very least, but when I telephone, he doesn't answer. Maybe he's in the shower, or having a shit. I go back into the kitchen. It turns out that what is on the radio is not what I expected, but one of those smug, unfunny sitcoms. Fuck knows who listens to them, but they probably live in Surrey. I twist the dial until I reach a music station. Some bed-wetter with a guitar. Fuck. Commercials. Bollocks. I turn it off.

I'm going to have to go over there.

———

I drive down the lane to Joe's house. The car wallows through the potholes and the loose change rattles in the ashtray. The headlights gild the verge against the heavy dark; a tumult of bramble whirling like razor-wire, the rigor mortis of last season's hogweed. A rabbit bursts from the undergrowth and zigzags down the channel of light ahead of me before disappearing into the hedge. It's cold. I turn up the heater.

When I pull up outside Joe's house, it looks like every light in the place is switched on, each window bright. I walk round the back – almost tripping on some unseen object as I go – and peer through the kitchen window. It's messy again, but not as bad as it was last time I was here. I knock, but there's no sign from inside. I rap hard on the door glass, and then for good measure hammer the wood with my fist. Still nothing. I try the handle and it opens. I'll have to tell him about that.

I check everywhere and see that I was right: every light in every room is on, even the lamps. But Joe isn't here. I sit down at the bottom of the staircase, on the second-to-last step. The coat hooks are on the wall in front of me and Joe's big, dirty duffel doesn't hang from any of them. I could stay here until he gets back, but when will that be?

I go out to the car and turn in the lane. It's narrow and I have to inch the car round, lock to lock several times, but eventually I face the right way. I can only hope that he hasn't taken the footpaths and bridleways – that even he wouldn't go out there in the pitch black. He must be in the village somewhere. I set off.

In the rearview mirror the lights of Joe's house still blaze away. Fuck it. That's the least of my worries.

Back in the village, I make a pass up and down the main road, but I don't see him plodding along, just some kids hanging out in the bus shelter. One of them almost runs out in front of the car. I brake hard and blow the horn, which invites muffled jeers and a thump on the rear wing as I go past. They're good kids, really. No, they're twats. Abortion should be compulsory.

I pass the pub, but he won't be in there. I crawl by the churchyard, but he's not among the gravestones or sitting on the bench. In truth, he's probably nowhere in particular: he doesn't like to stop, he likes to keep walking. I can't drive along every street in the village. The estates alone would take ages. Then there are all the terraces, and you can't even get a vehicle down the back lanes. Maybe I should just return to the house and wait for him to come home, but he doesn't have anything to come home to.

The park comes up on my right. Joe always thought the equipment was 'magnificent', but it was impressed upon him that it's unseemly for a man of his age to hang around a kiddies' playground, sitting on the swings and striking up conversations with five-year-olds. Still, under current circumstances it might be understandable if he were there now, trying to fit his fat arse down the slide. Simple pleasures and all that. He really liked the old park too, before it was ripped up and eventually replaced with one that met modern safety standards. I remember him pushing me on the roundabout once. He was stronger then, hadn't yet run to fat, and he pushed so hard and fast I thought I was going to fly off. Each time he gripped the bars and gave another heave I felt the surge deep in my insides. At first I liked it and the sensation gave me an erection. Then I started to feel sick, dizzy, and scared, but Joe had a big grin on his face and I didn't want to hurt his feelings by shouting to stop, so I just clung on. He kept going for ages. Eventually, someone's mum came over and told him to bugger off and let the other kids have a go.

I pull over and get out.

I can't see it from here, but the playground is in the middle of the park on a square of that special bouncy tarmac that will scuff your knees but won't break your skull. The night is moonless, and I'm in the glow of a streetlamp, so the open space behind the road is just a big black blank. I stuff my hands in my pockets and walk in what should be roughly the direction of the climbing frames.

After a minute or so, I hear voices to my left and slightly behind. I turn towards the sound and see the silhouette of the slide. I realize that I somehow veered away from and walked past the playground. I can't see the people, or hear exactly what they're saying, but ten to one it's a group of teenagers and no doubt they'll give me some cheek or other. There is a small flash and a bubble of light floats in the air for a couple of seconds, then disappears. I squint and can just detect the glow of the cigarette tip wavering at the edge of perception like the very faint stars you can see only when you don't look directly at them.

This is a waste of time. Even if Joe was here earlier, he won't be now; he finds groups of adolescents threatening, for obvious reasons. For my own part, I don't want them to realize that I'm out here, stalking around. That kind of attention is the last thing I need, so I turn back.

'Hold him!'

I stop. They're shouting now, excited. Then a huge bellow erupts.

'Joe!' I turn on my heel and run in the direction of the sound. My feet slip and slide under me and I almost fall, but the shapes of the playground loom up and then there are figures. 'Joe!'

I burst among them – three, four, maybe five, I'm not sure – and they scatter. Almost too late, I see Joe below me on his hands and knees, and I skid to a halt just before I crash into him. 'Joe. Fuck. What's going on?'

His face is a pool of shadows, and his voice is desperate. 'I'm the horse. Moo! Moo! I'm the horsey!'

'Joe, what are you doing?'

'They made me.'

Then someone's behind me, shouting into the back of my head. 'Don't fucking barge into me!'

I turn on them and we're face to face. 'What have you done to my friend?'

'Nothing. He's a mentalist.'

'What have you done to him?'

'He's a right fucking spastic; he was just swinging on the fuck-ing swing talking to himself.'

'That's his business. Leave him alone.'

'Is he your bum-chum or what?'

I bring my face right into his; our foreheads touch. 'You might think you're Jack the Lad, but I'm Jack the Man and I'll rip your fucking bollocks off, son.'

He takes a step backwards and I shove him the rest of the way. I turn to Joe – 'Get up' – and offer him my hand. He pulls himself to his feet, snivelling and mumbling under his breath.

'He's a fucking paedo.' Another voice from the darkness. 'He hangs out in the village hall with all the little kiddies.'

'I'm the horse!' shouts out Joe.

'Shut up, Joe,' I say. Then to the voice, 'I hear anything like that again, I'll take your fucking head off.'

'Fuck off, you fucking homo.' But they don't come any closer.

I grip Joe by the upper arm and steer him towards the road. I feel them follow us, but I don't stop.

'Is he your gay lover? Do you do fisting?'

I ignore them; I just want to get Joe away from here. Eventually, they give up and slink away. I put Joe in the passenger seat of the car, and when I get in myself, I turn the interior light on and look at him. There's a livid red spot just above his left eye.

'They stuck a cigarette on me,' he says.

'Aye, I can see that. Let's get you home.'

———

Joe sits at the kitchen table and forks beans on toast into his mouth. He isn't crying anymore, but his hand shakes, and droplets of tomato sauce spatter onto the tabletop and down his sweater. I let him get on with it. I can't sit there and feed him like a baby.

'They won't come here,' he sloshes.

'No, they won't. You shouldn't draw attention to yourself.'

Slosh. Chomp. He wouldn't eat like that if his mother was at the table.

'You can't go around acting like a nutter.'

He lowers his head over his plate and keeps eating.

'Is there any cream for that burn?'

'Dunno. It hurts.'

He fumbles with his fork and it hits the edge of the table, rebounds in a somersault that launches beans into his face, and then falls to the floor. He ducks down after it and almost slides off his chair as he goes. I get up and take a clean fork from the cutlery drawer and swap it for his. He grunts a 'thank you' and goes back to his dinner. He concentrates very hard on eating – wolfing it, hunched like a soldier whose mess tin contains hot food for the first time in days.

He finishes and looks up at me. 'Any more?'

'That was the whole can. If you have any more beans, you won't sleep for your farts.'

'Pudding?'

'I don't know, mate. There's naff all food in here. When did you last do the shopping?'

'Last Tuesday.'

I look in the cupboards and find a canned sponge pudding, from Heinz. 'I've never made one of these before.' I read the label. 'It microwaves.'

'They're magnificent, them. Can I have custard?'

'With last Tuesday's milk? You'll be lucky.'

'Don't want it, then.'

'Good.' I put the can away. 'Did they do anything else to you?'

'They kicked me leg. It didn't hurt, though. And they were making fun of me.'

'I'm sure they were. How did you get on to the subject of the fucking pantomime horse, though?'

He looks around the kitchen, as if the answer to the question might be hiding behind the fridge, then shrugs. 'I can't remember. They were all around me. They had nasty faces. I tried to talk to them, but it just made them worse. They told me to moo like the horse.'

'Horses don't even moo.'

'That's what I said! Then he kicked me.'

'Why were you out there?'

'Wanted to go on a walk.' He folds his arms.

I can see I'm not going to get far tonight. He hasn't even mentioned his mother. Even if he did, there's nothing I could say or do to make it better. The pure fuckery of it all settles on my shoulders like great coils of heavy chain. 'You should get some sleep. You're all jumbled up.'

'They won't come here,' he says again.

'No, they won't. And if they do, they'll find me waiting for them. I'll sleep on the couch, all right?'

'I'm tired.'

'Then go to bed.'

28

It's still dark when I wake, but I check my watch and I'm glad I did; it's almost six. If I'm to get to this job anything like on time, I need to leave now. I wonder if I should go and tell Joe that I'm away, but he's better off asleep, so I pull on my trainers and slip out without waking him. I drive home, feeling queasy. I make some sandwiches and get my stuff together, and I'm on the road by six thirty. I stop at the Spar for a large box of ibuprofen and then drive out of the village.

Years of the three of us getting lost in that van – stewing in our farts and bad tempers – has left me with a deep distrust of other people's directions, but Lee's turn out to be accurate. Each turning is exactly in the place he said it would be and is signposted in exactly the way he said it was. When I miss one, it's my own fault for going too fast. I arrive at my destination with hardly a swearword uttered.

I park on the verge of a private lane with a hardcore surface that looks like it was only recently put down. No one else seems to have arrived yet; apart from a mini-excavator bearing hire-company stickers, mine is the only vehicle here. I'm too early. The sky is still a night blue, but the horizon glows red and against it stands a group of agricultural buildings. I switch off the radio and the latest atrocities drop away in the silence of the morning. For something to do, I strap up my bad wrist with the bandage they gave me in hospital and swallow double the recommended dose of painkillers. Then I sit and watch as the light in the east infuses the furls of cloud. I begin to hope that nobody comes and that I could just wait here until I didn't want to anymore and then turn round and drive home.

Fat chance. A car crunches up the track behind me, sweeps past, and parks up near the buildings. A man in a woolly hat gets out, stands and looks at me for a few moments, and then disappears into the shadows pooled around a stone barn. After a while, I hear the reluctant *chut-chut-chut* of a cold diesel engine being cranked before it coughs and spins into life. Shortly after this, a rectangle of light appears on the darkest wall of the barn – the one facing me – and I see the man cross the doorway, then cross back. I decide to stay where I am until Lee turns up.

When Lee said 'bright and early', it seems the emphasis was on the 'bright' rather than the 'early' because by the time he gets here it's broad daylight and getting on for nine o'clock. I am still in the car, half asleep, when he knocks on the window. I wind it down.

'You're sleeping on the job,' he says in mock horror.

'I've been waiting for over an hour.'

'Sorry, mate – bit of a hangover situation.'

'It'll get you nowhere, the boozing game.'

'Yeah, yeah...Let's have a cup of tea and I'll show you the ropes.'

'Sounds good to me.' I get out of the car and follow him down the lane to the buildings. Woolly Hat Man's car is still there, but I don't see any sign of him.

'We've only been here a couple of days,' Lee says as we walk.

'Who's "we"?' I ask.

'Me and Rupert.'

'You and who?'

'Rupert.'

'Who the fuck is Rupert?'

'You know – short bloke, black hair, face like a Rottweiler.'

I vaguely remember a man fitting that description who worked in Mac's gang. I never spoke to him, and he never made any attempt to speak to me. 'And his name's fucking *Rupert*?'

'Aye,' says Lee with a smile.

'Fucking hell, no wonder he kept himself to himself.'

Lee goes into the barn I saw Woolly Hat Man enter earlier and I go in after him. The inside is bright, lit by fluorescent tubes fixed to the beams. Judging by the noise, the generator must be just on the other side of the back wall. Otherwise the barn is empty, except for a battered old sideboard where the tea-making paraphernalia sits. Lee goes over to it and sloshes the kettle.

'So where is Rupert, anyway?' I ask.

'He's here. He came in with me, but he ran straight off to answer a call of nature. You look fucking horrible, by the way.'

'Thanks. No one's mentioned that yet; I thought I'd got away with it.'

'What happened?'

'I fell.'

'I'll bet you did, but who punched you first?'

'Are you making that tea or what?'

He grins to himself while he fills the kettle from a bottle of water.

'Here, I saw a bloke in a woolly hat poking around earlier.'

'That'll be the owner, Jethro.'

'*Jethro?*'

'Yip.'

'Fuck me. That's even worse than Rupert.'

'Careful, mate. He can't be far away.'

Involuntarily, I look around, but we're still the only people in here.

Lee shrugs. 'He's all right really.'

'Tea ready?' Rupert appears in the doorway.

'Just a minute,' says Lee without turning round to him. 'You two've met, right?'

Rupert gives me a nod and a grunt and seems to be satisfied with that, so I just nod back. The three of us stand around in awkward silence for a few moments until I ask, 'So what are we on with, then?'

'Fucking loads, mate,' and as Lee prepares the tea, he reels out a long list of jobs that include gutting the buildings, demolishing one entirely, digging out the floors, taking roofs off, cutting trenches. My eyes glaze over; all I wanted to know was what we're doing today. 'In other words, we've got our fucking work cut out,' he concludes – with a wide grin that reminds me a little of Mac – and then hands round the tea.

I hold my mug up to my face and let the steam condense on my chin. For now, Lee seems to have exhausted his repertoire of motivational banter, so we settle back into silence as we drink. I'm aware of the hands on my wristwatch ticking past nine o'clock and I begin to feel anxious to get to work. There's a flap of wings from above and I look up into the rafters but don't see the bird.

'Are you going to get anything done today?' A different voice.

Lee speaks up. 'Aye, we're just giving the new man his, uh… orientation, Jethro.'

I don't turn round to see him; I'm afraid I'll laugh.

'Well, you've got the list.'

'Yes, we do. It's all in hand.'

Lee waits until Jethro has gone and then turns to Rupert and me. 'Right. I suppose we'd better get to it, then.'

I think I expected more ceremony, or some sense of occasion. This is the first time in my adult life I've ever worked without Barry and Geoff. As it happens, we just troop over to the other barn, climb into its loft, and begin ripping up the floorboards in preparation for removing the timbers that support it. We start at the wall and work back towards the ladder, discarding the boards by dropping them through the gap we've created and wearing masks so we don't inhale the dust thrown up by years of crusty dirt and bird shit. Soon I'm filthy, but it makes me feel cleaner.

Rupert is shorter than me, but strong, and working side by side, we fall into a rhythm disrupted only when one of us has to stop to tease out a tricky nail. My wrist seems to hold up pretty well, and I just ignore the stiffness in the rest of my body. Rupert and I make good progress, and it becomes apparent that Lee can't keep up with us.

'Fucking hell, lads,' he says at last. 'Don't get too keen. You're just making a rod for your own backs.'

'You could have done without them last few pints, mate,' says Rupert, without stopping work.

Eventually, Lee gives up and climbs down the ladder to concentrate on dragging the old timber out to the skip.

Rupert looks at me. 'He was still pissed when he picked us up this morning. I was shitting meself. All over the road, we were.' I'm relieved to hear that Rupert's voice is nowhere as posh as his name.

'He looked mostly all right to me.'

Rupert shrugs and carries on working. Either he's exaggerating or I'm far too used to spending time with heavy drinkers. I jam my crowbar in the gap between two planks and lever one up, and we fall back into the rhythm of work.

Even at our speed, it's going to take us all day and probably some of tomorrow to entirely remove this floor. We break for lunch and go back into the other barn, and I eat my sandwiches while sitting on a fold-out deckchair. We don't talk much, just chew in satisfied silence, and I'm happy with that. The morning's labour has improved my state of mind, and for the first time in years I feel relaxed at work. It's a novelty; I hadn't realized until now just how tense Barry's constant whingeing made me. Once I've finished my food, I make my excuses and go outside to find somewhere to have a slash.

I go into a neighbouring field, and once relieved, I walk back along the line of the hedge to where I climbed over. Although it's only just after noon, the sun is weak and low among the hazy cloud. I can look right into it without hurting my eyes; it appears as a perfect disc, stamped out of some impossibly smooth material. I stop and watch it. Without seeming to grow bigger, it floats up until it's all I can see. Then it doubles and the two discs move round each other like the effect of a coin on a tabletop set to spin off kilter.

'Now then.'

I turn round, suddenly dizzy, and a human figure shimmers on the other side of the fence. Jethro. I blink. Black spots dance over him.

'All right,' I say.

'Where've you come from, then?'

It takes me a moment to work out the intent of this question and then I explain where I live while trying to look at him sideways so I can at least see the shape of him.

He makes a gravelly, descending hum from the back of his throat and pauses. If he was smoking a pipe, he would be thoughtfully chewing on the stem right now. 'Aye, I know that area.'

'Oh. Then I'm sorry for you.'

He grunts. 'My brother-in-law lives around there. Do you know him?'

'Uh…' I squeeze my eyes hard shut and then throw them wide open, but it just makes the black spots move faster. 'What's his name?'

'John Smith.'

'Um. No. I don't know him.'

'Ah well, nice talking to you, then.'

As my vision returns, I see him ambling away, woolly hat still pulled down firmly over his head. 'Fucking hell,' I mutter to myself, then climb the fence and walk back towards the barns and the rest of the day's work.

29

On the way home, my stomach rumbles. I'm looking forward to dinner. A couple of rounds of fish-finger sandwiches and a four-pack will sort me right out – now I'm working again, I can afford to treat myself – and I stop at the shop to buy the necessary ingredients. I'm just leaving with my purchases when I almost bump into Barry.

It's an underwater moment, slow and without thought. He sees me, twists his body away, drops his head, and slips past. I step out into the cold air and just keep walking. It's not until I sit in the car that the world spins back up to speed. He didn't say a thing. He didn't even try to gloat. Fear? God knows, and anyway, there is nothing I could or should do about it now. I turn on the radio and drive home.

There is something on my doorstep. At first, I think it's a black refuse sack, but when I get out of the car, I see that it's a person huddled up, back against the door. I walk over.

His chin is buried in his chest, and his hood is pulled right up so only the peak of his cap sticks out, but I know it's him; I recognize his coat and his ropey old Hi-Tec trainers. Why does the world keep chucking shit at me when all I want to do is have some scran and go to sleep?

'Joe, what are you doing?'

No response. I squat down next to him and shove him in the shoulder with the heel of my hand. He looks at me.

'All right, mate?'

'Where've you been?' he asks.

'At work.'

'With big, fat Geoff?'

'No. I've got a new job now. Why are you here?'

'Dunno. Can I come in?'

'Aye.' I stand and put the key in the lock. 'Get up, then.'

He does as he's told and I let us in and turn on the light. He walks past me and flops down in my armchair. 'I'm hungry,' he says.

'Did you just come over so I'd cook your tea?'

He shrugs.

'Fuck's sake, Joe.'

'What's on telly?'

I toss him the remote control. 'Help yourself. Fish fingers all right?'

'Yuck. They're just the scrapings off the floor of the boat.'

'Did your mother tell you that?'

No answer.

I take the box out of the carrier bag and hold it up to him. 'It's Captain fucking Birdseye. Prime minced cod in golden breadcrumbs.'

'Don't care. It's kids' food.'

'Is it now? Jesus.' There is a packet of bacon in the fridge. I was saving it for the hangover I intend to have in the morning. 'Bacon butties, then?'

'Aye. That's magnificent, that.'

I go into the kitchen, put away the beer and fish fingers, and start making our tea. As I heat the oil in the frying pan, I hear Joe turn on the telly; it's one of those bloody quiz shows. He turns it up far too loud, but I can't be bothered to complain. Once the bacon is sizzling, I look in on him. He is hunched over with his chin in his hands and he stares in the general direction of the screen, but gives no sign of being involved in the programme. If I didn't know he had switched it on himself, I'd wonder if he was even aware of it.

I carry through the sandwiches. He accepts his wordlessly and takes a huge bite, tearing the bacon with a twist of his head. I pick up the remote and turn down the volume. He ignores me.

'Are you lonely at home?' I finally ask him.

'I don't like it there.' Flecks of semi-chewed bread spray off his lips.

'What do you mean?'

'It's all…empty. And I don't like the noises.'

'Every house makes noises, Joe.'

'Ours didn't used to.'

'Yes, it did – you just never noticed.'

'Well, they're different now.'

'A lot's different now; it's going to take a bit of getting used to, mate.' As I say this, I realize that I've assumed he will stay where he is and live alone in that house. Looking at him now – in the same clothes he's worn for days and clearly starving again – I can see just how unlikely that is.

'I hear her say things to us. She's not even there, man.'

I feel cold. He doesn't look at me, but gazes into the space above the TV. Then he blinks and bites his sandwich again. I get up, open the vent on the night storage heater, and turn my hands in the hot air. The wall in front of me is looking tired. I need to repaint in here. In fact, I need to repaint the whole house, but I just can't see myself getting down to it. Not that it matters – there's nobody else I need to please.

Joe must have finished his sandwich, because he asks, 'Is there any ice cream?'

'Ice cream? Do you think I'm made of money? I don't even have a freezer.'

'Then why have you got fish fingers? They're frozen.'

'Because I was going to eat them now!'

'You should get a freezer. It's nice to have ice cream.'

'You need to overcome your fucking pudding obsession, mate. It's bad for your teeth.'

'You're supposed to brush them.'

'Look, shut up a minute, would you?' I study my knuckles; a couple of them are split open. I sigh and turn to face him. 'There's only the one bed, so you'll have to sleep on the couch.'

'That's magnificent, that.'

'And I'm getting up early.'

He folds his arms across his chest. 'So am I.'

'Fine.'

I stuff the last of my sandwich into my mouth, take the plates into the kitchen, and return with a beer. Joe looks at me hopefully, but I don't acknowledge it. If he wants anything else, he can fetch it himself. I drink and watch some fat idiot get all the answers wrong and go home with nothing.

Eventually, Joe says to me, 'Are you going to rehearsals tomorrow?'

'What? Oh…for the pantomime. No. Why would I do that? I'm not even in it.'

'You're helping, though.'

'I'm just screwing stuff together and painting things, mate. Anyway, if you're going to be mixing with people, you need to have a wash and change your clothes.'

He grunts.

'I mean it. Go home tomorrow morning and sort yourself out, all right? They won't want you around smelling like that.'

'I don't smell.'

'You do, and you've still got food stains on your jumper from last night. There's mud on your knees…Have you even changed your underpants this week?'

'Shh! I'm trying to watch telly.' He leans forward and squeezes his arms round his chest. I want to throw something at his head, but it won't help, so I down the rest of the beer and go to get another one.

From the kitchen, as I slurp the foam from the top of the can, I can just see the back of Joe's head bobbing up and down as he rocks in the chair. If he carries on like this, he'll turn into one of those maddos who sleeps rough and finally ends up getting their brains smashed out when they cross paths with some drunk on a Saturday night.

———

The following morning, I get up and swallow four painkillers, two glasses of water, and a mug of Nescafé. Then I wake Joe.

'Cup of tea?' he mumbles.

'No, we've got to get going.'

'I don't want to get up.' He rolls away from me, but I grab his wrist and start to haul him to his feet. He growls, but eventually co-operates and stands there rubbing his eyes. 'Can I stay here?'

'No. Come on, you'll make me late.'

I manage to get him into the car before he becomes fully alert, and then he says, 'I don't want to come to work with you.'

'I'm not taking you to work, you dozy bugger. I'm taking you home.'

'I don't want to go there either.'

It's too late for him to do anything about it, though: I'm already driving. We go out of the estate, onto the main road, then down the lane, where I drive faster than I normally would and we bounce up and down in our seats. Joe reaches up and grabs the handle over his door.

'When you go in, I want you to have a wash and put on clean clothes. First thing you do, right?'

'Why can't I do it at yours?'

'Where's your toothbrush?'

'My house.'

'Where are your clothes?'

'My house.'

'Well, then.'

This exchange distracts me from the fact that we've reached our destination, and I brake sharply. The front wheels lock up and we slide for a few feet before a crunching halt. Joe tuts at me.

'Never mind that,' I tell him. 'Just go and do as you're told.' I almost add 'please', but I suck it back; I don't want to sound desperate.

'Keep your hair on.'

'Yeah, yeah, and the rest. Get out.'

'Rude.'

'You start taking care of yourself like a civilized human being and I'll start treating you like one. Deal?'

He emits a heavy sigh, then opens the door and swings himself out of the car. I watch him in the wing mirror for a couple of seconds, then wind down the window and call him back. I rummage in my pocket; there's some change and a battered fiver. I stuff the note into his hand. 'When you get hungry, don't try to make anything. Just go to the Spar and get yourself a couple of pasties and a bottle of Coke.'

'Thank you.'

'Don't blow it on cider.'

'I don't like cider.'

'I was joking. See you later, alligator.'

He just shuffles away. I see that his neighbours' lights are on. I wait until I'm sure he's gone inside, then I get out of the car, knock on their door, and ask them to keep an eye on him.

30

Later that day, we finish our allotted jobs by about 4.15 p.m. It's getting dark, so it seems a little late to start a new task and we troop back to the other barn and settle down with a cup of tea. Jethro was around for a while in the morning, but buggered off muttering darkly about cowsheds, bio-security, and vet visits. We haven't seen him since. Lee sits there looking at our 'list' like he wants to wipe his arse on it.

'Aye, there's no point starting on any of this. We'll barely get moving before we have to lock the tools up again.'

'Suits me,' I say, and shift in my deckchair, which creaks alarmingly but doesn't collapse.

'Pub, then?' asks Rupert.

'Better give it another twenty minutes or so in case he turns up again,' says Lee. 'Don't want to look like we're taking the piss.'

'I don't think I can come, anyway,' I say.

Lee and Rupert look at me in mock horror. 'You don't want beer?' says Lee.

'Aye, but something's come up.' In truth, I'm worried about Joe. The state he's in at the moment, I feel like I should be at home so that if anything happens, I can intervene. Then again, his neighbours did say they'd keep an eye on him and he's going to the village hall tonight anyway. I'm not that keen on him being around those people in his current mood, but at least they know who he is and, like Mr Green said, I can't babysit him.

'I'm sorry, mate, but if you're going to keep working here, you need to have your initiation.'

'Well, I'm driving anyway, so I can only have a couple.'

'Doesn't matter – it's still compulsory.'

'All right, all right, I'm persuaded.'

'Cracking.'

———

About forty-five minutes later, we park our cars outside a village pub and it doesn't look promising. In fact, it looks closed. We get out and gather at the front door. I try the handle; it's locked.

'Bollocks.'

'Lights are on,' says Lee.

We walk over to a window and peer in. There's a man behind the bar polishing glasses, with a stack of drip-trays in front of him. Lee raps on the glass. The man starts and looks round. Lee knocks again. The man sees us and frowns, then points at his watch and waves us away. Lee makes a beseeching gesture with the palms of his hands. The man shakes his head and goes back to polishing. Lee knocks again. The man gives us a long-suffering glare, then puts down the glass and cloth, and comes to the door. We walk round to meet him. The door opens a crack and his head pops out.

'Not open till seven,' he barks.

'Aw, come on, it's been a hard day. We only want a couple each,' says Lee with his best smile on.

'I'm closed.'

'We'll be good. You can't turn away custom, can you?'

The man grunts and looks at our trousers. 'You can't sit in the lounge like that.'

'We'll stay in the bar.'

'Fine. But any monkey business and you're out on your ear.'

I'm not sure what monkey business he thinks we might get up to, but watching Lee butter him up makes me feel quite happy. It's nice – for a change – to be around someone capable of genuine charm. We murmur our promises of good behaviour and the man lets us in. Lee buys three pints of bitter and we sit down round a table in the bar, next to the unlit fire.

'Rule one,' he says, 'is always get on the right side of the local landlord.'

'Good policy,' I say.

Lee holds up his glass. 'To Mac.'

'Aye. To Mac.' We lift our glasses and toast, and then I add, 'And to a brighter future.'

Lee smiles at me across the table. 'Oh, yeah?'

'Yeah.'

Lee and Rupert look at each other.

'What?' I ask.

Lee laughs and tips his glass at me. 'Nothing, mate. You're sound. You're in.'

And despite all the other shit I've got to deal with, I'm grinning like an idiot.

———

I said more about things than I probably should have – enough to make their ears prick up – but at least I skirted round the part that concerns Laura. Now I'm driving home, having drunk more than I probably should have, and I'm wondering how she is. I haven't heard from her for a couple of days. Having a drink with Lee and Rupert made me feel part of something again, and despite everything, I seem to be in quite a good mood. Maybe I should go over there and see if I can cheer her up. Not that I can remember ever cheering up anybody in the past, but it's worth a try.

I swing by the offie on the way home and buy a bottle of wine. I never drink wine by choice, so I just get one that costs £4.99; it seems like a reasonable price point. Then I go home to change out of my work clothes, where – to my relief – there is no sign of Joe. Clean and dressed once more, I walk over to Geoff's house.

She answers the door. 'Hello.'

'I thought you might like something to take your mind off things.' I hold up the wine.

'Is alcohol your answer to everything?'

'Ummm…'

'No, it's a nice idea. Come in.'

I follow her in. 'How've you been?'

'I'm alright. Just getting on with things. I'm going back to work tomorrow. I mean, I have to. I can't just sit here going crackers.'

'Aye, I'm back at work too.'

'I was going to say you seem in a better mood than last time I saw you. Let me have a look at your face.' We stand under the main light of the living room while she tuts over my bruises. 'Well, at least you're healing.'

'Course. It'd take more than that to sideline me.'

'You silly bastard. Sit down. I'll get some glasses.'

I do as I'm told. A couple of framed photographs of Geoff and Laura together stand on the mantelpiece. Ordinary objects, but to see them under these circumstances has a sharpness to it. I suppose they've always been there, but I don't remember noticing them the last time I was over here. I was probably too engrossed in other problems. I feel drawn to stand up and look at them more closely, but then Laura returns with two glasses.

She must have clocked the direction of my gaze because she stops next to one of the photos and says, 'That was in the Lake District, last year.'

'Oh, aye, I remember you going there. When he came back, he complained you made him walk up hills.'

'Yeah. He wasn't convinced. It's a screw-cap, isn't it?'

'Yeah. Only the best.'

She sits next to me. We open and pour the wine and say our 'cheers', and she sips hers with a wrinkled nose and says, 'It's not bad.' I try mine; it just tastes like wine, so I agree with her.

We chat for a while about this and that. She doesn't offer further information about Geoff – and I don't ask for any – so I assume she hasn't heard from him. I'm just happy to talk to someone about anything other than Geoff or Joe. She asks me about my new job and I tell her that I like it so far, and almost add, 'It's better than working with Barry,' but think better of bringing up that subject. 'It's varied,' I say. 'We've got all kinds of jobs to do, and it's a nice spot.'

'Sounds like you're happy with it.'

'I am, actually. Yeah. I am.'

She drinks her wine quickly – faster than me – and pours herself a new glass, gives me a top-up. It starts to go to my head. I remember that I haven't eaten. 'Careful, you'll get me plastered.'

'That's funny, coming from you.'

'I'm not that bad.'

'You could have fooled me.'

I look at my glass and tip it so the wine laps up the side, then slips back. Its surface glimmers in the light. Laura brings her face closer to mine and says, in mock-mothering tones, 'Awww, I'm sorry. Did I hurt your feelings?'

I feel her breath on my ear. I pull away a little and open my mouth, but I don't have any words to say, so I face her for a dizzy moment, trapped between silence and speech. We are still, and then I don't know who moves first, but our lips are together. I put my hand on her face. Her tongue flickers against mine.

'Jesus!' I pull away.

'Wait.'

'No. You're his *wife*. I've got to go.'

31

Geoff reclines on a lounger and sips his third beer of the morning. He isn't used to the heat and humidity yet; the air coats him like baby oil. They told him this was the *cool* season in Thailand. On the other side of the pool, a woman takes off her bikini top and Geoff watches her through his sunglasses. He likes the look of her, but is suddenly aware of the size of his own belly. In England, he would never have thought of it, but out here it feels ridiculous. Four days in and he hasn't met anyone else who even approaches his size.

Still, for four days he has barely moved. The heat slows him down, but the truth of it is that this place overwhelms him. During the taxi ride from the airport, the sheer weirdness of everything gave him a headache, while the traffic almost gave him a heart attack. Welcome to Paradise. It made him wish he'd gone for Spain after all, but Spain just didn't seem far enough away. He hasn't left the hotel compound since he arrived. It's comfortable here.

The topless woman rubs on sunblock. Her hands circle her thighs until the streaks disappear and her skin glistens. Geoff watches as she works her way up her body, and when she seems to linger over her tits for slightly longer than necessary, Geoff isn't sure if he is imagining things. He gently squeezes his dick through the pocket of his Hawaiian-patterned beach shorts. This is no good, he thinks. What I need is a whore.

That's something Geoff has never done before, although he knows Barry has. He had suspected Jim too, because Jim definitely never gets laid any other way. Or at least that's what Geoff thought until he found out about…No. Geoff shakes the image out of his head. The point is that Geoff always thought it was too dirty – something he would never be desperate enough to do – but now that money is no object, it doesn't seem like such a bad idea. Besides, with what that bitch has put him through, he feels entitled to it.

He motions for another beer and, while he waits, peels the label on the bottle already in his hand. He saw them on the street on the way over here. Just glimpsing them through the window of the taxi, he knew instantly what they were even though he has never used one or ever been to this country before. In fact, they were the most familiar thing he saw during the whole drive. Apart from the beggars. They seemed pretty familiar too.

'Sir, beer.'

The kid with the tray. Geoff feels sorry for him, working in this heat in a jacket and tie. 'Thanks. If I'm Sir Beer, you must be Squire…' Geoff trails off as he realizes that he doesn't have a punch line and that the kid doesn't understand a word anyway. 'Never mind.' The kid just stares at him blankly and holds out a chit to sign. Geoff waves it away. 'Later. I'm not going anywhere, am I?'

And he isn't going anywhere. He just isn't ready to go outside yet, not alone anyway. What he'll do is go and talk to the man at the desk, the one who smiled a lot and promised to make his stay pleasurable. He'll go and see the smarmy little fucker and he'll use his new magic words. 'Be discreet.' That's what the accountants promised to be, and they bloody well were. Geoff winced at their fee, but they were worth it: they fixed everything. It turns out that 'be discreet' is powerful voodoo once you've got the cash to back it up.

On the other side of the pool, the topless woman has been joined by a topless friend. Now they're putting sunblock on each other. Geoff smiles, stretches, and settles back to enjoy the view. Tomorrow, someone is coming to talk to him about getting a place to live.

32

For the next week, Joe spends almost every other night sleeping on my couch. He turns up in the evening – or just waits on my doorstep until I get back from work – bedraggled, hungry, unable to cope. I take him in, let him share whatever I'm eating, get down the spare blanket, and in the morning take him home. Then he's all right for one night, but the next day, he's always back. He knows that she's dead, but he also thinks she still talks to him. I don't understand how he can believe those two things at the same time, but he does.

I'm worried he's losing his marbles; he only had a couple of ordinaries to begin with.

The day of his mother's funeral arrives. We take our seats and the humanist minister at the lectern burbles on and I can't follow what he says, because it just doesn't matter. He didn't talk to us about what to say. There are only four mourners in the chapel: me, Mr Green, Joe, and, alone on the other side of the aisle, Mrs Joe's brother. He sits straight-backed in his double-breasted suit, eyes fixed on some point on the wall. If he's listening to the sermon, he gives no sign. There's no movement, no expression. He looks more like an old soldier than a man who made a living running a removals firm.

There are no hymns or prayers. She didn't go in for that stuff. Why would she? And so we simply have a moment's silence before the curtains open and the casket is swallowed. As we walk out, the only sound is of our footsteps on the hard floor of the aisle. The minister offers his hand at the door. I ignore him.

Outside, Mrs Joe's brother gets into his car and drives off. Since he went to the house that night last week, he has made everything a mere formality, perhaps out of shock or maybe just the sense that the best he could do was be rid of a bad job as quickly as possible. Amazingly – after four decades or more – Joe recognized his uncle on the doorstep and promptly flipped out. Somehow, he chased him to the next-door neighbours' house. It was then I got the call. Thank God I was in. I arrived to find Mrs Joe's brother hiding in the young couple's living room while their kid screamed blue murder. Joe was in the lane, yelling his mother's view of various family disputes that surely aren't important to her now. Joe never did learn the lessons of what really matters and when, so I had to pin him to the wall and let him kick my shins, while his uncle scuttled to the car and screeched away. Later, I found his wing mirror lying in a puddle, and a great scratch down my driver's-side door.

'Do you think we'll see him again?' I ask Mr Green, as the black Jaguar sweeps past us.

'I'd say that was fairly unlikely, son.'

'Can we trust him with the solicitors and that?'

'We'll have to, won't we? It's officially none of our business.' He fumbles with the car door handle; I go over and help him. 'Take me to the pub,' he says.

'Are you sure? What about him?' I nod over at Joe, who just stands with his hands stuffed into the pockets of his coat, staring at his feet.

'Bring him with us.' Then he throws his walking stick onto the back seat and slowly climbs in after it.

I close the door for him and call over to Joe, 'C'mon, mate. It's time to go.'

'No one came,' he says.

'Don't worry about that. You were there – that's all that matters. Come to the pub with us.'

'I'm barred.'

'That was ten years and two landlords ago. They won't remember. Anyway, it wasn't your fault. Get in.'

'Is *he* going?'

'Your uncle? No.'

'He's a nasty piece of work, that one.'

'He's gone. Forget about him.'

He looks over his shoulder to the crematorium, looks back at me. 'I don't want to leave her.'

'She's not here, mate. She's not here. Come with us.'

For the first time today, he starts to cry, but he gets in the car and we drive away.

———

At the pub, I buy the drinks: a pint for Mr Green and a shandy for Joe, whose mother never let him get drunk. It's about six o'clock – Mrs Joe's was the last funeral of the day and the drive back took half an hour – so the pub is still sparsely populated, but people are drifting in. The three of us drink, Joe quietly, Mr Green and me earnestly, and mull over our individual regrets. In here, Joe looks like a rabbit who finds himself in the fox's den. I could reach out and put my hand on his shoulder or something, but I don't. After a little while, he gets up and goes to the toilet.

Mr Green leans over to me. 'Lydia came to see me the other day.'

'Who?'

'The panto lady.'

'Oh, her.'

'Aye. She says that Joe worries some of the others. Wondered if we'd mind keeping him away from rehearsals in future.'

'He'd be heartbroken. I hope you told her to go and do one.'

'I was slightly more diplomatic than that.' He sucks his teeth.

'So he's not kicked out?'

'No. Not yet.'

'Good.'

'She asked me about you too. It seems somebody has been whispering to her about your chequered past.'

'Jesus.'

'Well, I told her you're "fully rehabilitated" and "an upstanding member of the community". She liked that. I think she's a *Guardian* reader. Listen…' He pauses, taps the tabletop. 'I called Social Services.'

'About Joe?'

'Of course about Joe.'

'Right.' Joe is scared of the authorities, and I'm not sure I like the sound of this. 'So?'

'So nothing. They listened sympathetically, issued forth some platitudes. You know what a platitude is, don't you?'

'Yes, Mr Green, I know what a platitude is.'

'Good. Well, I just wanted you to know that I've set the wheels in motion, or I'm trying to at least.'

'Right.'

'Don't worry – they're not going to drag him away by the hair. They're not that efficient, for a start. I was a teacher, so I've dealt with these people before. It'll be hard enough to get them to do anything, let alone something drastic. They're overworked and under-resourced.'

'Well, as long as you know what you're doing.'

'Unfortunately, in this regard I do.'

I pick up a beer mat and turn it over in my hands because they're itching for something to do. I suppose I should be glad; if

Joe gets help, maybe he'll stop coming to my house at all hours. Then again, that assumes the 'help' is any *help*.

'Relax,' he says to me. 'I'll handle them. You just keep doing what you're doing.'

'That's what I'm scared of.'

'That and everything else, I should imagine.'

'Aye. That and everything else.'

Joe gets back from the bog and slumps once more into his chair. He keeps looking around himself as if he expects attack from any angle. Under the table, I nudge his shin with my toe. 'Chill out, mate. Nobody's going to bother you. You're with me.'

'It's not civilized in here,' he pronounces.

'Joe, that's the point. If it were civilized in here, no bugger would come.'

'It's full of ruffians,' he says, and sips at his shandy.

Mr Green reaches into his inside pocket and withdraws his wallet. He inspects its contents, then pokes a tenner into my hand. 'I think you and I need a large whisky each.'

'I think you might be right.'

I know he's just had a stroke, but that's his business, and if he wants to drink himself to death, I'll be right behind him. I'm watching the barmaid push a glass to the optic when the muscles in my shoulders and neck suddenly stiffen. A familiar voice comes through the door behind me. If this were a western, I'd lower my hand to my hip and prepare to spin on my heel the moment the talking stops. Instead, I quietly ask for a bag of cheese and onion crisps and some dry-roasted nuts.

Back at our table, I push the snacks towards Joe and sip at my whisky. Barry sits with his back to us, so I don't think he has seen me yet. His companion is at the bar and he looks familiar, but I'm not sure: a big guy with a hint of belly hanging over the top of his jeans. I've seen him around. He looks like a ruffian.

He swaggers back to Barry with a pint in each hand, sits down, starts to drink. It's not far from here to there – maybe eight or nine paces. They're laughing at something. I could cover that distance quickly; Barry wouldn't see me coming, and his mate wouldn't have time to work out what was happening. I could punch Barry in the back of the head and break my glass in the other guy's face before he was even on his feet, but that's not going to happen.

My knee judders up and down.

'Are you all right?' Mr Green is talking to me.

'What? Yeah. I'm fine. It's just…nothing.' I pick up the whisky and wish I'd got a pint instead; I need something wet.

'You looked like you were miles away.'

'No such luck.'

'Do you know those men?'

I look round. Barry turns in his chair, smiles, and tips his glass towards me. I do nothing. He gets up and saunters over.

'All right, mate?'

I say nothing.

'Sorry I didn't stop the other night. I was in a rush.'

What you mean, I think, is that you didn't have back-up. I look past Barry, to the big guy; he's watching, arms folded.

'I hear you're back in work. With that lad from Mac's lot. What's his name? Lee.'

'How did you know that?'

'Ways and means.'

'Shut up, Barry. You're all piss-steam.'

'Am I now?' He looks at Joe. 'I see you're still doing your bit for charity.'

'Baz, we've just been to a funeral. If you want to talk to me, you know where I live. Now get lost.'

'Nasty bruise, that.'

'Thanks for your concern.'

'You're welcome. I'll see you later.'

He goes and sits with his mate again.

Mr Green looks at me. 'What was all that about?'

'Nothing for you two to worry over.'

Joe has gone very still and small.

'Are you all right, mate?' I ask him.

'I don't like him,' he says quietly.

'I know you don't. I'm not that keen on him either. C'mon, drink up and we'll go and have some dinner.'

33

It rained heavily at work today. I get home soaked through, cold, and clarted up with mud. I peel off on the doormat and scurry naked upstairs and straight into the shower. I stand under the hot water for a long time. I can afford to relax because I know that Joe won't turn up this evening; he has another rehearsal at the village hall. He doesn't need to go to every one – he's just the back end of the horse, after all – but he does. God knows how he occupies himself; sits and watches, I think. If it makes him feel there is still a world he's part of, though, then I won't let anyone stop him doing it.

Anyway, he's not here now. I put him out of my mind. The water flows over me, and I think of Laura. I tried hard to forget that kiss, but I dreamed of her last night. I feel guilty about it, but the days have turned to weeks and still no word from Geoff, so who's the traitor now? Wasn't this always there, anyway, ever since she first came here? Perhaps this was waiting to happen. Perhaps it's actually *right*. And yet I still can't understand why she would want to. Why she would want me, of all people.

Here I am, though, wanting her too. It's as if all the action, all the moving, all the change of the last few weeks has hauled my body and mind up to speed and suddenly my sex drive is back.

On the way over to Laura's, questions and doubts grow in the cold
and the dark. I stop and find it difficult to take another step. My
legs are very heavy. I rake my knuckles over my chin. At the very
least, I need to know. I force myself to walk again.

'You've been quiet,' she says, on opening the door.

'I'm sorry. I couldn't…I've been…'

'Yeah. I know.'

I watch a cat emerge from the shadows of a small, neat lawn,
trot over the road, and disappear into the shadows of the small,
neat lawn opposite. I look back at Laura. I feel my jaw working,
as if I need to chew the words to make them soft enough to come
out. 'Look, did you…? When you…? Oh fuck.'

'What?'

I feel like I'm taking a desperate, running jump at a large, deep
hole. 'When you kissed me, did you mean it?'

'When *I* kissed *you*?'

'When we kissed each other, did you mean it?'

'Oh God. Yes, maybe.'

'But…how could you?'

'Oh, don't come with that. He's not coming back, is he? And
you came over here with a bottle of wine. Don't tell me that—'

'No, I mean, how could…*me*?'

'What?'

'I *used* you.'

She steps out, quickly, looks up and down the street. 'Get
inside. Now.'

I do as I'm told. She closes the door behind me, shoves me
against the wall. 'Is that what you think? Is that what you've
thought, all this time?'

'That's what it is, really. That's what it always is when you—'

'Go with a whore?'

'Yes.'

'And I'm your victim? A punchbag? A fuck-toy?'

I can't answer that. I just shrug.

She grabs the front of my jacket in her fist, pushes her forearm across my chest, and looks up into my face. 'Yes, I was young, and yes, I was stupid. I was too young and too stupid to know that what I thought I wanted was all just shit, but that's the same thing as wanting it anyway, so don't tell me you used me.'

'But it was horrible. That house. Those people.'

'Yes, but I didn't see it like that at the time, and once I did, I got away.'

'Jesus. I'm so sorry.'

'No. You don't understand. I left that bastard, but I didn't stop escorting – not then. I kept going and I did it for myself and I used the money for something good. So I'm not sorry, and you shouldn't be either.'

She lets go of my jacket. I watch her eyes and they are full on me. 'It was Barry,' I say. 'He made me visit you that day. I didn't do it for my own sake.'

She smiles at me. 'I know. He told me that part himself. He wanted to make it clear to me who was the boss.'

'The bastard.'

'Are you still glad you kept the secret?'

'Yes.'

Then we stand there together in her hall, saying nothing. Whatever force drove me to her door is all gone and everything I expected to hear is not quite the truth after all. 'So what now?' I say.

She pushes open the door to the living room. 'Come in?'

I find it difficult to move, but then her hand slips into mine and I go with her. She takes me to the couch and we sit down together. She puts one hand in my hair and rests her forehead against the side of my head. Her breath smells like milk. I hear her tongue move behind her teeth and she says, 'Do we understand each other now?'

I don't know what the question means, but I say, 'Yes.' Then with a steady pressure from her hand she turns my face to hers. We kiss. She *tastes* of milk too. And I don't think about whether this is wrong anymore, because she is very soft and warm, and I just want to go further into her. What else have I got?

———

Much later, I walk home and I can still smell her perfume. It seems to be all over my face. I feel idiotic and empty, but I know we'll do it again. Why shouldn't we? I come round the corner of my street and think I see movement in front of my house. I stop, look. Nothing. Maybe another bloody cat.

I get to the door and struggle with my keys for a moment. It opens, but I feel something behind me and turn. Too late. I tumble backwards into the house, and a heavy weight thumps down on me. I try to shout, but my mouth and nose are muffled by stale-smelling fabric. I kick out, but hit thin air. Someone is actually lying on me. Then he's up on all fours and his face is in mine, showering me with spit.

'They're after me!' Joe hisses. 'They're after me!'

34

I put him in the armchair and manage to piece together his story. It goes like this:

Joe doesn't like Lydia, the new director, because she never gives him anything to do. Tonight was no different, and Joe sat at the back while the others practised their singing. It wasn't too bad, because Joe enjoyed listening, and when they confused the words or stumbled over the tune, it made him laugh. One of the Ugly Sisters called Joe a 'knob', but Lydia said, 'Just concentrate on learning the song, for God's sake,' which Joe felt to be the most sensible thing Lydia has ever said.

After a while, the plastic seat made Joe's bum go numb, and he started to need a wee. Joe put up his hand. Nobody looked. Joe's shoulder started to ache. Still nobody looked. Joe drummed his heels on the floor. Eventually, Lydia asked him if something was wrong. Joe said, 'I need a wee,' and the rude Ugly Sister said, 'Oh, for fuck's sake,' but Lydia said, 'Then why don't you go to the toilet, Joe.' Joe said, 'Thank you,' and went.

'Joe, is all this relevant?' I ask now.

'You what?'

'Just tell us the part where you get into trouble, man.'

'All right, keep your hair on.'

On his way back from the loo, Joe heard a strange noise from behind a half-open door. It opened into the carpeted room that is used as a crèche during the weekly mothers' coffee morning. There were two young children in there – a girl and a boy – and when Joe walked in, he couldn't believe his eyes.

'It was one of them blocks what stick together,' he tells me.

'Lego?'

'No, the spiky ones.'

'A Stickle Brick?'

'Aye, them.'

'He was poking her cunt with a Stickle Brick?'

Joe turns red and nods, mutely.

'Jesus Christ, Joseph.' A moment of silence. 'You know, there's people on the Internet would pay good money to see that sort of thing. Did you get any pictures?'

He shoots out of his chair. 'You're disgusting!'

'Settle down, man. I'm joking. What did you do?'

'I picked him up and I said, "Stop it," but he started to scream and then his mam ran in and called me a "fucking pervert"!'

'Fuck. And then what?'

'I ran away.'

'You did what?'

'I legged it.'

'With him still under your arm?'

'No. I dropped him.'

'Oh, Joe, you total knobsack. Why didn't you just explain?'

He collapses back into the chair and shrugs, distraught. He knows he's fucked up.

I go and look out of the front window, but the street is quiet. It's only a matter of time until the police come to find him. I decide not to mention that fact and say, 'Well, no point worrying about it now. Do you want to watch some telly?'

———

Joe stays over, of course. In the morning, I get up and call Lee. 'I've got some personal problems to deal with. I can't come in today.'

'Never mind,' he says. 'We'll cover for you.'

'Thanks, mate.'

I wake Joe and we eat some Coco Pops together, neither of us saying much. I expect a knock at the door at any moment, but for the time being nothing happens, so we just slob out in front of *GMTV*. Joe pays close attention to a segment about a rat that's been trained to type the Lord's Prayer. Through careful conditioning by its handlers, the rat has learned not only the relative positions of the keys it needs to press, but the actual form of the letters stamped on them, so that even if you give it a differently shaped keyboard, it can still perform the feat. Apparently, it did all this for chocolate. Thy kingdom come.

I close my eyes and try to think of Laura, but I just keep seeing Stickle Bricks.

At 10.58 a.m., they arrive.

Joe sits bolt upright.

'Relax,' I say. 'It's probably just the milkman or the window cleaner.' I know that's not true, but the only hope of averting total disaster is to keep him calm for long enough for the police to establish that he's innocent. I go into the hall and open the door. There are four officers and two squad cars outside.

One of them says my name, more as a statement than a question. I nod. 'That's me. Look, I've heard what happened, and he didn't—'

'We're looking for a man called Joe.'

'Here's here, but—'

I sense movement behind me and I turn, but the police officers barge past me into the house. I recover myself just in time to see Joe disappearing up the stairs, with the cops in pursuit. I hear the bathroom door slam and a policeman swear loudly. I follow them up. One of them is slapping on the door with the palm of his hand. 'Come out. We need to talk to you.' Then he sees me. 'He's locked himself in!'

'Stop hammering. That's not going to work.'

'Fuck off, you bastards!' Joe, from inside the bathroom.

'You're scaring him. He's not going to come quietly if you scare him.'

'Can you get him out?'

'He's innocent, you know.'

'Well, if you get him out, we can sort that, can't we?'

'Move,' I say. The filth look surprised to be given an order by a civilian, but they step back anyway. I go to the bathroom door. 'Joe?'

'Get them away! I'm not going to prison! No, no, no, no, *no*!'

'You're damn right you're not going to prison – you've done nowt wrong.'

'We'll be the judges of that,' says a policewoman.

'Shut the fuck up!' I tell her.

Next thing, my face is in the wall and my arm is up my back.

'Stop! You don't understand him!' I gurgle through the pain, but it's way too late for talking, and out of the corner of my eye I see a cop aim an almighty kick at the door. His foot goes right through it and he falls on his arse, but his colleague comes, reaches through the hole, and unlocks it from the inside.

'Fuck,' I hear him say. 'He's gone through the fucking window.'

———

Joe was sedated and taken to hospital under police guard. They didn't arrest me in the end, but asked me to help. They realized once they saw him there – lying on the ground, gibbering, and crying – that they were going to need me in order to get any sense out of him. So we followed along in the squad car, and now I'm sitting in a corridor with a grim-faced copper on either side of me, waiting for information on the extent of his injuries.

As we sit there, one of them asks me questions. I tell him the story Joe told me and watch his face, but it doesn't betray a thing. He just writes in his little book. He doesn't trust me, because he knows about my record. As far as the police are concerned, I'll always be a marked man.

'The real world's scary to him,' I try to explain. 'He lived with his mother all his life and she protected him from everything. It's not surprising that he ran away. It doesn't mean he's guilty, just scared.'

'So you admit that he's a bit strange?'

'Well, yeah, but…' I'm not doing any good. I shut up. Anyway, the policeman seems to have asked everything he wants to ask for now, so we go back to sullen silence.

Time ticks by very slowly in a hospital.

Eventually, a doctor turns up and talks to the police.

'He's a lucky man. Just a twisted ankle and a badly bruised knee. I've treated people who broke their necks in shorter falls than that.'

'Can we talk to him yet?' asks the policeman who questioned me earlier.

'Yes. I'll take you to him.'

The cop turns to me. 'You'd better come too.'

I follow them through the ward, and then the policeman's mobile phone rings.

'That should be turned off,' says the doctor.

The policeman holds his hand up to the doctor's face and turns to the wall. After a muttered conversation, he sighs, switches off the phone, and slips it back into the pouch on the front of his stab jacket. 'You're in luck. The little lass corroborates your story – says it was the boy that fiddled her.'

Relief. 'Thank fuck for that.'

'Aye, well, we'll be seeing you.'

And with that, the two policemen just turn and walk away.

'Hey,' I call after them, 'what about my bathroom door?'

They don't even stop.

35

When I call Laura from the hospital phone box, she laughs. 'For fuck's sake. You and hospitals. What are you doing there this time?' I explain the situation and she stops laughing and agrees to come and get us.

Joe gets a crutch, but he just can't co-ordinate his body with it, so he leans on me all the way to the exit. When we get outside, I sit him on a bench and we wait. He's a bit buzzy from the painkillers, and watches a crisp packet in the wind with all the concentration of a snooker player lining up a shot on black.

'You're a lucky cunt, you,' I tell him.

He just shrugs. He's not lucky anyway, but he may as well be told it. It might help.

It's dark outside now, but there's a streetlamp above us and Joe looks pretty old in its light. I begin to panic at what I find myself saddled with – this ageing idiot I have to care for – so I go and sit next to him and put my head between my knees. I'll ask Mr Green about Social Services again; maybe this latest fuck-up will persuade someone into action.

'I don't want to be in the panto anymore,' Joe announces.

'Probably a good idea, mate.' At least he sees sense. I sit up straight, about to offer him some sort of sympathy, but as I open my mouth, Laura pulls up next to us. With some difficulty I help Joe into the back seat.

'You'll not get much in the way of conversation out of him,' I say as I get in. 'He's full of pills, aren't you, Joe?'

No response.

'Well, let's get you home, then,' she says, and we drive off. I hope I've seen the last of that hospital for a good, long while.

By the time we get to the dual carriageway, Joe is asleep. His big, wet snores fill the car.

'It's good what you're doing for him, y'know,' Laura says.

'I don't know that I'm doing any *good*, but it's a right pain in the arse.'

She reaches over and puts her hand on my thigh. 'Don't worry. You're doing the right thing.' She stops and takes a breath, glances at me.

'What?'

'Oh, nothing.' She sighs, and we drive the rest of the way back to the village in silence.

We pull up outside my house and I turn in my seat and shake Joe's uninjured leg. 'Wakey, wakey. We're back.'

He opens one eye, then the other and looks around. I watch the expression on his face firm into one of full consciousness and then he says, 'No.'

'No, what?'

'I want to go home.'

It hadn't even crossed my mind that we should take him back to his place; I've almost become used to him snoring on my couch.

'I thought you didn't like it there.'

'It's my house.' He shrugs.

'But you'll need some dinner – you must be starving.'

'I'll cook some beans, then.' He looks me right in the eyes.

'All right, then, we'll take you there.' I turn to Laura.

'That's fine by me,' she says, and starts the car again.

As we drive, I keep glancing back at Joe, but he's just looking out of the window, expressionless. Did he hear what I said, when I called him a pain in the arse? No. He was definitely asleep.

When we reach his house, I help him out of the car. 'Have you got your key?' I ask.

He pats his pocket. 'Safe and sound.' Then he starts to hobble off without me. I pick up the crutch and follow him.

'You should keep your weight off that ankle,' I say.

'Don't fuss,' he mutters, and unlocks the door.

'You're going to be all right, then?'

'Aye.'

'All right. Well, see you.'

'See you.'

And with that he goes in and leaves me standing in the yard. I walk back to the car.

'Well, he doesn't seem that dependent on you right now,' says Laura when I get in.

'That was weird.'

'Maybe what happened made him realize he needs to take care of himself.'

'I thought I'd be wiping his backside before long.'

'Well, let's hope he keeps it up, eh?'

'Aye. Let's hope.'

'Come on, don't be so miserable. He'll be all right. He doesn't seem as daft as you make him out to be.'

'He's not. I suppose it's good that he at least wants to try.'

'Course it is. Come back to mine?'

'Yeah. I'd like that.'

———

When we get back to her place, Laura tells me I look hungry and makes me a sandwich. I wolf it down; I was starving. She sits on the other side of the table and watches me eat with a slight smile on her face, saying nothing. I carry my plate into the kitchen and wash it, and when I come back, she is still sitting there. She looks up at me. I feel like something important is unsaid.

'Is there something you want to tell me?'

She bites her lip. 'Not yet.'

'Not *yet*?'

'Come upstairs.'

In the bedroom, there are two cardboard cartons on the floor, sealed with parcel tape. She nods at them. 'Geoff's clothes – the ones he didn't take. I packed them up this morning. I was going to carry them down to the garage.' She shrugs.

'I'll do it.'

'They're not heavy.'

'I'd like to anyway.'

'Leave them for now.' She pauses. 'Look, he's not coming back. And if he does, we'll just tell him to fuck off, all right?'

'All right, then.'

'His stuff doesn't matter; you can burn it all if you want. Right now, I want you to concentrate on me.'

She undresses and I watch her. My body hums with the sound of an orchestra warming up, the growing excitement of having something so beautiful all to myself. For now, at least.

This time I go down on her. I don't have much experience of that, but she kneels over my face and tells me what to do. As she comes, I find myself moving in time with her and every movement seems just right. Then she rolls away from me and lies on her back, shuddering. After a time, she opens her eyes and reaches out to me, pulls me onto her.

Later, we lie together cuddled up under the duvet, and she says to me, 'I was your first, wasn't I?'

'Well, yeah. I'd never had a girlfriend before I went inside, and you don't get many opportunities in prison. None you'd want, anyway. I suppose it's part of the punishment.'

'And has there been anyone else? You know, since the first time we met.'

I struggle to find an answer to that. I want to curl away from it, like a worm from prodding fingers.

'It's just that you act like this is all new to you, like you don't quite trust it.'

I almost say, 'Of course I don't trust it,' but instead come out with, 'Well, you'll just have to keep up the persuasion.'

She bites me gently on the shoulder. 'But am I your only one?'

'No,' I say. 'There were others. Just not *girlfriends*.'

'One-night stands?'

'Aye. We used to go out on the town sometimes, me and Baz and Geoff.'

'Oh, out on the pull. I see.'

'Well, it's not as if I made a very good average, is it?'

'It's quality that counts, not quantity.'

'Well, there wasn't much quality involved.' I don't know what I can tell her about it. 'It just…It never worked out very well. That's all.'

If I was expecting sympathetic noises, I'm not going to get them. She narrows her eyes at me. 'Were you trying to pretend you knew what you were doing?'

'Yeah.' I shrug. It's true, in a way. 'Yeah, I was.'

'Well, that was your first mistake.' She swings her leg across my body and kneels above me. I relax and let her pin me down. She's no older than me, but so full of experience that I really do feel as if she's schooling me. How did she go through what she went through and end up like that, when I ended up like this? 'So what you're telling me,' she says, 'is that you need an education? I can corrupt you just how I want because you don't know any better?'

I sit up and put my face on her neck, feel her pulse against my lips. 'I don't know about that.'

She pushes me back down. 'Did Geoff ever chase women when you went out?'

'Not very successfully.'

'I mean after he was with me.'

'No. We'd stopped doing that kind of thing by then. If you want the truth, he always said you were a dirty bitch and you were all he needed.'

'Hm. You wouldn't think it from looking at his Internet history.'

'He was always daydreaming about this or that. It was how he lived. He would never…' I stop.

'You've just realized you're talking like he's dead, haven't you?'

'Aye.'

She climbs off me. 'There's something I've got to show you.'

She leaves the room and goes downstairs. She reappears with a piece of paper, which she hands to me. 'Look at this.'

'Mortgage Statement,' it says.

'Why?' I ask.

'Look at the numbers.'

I follow the column of figures down the page and they end with a zero. I look back up the column and realize what it means: the entire balance of the mortgage – plus the penalty – was cleared with a single payment last week.

'Christ. Geoff did this?'

'Who else?'

'Where did he get the money?'

'I've no idea.'

'How long have you had this?'

'It just came today.'

I look back at the statement, but it still ends with a big, fat nought. 'Fuck me. I thought it was Barry that was on the make.'

'Do you think Geoff's into something dodgy?'
'For sixty-odd grand, do you really think he isn't?'
'I'm scared.'
'So am I.'

36

'Come here, you little slut.' The American at the corner table reaches out and pulls the whore into a wet, hard kiss. She twists away and giggles half-heartedly, but from where Geoff is sitting he can see that she isn't comfortable. Her shoulders are stiff, and she keeps looking around the club. The American stuffs more cash into her stocking top. He's been doing that all night. Geoff tosses back his shot and waggles the glass at the barman for another.

He turns to the Australian backpacker next to him at the bar. 'Look at that cunt over there. He's fucking mauling the poor lass.'

'Are you sure you're in the right place, mate?'

'Course I'm in the right place; I'm no prune. I'd just like to see him treat her with a bit of respect and some fucking…what's the word?'

'Decency?'

'Aye! Decency. He's having his fun. Why does he have to treat her like shite and all?'

The Aussie shrugs. 'She's getting paid.'

'I don't like him.'

'You're pissed as a fart, mate. You should get out of here and go to bed.'

'I'm not going anywhere.'

'Suit yourself.' The Aussie picks up his drink and wanders off through a bead curtain into the brothel at the rear. As the beads swing back into place, Geoff just catches sight of him linking arms with the little girl in the hot pink skirt, the one who sucked Geoff off earlier. She was really gentle and Geoff had liked her a lot. He hopes the Australian isn't a bastard to her.

'Where's the goddamned waitress?' That American again – he's so loud. 'Well, fuck her.' He turns to the whore. 'Go to the bar and fetch me a drink.'

The whore looks momentarily confused and opens her mouth to speak, but the American grabs her by the shoulders and speaks loudly right into her face. 'Go. To. The. Fucking. Bar. And. Get. Me. A. Goddamned. White. Russian. Do. You. Under. Stand. You. Dumb. Bitch?' The whore nods quickly. The American pushes another note into her bra and pats her on the cheek. 'Good girl.'

She walks up and briefly speaks to the barman in their gobbledygook language. Geoff hasn't even worked out what 'please' and 'thank you' are yet, which makes him feel like a twat, but English has worked for him so far. 'You all right, love?' he asks the whore.

She looks him up and down. 'You shouldn't get so drunk in here. Not good place to drink alone.' Then she turns her back to him and stands there studying her false nails, while the barman finishes the cocktail. Geoff doesn't really blame her for playing along; the yank might be a total cunt, but at least he's flash with his cash. Still, Geoff hates people who treat others like that. They remind him of Barry, for a start.

The whore goes back to the American with the drink, sits close to him, and runs one hand up the back of his neck; her other hand disappears under the table. The American throws his head back, mouth open like a pussy cat. Geoff begins to think that the whore has re-established control of the situation, but suddenly the American is looking at her through slitted eyes. 'You know what we do to little exotic bitches like you in my country?' He's quieter now, but Geoff can still hear him. 'We grab them by their ears and we fucking skull-fuck them.' He holds up the first two fingers of his right hand and then jabs them straight into the whore's mouth all the way up to the knuckle.

The whore gags immediately and tries to pull away, but the Yank's too quick and too strong. He puts his left hand on the back of her head and holds her tight, his fingers still buried in her face. The whore throws up her hands, but there is nothing she can do, with her whole upper body shuddering and jerking in involuntary spasms. 'You'd better get used to that, you little bitch, because you can bet your bottom dollar that my dick's gonna go even deeper.'

The whore shoots to her feet with a huge retching sound, then collapses back onto the rolled vinyl bench with her hands at her throat, breathing hard. Her eyes are watering, but she's not crying.

Geoff looks at the barman. 'Are you going to let him do that?'

'Not unconscious. Not bleed. Not problem.'

'Fuck this!' says Geoff, slams the rest of his drink, and marches over to the American. 'Here, what do you think you're doing? Leave the poor lass alone.'

'What the fuck? Get the fuck outta here, man.'

'You are not going to treat her like that.'

'What the fuck are you, Scottish or something? I can't understand a goddamned word you're saying.'

Geoff pounds his fist onto the tabletop, so hard that the American's drink slops over the edge of the glass. 'I'm from fucking County Durham, son, and you're a cunt.'

The American seems to understand that. 'You motherfucker.' He stands up and Geoff begins to wonder if he's made a mistake: the bastard must be all of six foot five and certainly isn't skinny. It occurs to Geoff that violence was never really his strong point, and for the first time he wishes that Jim was here. The American glowers down at him. Geoff looks up into his eyes and sees the same stagnant little pools of pure fucking nastiness that Barry once looked at him with. Fuck you, he thinks. Then he straightens his back and says, with as much conviction as he can muster, 'I'm going to rip your fucking head off, mate.'

Geoff was expecting the American to swing for him, but he wasn't expecting to be attacked from behind. Something crashes into the back of his legs and Geoff drops to his knees with a thud that hurts like hell even after all that whisky. The table flies over, glasses shatter, and everything's a blur. The next thing Geoff knows, he's through the door and on his back in the street.

'Gobbbledy-gobbledy-gobbledy-gobbledy-gobbledygook!' the barman screams down at Geoff, and slashes a machete back and forth through the air.

Geoff flattens himself against the pavement, scared of losing his nose. 'All right, all right, I'm fucking going. Put the fucking chopper away.'

'Gobbledy-gobbledygook!' Someone kicks Geoff in the ribs, and they stalk back into the club, leaving him groaning on the ground.

Eventually, Geoff sits up. Passers-by sidestep him as if he were dog shit. He feels sick and he's shaking with fury. 'Bastards being bastards for no bastard reason,' he mutters to himself. 'Just to feel big. Bastards!' He wants revenge, but he can't go back in there. Then it dawns on him. There is one bastard he can strike back at. Those accountants said they were at his service, didn't they? And there'll be a fax machine in the hotel. Maybe those accountants can be persuaded to post a little note for him. He'll just tell them to 'be discreet'.

37

The next day, I go to work and, in the rhythm of cutting a trench, forget about the mystery of the mortgage. When I get home, I half expect Joe to be on the doorstep again, but he isn't there. I wash and then sit and read for an hour, waiting for him to turn up or call, but he doesn't. I pick up the telephone and I'm about to dial his number when I think: No. It's good that he isn't here, and if he needs anything, I'll be his first port of call anyway. I'd better just leave him to it for a while.

Instead, I phone Mr Green to alert him to events. He listens quietly and then says, 'Well, at least he's all right.'

'He'll be limping for a while.'

'Probably a blessing in disguise: now he might stay put instead of roaming the village getting himself into bother.'

'Aye, I suppose so. Did you get anywhere with the Social Services yet?'

'Did I heck. But there is one bright spot on the horizon.'

'What's that?'

'I spoke to Joe's uncle, to find out about the estate, and it turns out there's some money. Not a fortune, but more than you'd think. And some share certificates. And the house. It'll all be held in trust and Joe'll get maintenance. It's probably enough for him to live on.'

'That's great news.'

After I hang up, I just stand there, almost stunned by relief. Joe's going to be all right, and he's not going to spend the rest of his life reliant on me. I can sense the dark shadows of all the things that could go wrong lurking at the back of my mind, but I dismiss them before they even take form in my imagination. I feel myself smiling. I pick up the phone and call Laura; I want somebody else to be happy with me.

———

The rest of the week passes quickly – I spend my days at work and my evenings with Laura – and I don't see Joe again until Saturday. I go over to check that he knows to pay his bills. That's what I'm going to tell him, at least. In truth, I just want to satisfy myself that he really is OK.

When I get there, the house isn't spotless, but it's much better than I expected; he's obviously making an effort to look after the place. I make us a pot of tea and we sit at the kitchen table.

'That leg of yours dropped off yet?'

'Nope. It's better.'

'Good job.'

There's a small stack of opened post on the table, so I pull it over to me and start to sort through it.

'You're nosy,' says Joe.

'I'm just looking for the bills.'

'There's only electric and phone.'

He's right. I lay them out in front of me. 'Look, you need to take them into the post office.'

'I know. I've done it loads of times. It was my job.'

'Oh. Well, have you got any cash?'

'No.'

'I'll lend you some until we get you sorted out.'

'Why?'

'So you can pay these bills.'

'Needn't bother. I'll just go to the machine.'

'What do you mean?'

He looks at me like I'm stupid, then shifts in his chair, pulls his wallet from his back pocket, and takes out a debit card, which he holds up to my face. 'I. Know. The. PIN.' He pulls a spaz face at me and makes a gurgling noise.

'If the wind changes, you'll stay like that.' I grab the card from him and inspect it more closely. It's in his mother's name. I suppose when they're told she's dead, they'll want to close the account, but until then it'll do.

'You've been keeping the place clean.'

'My job now.'

'Aye, it is.'

I look into his face and he looks steadily back at me; it seems that he's equipped to survive after all. He may not be able to cope with the world at large, but his mother left him with enough knowledge to run the house. All he had to do was decide to use it.

There's only one other thing I can think of to check, so I get up and open the food cupboard; there's not much in it.

'Looks like you could do with getting some shopping in. Do you want a lift to the supermarket?'

'Aye, that's magnificent, that.'

———

Later, I go to Laura's. We order a pizza and settle down in front of a film I don't really want to watch.

I'm woken by knocking. My eyes flicker open and I'm looking straight up at Laura.

'Someone's here,' she says. I sit up. I must have fallen asleep in her lap.

'I'll get it,' I say automatically.

'Oh, no, you won't. I don't want people talking. Stay here and don't make any noise.' She goes out and closes the door between the hall and the living room behind her. Moments later, I hear her say, 'What do you want?'

I get up and cross the room, stand behind the door.

'Geoff's not here. You know he's not here. Go away.'

I reach for the handle.

'You fucking bitch, I'm not going to let you rip me off.'

Barry's voice. I throw open the door and step out into the hall. A moment of silence and then Laura falls back against the wall with her hands to her face. 'Oh Christ, no…' she murmurs.

Barry looks at her, looks at me, and then starts to smile. I cut him off before he speaks: 'Leave her alone.'

'Are you in on this too, or are you just fucking the dirty bitch?'

'What are you talking about?'

'Don't fuck me around – I know what's going on.'

'Well, I bloody don't. Are you going to fuck off yourself, or do I have to make you?'

'You're not going to scare me away. I've got proof.'

'Proof of what?'

'Proof that that fat bastard ripped me off!'

'Barry, I've no idea what you're on about.'

'Well, let me fucking educate you.' He reaches into his pocket and pulls out a wad of paper from which he unfolds a sheet that he holds out in front of him. I go over. 'Uh-uh. Look with your eyes, not your hands.'

'For fuck's sake, Barry.'

'Just read it!'

I read it. A scrawled note, Geoff's handwriting:

Check the numbers you nobsack. Ha ha ha.

'So what? What's that supposed to prove? I don't even know what it means.'

'Don't play fucking stupid.'

'I mean it. I don't know anything about this.'

He unfolds another sheet, hands it to me this time. It's full of rows of printed figures. One row is highlighted. 'That's off the Internet,' he says, as if it explains everything. His eyes gleam like those of a mad vicar, preaching fire and brimstone. I shrug at him.

'That fucking row there.' He jabs at the highlight. 'Don't you recognize them?'

'Of course I don't fucking recognize them.'

'They're our fucking lottery numbers!' He's shouting now. 'This is a list of all the numbers that have come up in the past two months, and ours are on there. Look – the jackpot was two point eight million, split between five winners. The fat fucker has taken us for over half a million quid!'

And then it hits me. The mortgage. The disappearance. This is why he didn't stay to sort things out; he didn't need to. And his words: 'Nothing I want to share with you.' Jesus Christ.

'How do you know they're our numbers?'

'Because it's my row and I remember them. I remember how I picked them: my birthday; your birthday; Geoff's birthday… Do I need to go on?'

'No. Shit. Show me that note again.' He holds it out. It looks like a photocopy or something. 'Is that the original?'

'It's what came through my fucking letterbox. Look, I want my fucking share. I've worked my hands bloody for years and I want my share.'

'I haven't got your share.'

'But that slut knows where he is.'

'She doesn't know anything.'

'She's been lying to you. She knows. I'll break her legs if I have to.'

I'm suddenly angry, but not with Geoff. 'Fuck you.'

'What? It's money, you idiot! It's yours too.'

'Hold on a minute. You don't have *real* proof. All you've got is that note. That could mean anything.'

'What are you saying?'

'I'm saying I'm not going to help you. I'm keeping my mouth shut. You can't prove we ever had a lottery syndicate, and you're not getting any of the money.'

'You're in on this! You bastard!'

He throws himself at me and I punch him in the teeth. He hits the ground like a sack of shit.

'Oh God.' Laura.

'He'll be all right – he always had a glass jaw.'

Geoff's letter is still clutched in his fist. I lean over and take it from him, stuff it in my pocket. Then I grab him by one ankle and drag him off the property. A woman crossing the road stops to stare.

'Just taking out the rubbish,' I tell her.

I leave Barry in the gutter, groaning.

Back inside, Laura is crouched against the wall with her head in her hands. I pull her to her feet. 'Did you know about this?'

'No. Honestly.'

'Why did you react like that when I came out? You said you'd never take Geoff back anyway, so why would it matter if Barry knows about us?'

'I don't know. I'm just…scared. I don't want that bastard to think he was right all along.'

She's telling the truth. I let her go. 'Where's Geoff's tool hod?'

'In the garage.'

I go out and look for it; it's sitting on a workbench just as he left it. The little policeman's notebook is inside, just as it always was: our numbers on the first page, then the running account of all the money we've ever staked. There are even some old tickets stuck between the leaves. This is the physical proof that Geoff ripped us off. I can't believe the fat bloody fool forgot to take it with him.

What the fuck am I supposed to do with it?

'What is it?' Laura comes up behind me.

'It's the account. Geoff organized the syndicate. Me and Baz never took it that seriously. Half the time we forgot to bloody pay him.'

'So Barry's right?'

'Yeah. Your husband's taken us for idiots.'

'Jesus.'

We both stare at the notebook.

'How much do you hate Barry?' I ask her.

'Completely. I've never hated anyone so much in my life.'

'Me too.'

I decide what to do. I take the notebook into the kitchen, tear out the pages, and drop them into the sink with Geoff's letter and Barry's list. I open the windows, close the door, and look around for a lighter. I find a pack of five in a drawer, shrink-wrapped, straight off a market stall. I pull one out. Laura follows me in.

'What are you doing?'

'Burning it all.'

'What about us?'

'We'll cross that bridge when we come to it. Anyway, you already got a free house out of the deal.'

'It's not your decision to make. I'm his wife; some of that money is mine.'

'There's no way I'm going to let Barry get his share, but if we don't get rid of this, that's exactly what will happen.'

'Jesus. I don't want to watch this.'

She walks out. I burn it.

38

I don't see her again for several days, but then she turns up at my house one evening after work. She stands on the doorstep, doesn't know what to say.

Eventually, 'Hello.'

'Have you forgiven me?' I ask.

'Maybe.'

'I wasn't sure I'd see you again.'

'Well, here I am.'

Yes. Here she is. We had fallen into a routine and then fallen out of it and I saw again how tenuous things are between us, but she has come back. And I'm glad to see her.

I lead her into the living room and we climb into my armchair together, Laura curled up in my lap. I stroke her hair and feel her heartbeat against my chest and her breath against my skin.

'Are we just making more trouble for ourselves with this?'

'I don't know,' she says. The only possible answer.

'And what about Barry?'

'I haven't heard anything else from him.'

'He'll be planning his next move. He won't give up yet.'

'I want to stay here tonight.'

'That's fine.'

———

A crash from below and I'm on my feet, breathing hard. I charge downstairs and skid into the living room. Broken glass glitters on the carpet, and the curtains billow in the wind. I flick on the light just as Laura appears behind me.

'Don't come any further. There's glass everywhere.'

'What happened?'

I point at the brick on the floor. 'That happened.' We look at each other. 'Barry,' I say.

She sags and turns away. 'For fuck's sake. Is this all there is? Is this what we get?'

'Laura—'

'I can't live in this shithole anymore. I'm sick of everything.'

She goes back to bed without another word. I stand motionless, staring at the glass. If I lose her because of Barry, I'm going to kill him.

I sweep away the mess and tape a bin bag and a piece of card over the broken window. Finally, I pick up the brick.

PAEDOS OUT

The words are scrawled on the flat underside in white chalk. This isn't for me; it's for Joe. I drop the brick. *But he's innocent. He's innocent.*

I run upstairs, turn on the lights in the bedroom, start pulling on clothes. Laura sits up.

'What are you doing?'

'I need to go to Joe's.'

'What? Why?'

'They're after him.'

'What do you mean?'

'I'll explain later. I've got to go.'

I get in the car and set off. My chest is tight, and I can feel my guts slithering inside me. Is Barry behind this? I don't know now. I reach Joe's place and everything looks quiet: no lights on, no people around, no strange cars, nothing out of place. I get out and knock on his door, but I don't wait long before checking if it's locked. It isn't – again – so I just go in. I walk through the ground floor, turning on all the lights as I go. There's no sign of anything untoward. All I sense is the living stillness of a house at night: the dirty mug on the coffee table, the cushions arranged at random on the couch.

'What are you doing?' Behind me.

I spin on my heel and face him. He stands at the bottom of the stairs in his pyjamas, all sleepy-faced. 'You need to keep the fucking door locked, Joe!'

'All right, keep your hair on.'

'I could've been anyone.'

'No, you couldn't. You're only you.'

I feel stupid. What am I supposed to do now? I can't tell him the truth; his existence here is fragile enough. If I scare him, everything will go to shit again. 'Look, just keep the door locked,' I say.

'I'll put the kettle on.'

'Don't bother – I'm going.'

'You're crackers, you.'

'I'm coming close, mate.' I walk back into the kitchen and pause at the door. 'Look, has anyone been here apart from me?'

He shakes his head. 'Nope.'

'Right. Lock the door behind me and go back to bed. Call me if you need anything.'

He yawns, loudly. I leave his house, sit in the car, and watch his windows go dark. I wonder why someone put a brick through my window but left Joe alone. Maybe whoever it was thought Joe was still staying with me, or maybe he just couldn't be bothered to come all the way out here, and chose a more conveniently located victim. Or maybe it really was Barry, using Joe as an excuse to get to me. If someone is spreading false rumours, though, I need to put a stop to it. The question is, how the hell do I do that? Especially if I'm part of the rumour.

I drive home, and when I get in, I find Laura sitting at the table, fully clothed with the brick in her hands. She holds it up to me.

'This is disgusting.'

'Yeah, I know.'

'Look, while you were gone, I was thinking. There's no reason for either of us to stay here. Let's go away.'

'My whole life's here.'

'Life? In a place where people do things like this? Why would you want to stay?'

'What about Joe? I can't leave him to face this on his own.'

'Just tell the police and have done with it.'

'Fuck the police. The police can't help.'

'Jesus. Sometimes I think you're just looking for more reasons to punish yourself for what happened. You could have so much more. You made one mistake! Geoff told me what happened that day. It was an accident. You were just trying to defend your mates, and all the rest of it – your mam dying, what your dad did to himself – was not your fault. This isn't your responsibility.'

'It's nothing to do with that!' I'm almost shouting now. 'I can't leave Joe.' Why doesn't she understand?

'You're just using that as an excuse. You don't have to let prison hold you back anymore. You could leave here. You could go to college, like you wanted to when you were a kid. I'll help you.'

'All that might be true, but it doesn't matter now. I need to be here for Joe.'

'Fine.' She puts the brick on the table. 'But I can't deal with it.'

'You don't have to deal with it. It's not your problem.'

'I'm scared and I'm going home. I'm sorry.' She gets up and leaves. I hear the front door close behind her, then I go to bed.

———

I wake up late the next morning and swear at my unset alarm clock as it ticks towards 10 a.m. I have to go to work; there's nothing else I can do.

When I arrive at the site, I find Rupert and Lee in the barn, just starting their lunch. They watch me walk in, but don't say anything.

'Sorry I'm so late.' I search for a realistic excuse, but I can't think of anything, so I just shut up. The kettle is still hot. I make myself a cup of tea and go and sit on my deckchair. Rupert puts the lid on his lunchbox and goes outside.

'He all right?'

'Dunno.' Lee shrugs. 'You'll have to ask him.' He takes a bite of his sandwich and starts to chew.

'Right. I'll get on with that digging out, then.'

'Suit yourself.'

Down the lane, I can see Rupert sitting in his car, eating and fiddling with his radio. I grab my pickaxe and shovel, and go into the other barn, where I'm supposed to be tearing out the years of compacted mud. Really, it's a job for the excavator, but Jethro wasn't prepared to let us knock a hole in the wall large enough for us to drive it through, so I'm doing it by hand. I swing myself into the work and lose track of time. The next thing I know, Rupert comes in and starts digging at the opposite end of the building. For the past two days, we've been working next to each other.

'You all right?' I ask.

No answer.

'I said sorry for being late.'

He swings his mattock into the floor with unnecessary violence and stalks out, leaving it jammed there with the blade buried almost to the handle.

'Fuck's sake,' I mutter, and start work again, but Lee comes in.

'Look, just don't talk to him, all right? He's got strong opinions on the subject.'

'What fucking subject?'

'You know what I'm talking about.'

'I bloody don't.' But the truth is, I'm starting to get an idea.

'Just keep your head down.'

He walks away. I follow him out into the yard and call after him, 'What's going on here?' I sound lame. I know what's going on here, and I'm only asking out of a last, desperate hope that I'm wrong.

'Look, I don't believe you had anything to do with what he did, but you cannat be protecting a bloke like that.'

'Christ. Where did you hear about this?'

'Jethro told us this morning, before you got here.'

'And where did he hear it?'

Lee shrugs. 'Friend of the family, he said.'

'Joe didn't do it. He's innocent. The police let him go because it was all a load of bullshit.'

'So you say. We heard he was caught red-handed.'

'So why isn't he in prison, then, if it was all so bang to rights?'

'Because he's mental. Special treatment and that. Anyway, even if he didn't do it, it's just weird you being mates with him. He's… fucking…y'know.' Lee looks less sure of himself now.

'Don't be so bloody daft. You know where this has come from? Fucking Barry, that's who. Do you really believe any gossip that comes from that bastard?'

'You'd better take this up with Jethro. He was looking for you this morning anyway.'

'Oh brilliant.'

'Here he comes now.'

I turn and see that Lee is right: Jethro's car is coming up the lane right towards us. I feel like I've walked into an ambush. He keeps driving right at me, and for a moment I don't think he's going to stop. He pulls up with about a foot to spare, the door flies open, and he throws himself out of the car. Without his hat, I see that he's completely bald.

'Well, if they're too scared to tell you, I'll tell you myself. You're sacked!'

'Are you completely insane?' If he comes any closer, I'll knock him out.

'I know all about you. I know the things you've done. And now this. Bosom bloody buddies with a paedophile? I don't want you on my property.'

'Who the hell have you been talking to?'

'Your mate Barry's sister-in-law is married to my wife's brother. Didn't know that, did you? But I've had your number from the start.'

Well, at least now I know how Barry knew I worked here. I realize that I'm not going to hit Jethro – there's no point – so I just say, 'It's not true. Joe didn't do anything.'

'I hope someone cuts your balls off.'

'What?'

'You're thick as thieves with him. You knew what he was. You've probably been covering up for him for years. You probably do it yourself – Baz says you've always been a weirdo.'

'Baz is a lying, evil bastard. If you've got any sense, you should know that just as well as I do.'

'Get lost, and don't come back.'

'Aye, I'm going. Don't worry about that.'

I walk back to the car and change out of my boots. I'm about to leave when Lee taps on the window. I wind it down.

'Look,' he says, 'I don't know who to believe now, but the way Jethro told it, there are certain people who aren't going to let this lie.'

'Neither am I.'

I drive off and leave him standing there.

39

She's an Englishwoman. Geoff hadn't expected that. It makes him want to keep quiet. He doesn't want to reveal anything about himself in case – despite the letter and his very good reasons for leaving – Laura might be searching and his name might be known. When they go out to the car, it turns out that she has a driver, so she gets in the back with him and just keeps chatting. Jesus fucking Christ, he thinks. Is this dippy bitch going to shut the fuck up or what?

'Geoffrey, I really think you're going to like this apartment, yeah? It's only like ten minutes from the beach, so you can go down there whenever you feel like it, but the complex is, like, really quiet, so you'll really feel like you've got your own space, do you know what I mean? And it's gated...'

Geoff's face is going stiff. Will living in this country frazzle his brain like it has hers? She's a bit younger than him, this estate agent – or 'realtor', as she calls herself – and Geoff usually finds women in business clothes sexy, but he doesn't fancy her. She's still talking. It's not even estate-agent-speak anymore, but some yet more witless brand of total bollocks and Geoff can't follow a word of it. Maybe, thinks Geoff, this is what being an ex-pat does to you.

He realizes that she has stopped talking and is looking at him expectantly. He has no idea what she just asked, but he starts to speak automatically and the first thing out of his mouth is, 'Call me Geoff. Everyone else does, like.'

'Oh. Oh right, yeah, great. Thanks, Geoff. So is the apartment just for you, or is someone coming out to join you?'

'Just me, love. I'm here alone.'

'Me too. I've been here almost two years now. It's just, like, so totally amazing.'

Geoff nods and looks out of the window.

———

Eventually, after showing him the flat, the estate agent shuts up and leaves Geoff alone to look around for himself. He breathes a sigh of relief and stands there for a while, looking out of the window and trying to collect his thoughts. It's nice. He's on the third floor. There's a balcony and below that gardens with palm trees and very green grass and a pool. The flat is just like he thought it would be: two bedrooms, living space, bathroom, kitchen. All very neat and clean and brand new.

He wanders through the rooms. He turns on the kitchen tap, watches water swill down the plughole, then turns it off again. He opens the bedroom wardrobe, runs his hand along an empty shelf, closes it. He flushes the toilet. It performs as expected. He could live here, maybe use the rest of the money to buy a bar and serve cold beers to hot tourists. That was one idea, anyway. This place has a spare room too, so that when the dust has settled a bit and he thinks he can risk it, he could have his mam and dad to visit.

He goes back out into the living room and feels the need to sit down, but of course there is no furniture. It occurs to him that he will need to fit out the flat himself. Then he realizes that he has absolutely no idea how to do that and immediately thinks of Laura.

This would be her domain: it's her who would have opinions about what kind of sofa they should have and where they should put it and all that other stuff. Without those opinions, this isn't a flat or a place to live; it's just a space. If the flat was already done out, Geoff could just accept it as it was and never give it a second thought, but to start totally from scratch? He doesn't have a clue. In his wallet, behind the loyalty cards, is a photograph of her. He'd forgotten it was there, but now he remembers it and has to beat down the urge to take it out.

'Shit,' he mutters.

'Excuse me?' The estate agent, from the other room.

'Nothing.'

She appears anyway and smiles at him. 'Are you starting to feel at home?'

Geoff feels too helpless to move or speak. Maybe he should go back to the hotel. Maybe it was a bad idea to come here alone.

40

I drive slowly past Barry's house. For some reason, I'd imagined him sitting in his front room right now plotting my destruction, but the van isn't in the driveway. He must be at work, wherever that is these days. I park just down the street and wait. I don't know what kind of sick stories he's been telling about me and Joe, but I'm going to beat it out of him.

By five thirty, it's dark and other people are arriving home, but no sign of Barry. Six o'clock comes and the van still hasn't appeared. I desperately need a piss. This isn't going well. I want to be here when he arrives, but if I wet myself, it might ruin the effect.

Back at home, having relieved myself, I come up with an idea. I pick up the phone, do 141 to withhold my number, and then dial Barry's. His wife picks up. I lower the pitch of my voice and try to soften my accent.

'Hello. Can I speak to Barry?'

'He's not in at the moment. I can take a—'

'Any idea when he'll be back?'

'Not really. He went to the pub after work. Who is this?'

'Thanks.' I hang up.

Now I know where Barry is, assuming that 'the pub' means the Admiral. I leave the house and start walking. The time is just after 7 p.m.

Ten minutes later, I get to the pub and walk round the back to check the car park. Barry's van is there: I've got the bastard. I lean against the wall in a patch of dark. A plan? I don't have one. My stomach boils, but my mind is a dead calm and all I know is that I need to go in there – right now – and bring an end to whatever it is he's doing. My body moves and I'm walking again, round the side of the pub, past the windows, and through the front door.

He's in the corner, behind the pool table with a group of men. There's a heavy cloud of smoke above them, their ashtray is full, and there are empty glasses everywhere around. I recognize the big bastard and a few other faces, and then Barry sees me. He rises to his feet and points. 'Speak of the devil.' They all turn to face me; I haven't felt this hated in years.

'What are you doing, Barry?'

'*We* are protecting this community.'

'You lot? You're what this community needs protecting from.'

'You'd better be careful what you say. There's a lot of angry people here.'

'You're just doing this to get at me because you can't get to Geoff. You know that Joe's innocent.'

'Is he fuck,' the big bastard butts in. 'I've spoken to that little boy's mother.'

'That little boy is the one that fucking did it, and you know it.'

'Bollocks. What was your mate doing in there in the first place? Fucking weirdo, he is. I've seen him around. I don't like the look in his eyes.'

'No one likes the look in his eyes: he's mental, but he's not a child abuser.'

Barry steps forward. 'We're not taking any chances with our kids.'

'Fuck off, Barry. You're an idiot. Frank,' I call over my shoulder, 'I think you should call the police – there's a fucking lynch mob forming here.'

No response. I turn. Frank is crossing the floor towards the door, keys in hand. I start to run towards him, but I'm tripped and fall into a stool. As someone hauls me up by my jacket collar, I catch sight of Frank retreating back to the bar, and the door firmly closed. Pairs of hands spin me round, but I don't have time to take in who they belong to because my feet are off the ground and the air rushes past my ears as they slam me down onto a tabletop. The whole world is suddenly light, making no sense.

The ceiling resolves itself above me. I try to move but my arms are pinned. Barry's face appears.

'Don't get in our way.' His breath stinks of beer and fags.

'Whatever you think you're going to do, you won't get away with it.'

The big bastard looms up next to Barry and shoves something under my chin. I don't know what it is, but it feels pointy. 'Now, there are no grasses in this room, are there?'

I don't say anything.

'I did the brick, in case you were wondering.' He winks at me and then turns away. 'Lock this cunt up.'

They drag me to my feet, propel me into the back of the pub, shove me through a door, and close it behind me.

Total darkness.

I turn and reach out, feeling for the doorframe and then the wall around it. Eventually, I land on the light switch and press it. I'm in the cellar. I try the door; it's locked.

'Just behave yourself in there.' A voice from outside.

'Fuck off,' I shout back, and heave an empty barrel across the room. It clatters off the wall and bounces back towards me.

'No good making noise – they've turned up the music.'

'Let me out!'

'Just relax. There's nothing you can do.'

Prick. But I don't see what other options I have. I sit down on the barrel and wish I'd got round to buying a new mobile.

Minutes tick by. It's coming up to 8 p.m. I've got to get out of here before it's too late. Then I realize what I have to do to make them open the door. It's simple. I walk over to the gas cylinders and turn them off. Then I unhook all the barrels one by one, sit back down, and wait.

Shortly afterwards comes a hammering on the door. 'Stop messing around in there!' Frank's voice. 'Turn the beer back on – I've got a pub to run!'

'Come in and do it yourself.'

'Don't fuck me about!'

'I'm not fucking you about; I'm offering you a deal. You've got two minutes to open that door or I'll start breaking things.'

'You fucking will not.'

'What do these big plastic valves do? The ones on the wall with the red balls floating in them? They look important.'

Quiet. I go over to the door and listen at the keyhole.

'We're not letting him out.' Another voice.

'We have to. If he starts breaking things, it could take me days to get the parts.'

'That's right, Frank!' I shout. 'You'll be the pub with no beer. Have you heard that song? It's a good one.'

The door swings open and I'm staring down the barrel of a handgun.

It's one of Barry's followers, a skinny kid in a pink shirt. He can't be any older than nineteen. Frank stands behind him, looking like he's going to shit himself. It takes me a few moments to understand what I'm seeing. Then I start to laugh.

'That's a fucking air pistol.'

'It'll still kill you if I shoot you in the head.'

'You're a moron.'

He shoots me in the arm.

At first, there is no pain. Then it comes. I'd always imagined that being shot would feel sharp, but in fact it feels like someone hit me in the bicep with a hammer. I put my left hand to my right arm and bring away blood. I look up at the kid. Our eyes meet for a second or two. He breathes in and then runs away.

Just me and Frank.

'Fuck,' he says. 'Are you all right?'

I chin him. It's with my left, but he's old and fat and it's enough to knock him down. He grovels on the floor with his hand over his mouth. I step over him and walk out into the pub. I stiffen my back, look ahead, and try to put one foot in front of the other in something like a straight line. No one tries to stop me as I make for the door. Barry and all his mates have gone.

Outside, I lean up against the wall. I touch the wound again. It hurts. My fingers tingle numbly, and although they move when I tell them to, they don't feel connected to the rest of my body.

It was only an air gun; it can't be that bad, I say to myself, but I know that it can if he hit an artery. There's definitely more blood than I ever like to see on the outside of my body. Fuck it. I need to warn Joe, and if they've gone straight there, I need to go now.

I start to move. The fresh air seems to do me some good; things sharpen up and the shock dies away. I can't go down the lane, because that's the way they'll take and I would just walk straight into them. I need to loop across the fields and head them off. I pick up my pace, break into a jog. I can do it. I run.

I head down the street and then take a left onto the road that leaves the village. I pass the phone box. I could stop and dial 999, but every second counts now, and if they get to him before me, who knows what they'll do in the time it takes the police to arrive. I keep running and eventually the houses stop and the hedgerows begin. Then I'm at the stile. I climb over it, slipping as I step off and falling onto one knee. Automatically, I put my right hand down and scream in pain and anger when I push myself up, but I'm on my feet again and moving forward.

From here, I can run in pretty much a straight line to Joe's house, avoiding the lane. I'll have to climb some fences, but the sky is clear and the moon is bright, so at least I can see where I'm going. I try to keep my pace up, but I'm straining now and my legs just won't move as quickly as I'm willing them to. I hop another fence, lose part of my jacket on the barbed wire, and by the time I see the lights in the houses on Joe's terrace, I'm knackered and stumbling.

Finally, I reach the hedge that runs along the lane and scramble through a thin patch on my hands and knees. I stand up. Joe's house is dark. I go to the door. It's locked. Of course it is; I told him to do it. I knock, but he's obviously not in.

'Oh, Joe, you fucking idiot. Don't be out walking.' But I know in my stomach that's exactly where he is. Now I have no choice but to call the police. I'm about to go and ask his neighbours, and then I hear yelling from down the lane.

I run towards the sound. Pitching forward in exhaustion, my legs and arms flail. It's further away than I thought, the sound carrying in the cold night air. I've got to get there. Then the noise stops and the only sound is my own breathing and the thump of my feet on the frozen ground. I come round a bend.

There is a body in the lane. They caught him at a break in the high hedgerow and did it by moonlight. He lies crumpled, like casually discarded clothes. The search is over, and all around me the night is suddenly vast and cold. I watch, I breathe, and then I run the last few feet and drop to his side.

'Joe.'

Epilogue

THE FOLLOWING YEAR

I stayed because I wanted to see Barry convicted. It took a couple of months to go to trial, but I got my day in court and he got sent down. Then I stayed because I didn't know what else to do. It was Laura's letter – the last thing I ever heard from her – that made up my mind.

> I'm sorry I left without saying anything. You must have realized that I went to Geoff. He got in touch just after Joe died. I needed to get away, and he had a plan. I've explained everything to him, and he understands the truth now. I couldn't stay in that place any longer. It's horrible. There's nothing left there for you or me, but I couldn't wait around for you to work that out. You should leave too. Please. Go and do something new. You deserve it.
>
> Love,
> Laura

I arrive in London in the spring, get a room in a doss house, and walk into a job agency. The venetian blinds are dusty, and the plants are fake. They find me a job me then and there.

'Flats,' the man says. 'New ones are going up all over the place. We've more work than we know what to do with.'

I don't like him. He keeps clicking the top of his biro and I want to take it off him and jam it up his nostril. I take the job, though. I fill in the forms but leave out my criminal record because it's obvious to me that these people will never check.

The job is easy: some huge old building, once a factory and now becoming apartments. There are so many men crawling all over the place that you could just lose yourself in a quiet corner and do nothing all day. Of course, I don't do that. I want the work; it keeps Laura out of my head, just about.

I pal up with a Polish guy called Adam. He's new too and we're both as skint as each other. For the first two weeks, until we get our pay packets, we pool our money and share lunch: one half of a pre-packaged sandwich each.

He picks a chunk of pickle out of his beard and puts it in his mouth, looks at me with serious eyes. 'Tastes like fucking shit,' he says.

'So what's the food in Poland like?'

He shrugs. 'Tastes like fucking shit.'

'What did you do for a job back there?'

'Psychiatric nurse.'

'Nice.'

When the money finally arrives, his is well short, so I help him nick a carton of new smoke alarms. We take them out of the boxes and tape them to his body under his clothes. He walks off the site, stiffly but without arousing suspicion, and the next day, he turns up with a loaf of fresh bread and a full pound of deli ham. We feast, sat on top of a stack of plasterboard. A couple of weeks later, he stops coming to work. He must have found something else.

It's late summer by the time I've saved enough to put a deposit on a flat. A studio, they call it. I call it the rabbit hutch. It's above a shop in Acton. There are rats in the walls, but at least it's not damp. It gets so hot some days that I have to take all my clothes off in order to stay indoors, but I know it won't stay this way; come winter, I'll be freezing. I make the most of the weather and spend the weekends in the park or walking around the city, letting the people flow all around me. It's exciting.

One night about three weeks after I move in, I hear someone hammering at the outside door. I open the window and look down. Adam is standing on the pavement. He reaches into a carrier bag, pulls out a bottle of vodka, and waggles it at me.

'It's my birthday!' he shouts up.

'Where've you been?'

'Scotland. Raspberry season. Then strawberries. Then black-currants. Fucking shit.'

I go down and let him in. He tells me my flat stinks. I ask him how he found me. 'Just asked around,' he says with a shrug.

We drink hard, then go to the pub and carry on. Adam talks about all the women he's fucked. I talk about all the women I haven't fucked. We stumble back late with kebabs and sit cross-legged on the floor, stuffing our faces. When we're finished, he licks his fingers, then spies a pile of library books and pokes at them.

'Ha. You're an educated man.'

'I'm bloody not.'

'Good books, though.'

'You know them?'

'Some. I read them at college.'

'You went to college?'

'Of course. I *am* an educated man.'

'And you've ended up fruit-picking and hod-carrying? It doesn't seem worth it.'

He sits up straight and looks me in the eye. 'Listen, that's just something idiots say. Education, it sets your brain free. And when your brain is free, there is always hope.'

'Always?'

'Almost always.' He laughs and lights a cigarette. I hand him an empty can for an ashtray, and he sits for a couple of minutes. 'It's worth it, man. It's worth it,' he says eventually.

'Aye. I could do with some hope.'

'Well, you did not come to London for this, did you?'

'I'm too drunk for this conversation. Let's put some music on.'

––––––

I wake up the morning after with a filthy hangover. Work is not going to happen. I take a shower and brave a cup of coffee. I keep it down, but only just. The room stinks. I can't remember Adam leaving, but he left a note for me. Some of it might be Polish, but all of it is in unreadable, drunken handwriting. The only bit I understand is scrawled in block capitals: 'DON'T FORGET THE HOPE!' Daft bastard.

I take some painkillers and listen to the radio until I feel able to move again. Then I go to my sock drawer and take out the thing I didn't show him last night: a blank Open University application form. It has been there for weeks, waiting for me. I spread it out on my tiny desk. It's long, and the type is small, but the first box only wants my name. That's simple enough. I write it in, slow and careful.

Well, it's a kind of hope, isn't it?

Acknowledgements

My family. Jane Rogers for her support and advice throughout the writing of this novel. Juliet Mabey and all at Oneworld for publishing it. Euan Thorneycroft, my agent, for taking the chance on me. The writing group in Sheffield for feedback and comradeship. Ellen Cartsonis and family for everything.

Thanks also to Marko Hautala, Sophie Hoskins, Elisabeth Garton, David Harsent, Sara Quin and anyone else who ever read a draft, in part or in whole, and offered constructive criticism or simple encouragement.